ROB THOMAS

Rob Thomas is the creator of the television series *Veronica Mars* and the co-creator of the television series *Party Down*. He lives in Austin with his wife and two children. He hasn't fully recovered from Ray Allen's three-pointer in Game 6 of the 2013 NBA Finals.

JENNIFER GRAHAM

Jennifer Graham graduated from Reed College and received her MFA from the University of Texas at Austin. Her short stories have appeared in *The Seattle Review* and *Zahir*. She currently lives in Austin with her husband.

ALSO BY ROB THOMAS

Rats Saw God

Slave Day

Doing Time: Notes from the Undergrad

Satellite Down

Green Thumb

veronica
MARS

THE THOUSAND-DOLLAR TAN LINE

veronica **MARS**

THE THOUSAND DOLLAR TAN LINE

Rob Thomas

and

Jennifer Graham

Based on characters from the series *Veronica Mars*, by Rob Thomas

Vintage Books

A Division of Random House LLC | New York

A VINTAGE ORIGINAL, MARCH 2014

Produced by Alloy Entertainment
1700 Broadway, New York, NY 10019
www.alloyentertainment.com

Based on characters from the series *Veronica Mars*,
by Rob Thomas.

Library of Congress Cataloging-in-Publication data
Thomas, Rob.
Veronica Mars. The Thousand-Dollar Tan Line /
Rob Thomas, Jennifer Graham.
pages cm.
1. Women private investigators—Fiction. I. Graham,
Jennifer. II. Veronica Mars (Television program)
III. Title. IV. Title: Thousand-dollar tan line.
PS3620.H639V47 2014
813'.6—dc23
2014001174

Vintage Trade Paperback ISBN: 978-0-8041-7070-3
eBook ISBN: 978-0-8041-7071-0

Thomas author photograph © Eric Doggett
Graham author photograph © Jennifer Gandin Le
Book design by Claudia Martinez

www.vintagebooks.com

Printed in the United States of America
10 9 8 7 6 5 4 3 2 1

For all the Veronica Mars Kickstarter backers. You're like the people who clapped loud enough to bring Tinker Bell back from the dead. Except instead of clapping, you sent money. And instead of a tiny blond fairy, you resurrected a tiny blond detective.

ACKNOWLEDGMENTS

First off, thanks to Rob Thomas, for imagining a world with Veronica in it and for giving the rest of us a chance to play there.

Enormous thanks to Lanie Davis. I could not have pulled this off without your expertise and your support. Thanks as well to Bob Dearden and Deirdre Mangan, who provided invaluable help in developing this story, and to the gang at Random House—particularly Andrea Robinson, Beth Lamb, and Anne Messitte—for all their hard work.

Thanks to Matt Donaldson and Cara Hallowell for their fight choreography, to John Preston Brown for his knowledge of the criminal element, and to Jack, Donna, and Zac Graham for their years of encouragement and care. I also had a ton of cheerleaders on this project and owe particular thanks to Alec Austin, Sarah Cornwell, Izetta Irwin, Jennifer Gandin Le, Patrick Ryan Frank, and Kyle John Schmidt, all of whom kept me going at various points of the process.

—JENNIFER GRAHAM

veronica MARS

THE THOUSAND-DOLLAR TAN LINE

PROLOGUE

The buses began to roll into Neptune, California, late Friday afternoon and didn't slow up until Monday. They arrived dusty, windshields speckled with dead insects and fractures from stray flying stones, the chaos of the interstate. They pulled in along the boardwalk, trembling with pent-up noise, shivering like dogs waiting for a command.

Their routes mapped out an arterial network, connecting the little seaside town to all the university cities in the western United States. To L.A. and San Diego; to the Bay Area and the Inland Empire. To Phoenix, Tucson, Reno; to Portland and Seattle, to Boulder, to Boise, even to Provo. Bright, excited faces peered from every window, pressed to the glass.

One after another the buses' folding doors clattered open, and students poured out into the streets. They looked around at the sand and the surf, the carnival rides lit up along the boardwalk, the foot-tall drinks. Some had just finished term papers the night before; others had stayed up all night studying for tests. Now, suddenly, they'd awakened in a fairyland that had popped into existence, just for their pleasure. Screaming with laughter, they flooded the town. They stumbled through the streets, blind drunk, trusting that the magic that had brought them here would keep them from falling.

And for exactly three nights, it did.

By Wednesday morning, the coastal town that sparkled at night looked . . . mundane. Not just mundane. *Dirty.* Pools of spilled beer collected in the seams of the sidewalk, and the rank tang of overfilled Dumpsters wafted out from the alleys. The ghostly forms of used condoms littered doorways and bushes, and shattered glass covered the street.

The Sea Nymph Motel was eerily silent when eighteen-year-old Bri Lafond stumbled in. Almost all of the guests were spring breakers, and the party didn't get started until early afternoon. She had been at a rave on the inland edge of town, and by the time the party had wound down at 4:00 a.m. she hadn't been able to get a cab. She'd still been high enough that the idea of walking back to the motel had seemed feasible. Now, bone tired, she trudged through the sandy courtyard to the room she and her three best friends from UC Berkeley had rented. It was one of the cheapest available, facing the Dumpster in the parking lot. Now she didn't care, fumbling with the lock and wanting only to fall into one of the two doubles they'd been sharing all week.

The room's blinds gaped open, letting in a ray of pallid light. Leah was sprawled across the bed with her head shoved under a pillow, still wearing a sequined dress from the night before. Her legs were bruised and smudged with dirt. Melanie sat with her back to the headboard, sipping from a paper Starbucks cup. She wore board shorts and a bikini top, her long blond hair tousled and smears of makeup caking her eyes. She looked up when she heard the door open.

"I have a surf lesson in, like, half an hour, and I'm still drunk," she said. She looked at Bri, her eyes focusing with difficulty. "Where've you been? You look like shit."

"Thanks a lot." Bri leaned down to unzip her boots, her feet throbbing. "Where's Hayley? Is she surfing too?"

"Haven't seen her." Melanie closed her eyes and rested her head back against the wall. Bri froze, one boot off, the other still pinching her toes. She looked up.

"Since when?"

"Since . . . since the party on Monday, I guess." Melanie opened her eyes. "Shit."

Bri blinked, then tugged the other boot off her foot. She sank to the bed and gently pushed Leah's shoulder. "Hey, Leah. Wake up. Did you see Hayley yesterday?"

Leah gave a low moan from under the pillow. For a moment she curled into a tight ball, her arm circled protectively over her head. It took them a few more minutes of prodding and cooing her name before she finally pulled away the pillow and looked blearily up at them. "Hayley? Not since the . . . the party on Monday."

A bleak, empty feeling expanded into every corner of Bri's body. She scrolled back through her messages. There was nothing from Hayley since Monday afternoon.

> Invited to a party in a MANSION tonight.
> Wanna go?

They'd spent three hours getting ready, Hayley wearing an uncharacteristically low-cut tight dress that showed miles of smooth, tan leg. She kept insisting they look their best; she'd been invited by some guy who bought her a mai tai in the Cabo Cantina and told her to bring her hottest friends.

They'd all gone, walking up a winding private road where a pair of burly security guards waved them in. The house was sprawling and modern, a boxy, sculptural structure. Every room burned with light and luxury. Melanie melted into the crowd instantly, gyrating her hips to the music. In the kitchen, Leah caught sight of a guy from her biology class and beelined toward him. Hayley and Bri pushed through the house to the back patio to get their bearings. An enormous pool glowed aquamarine below them, and out beyond that the beach stretched black in the moonlight.

Hayley's eyes shone, reflecting the bright colored lights of the patio. All weekend, she had alternated between sadness and outraged defiance. She'd be in tears one minute; the next, she'd spin on her heel to face one of her friends and snap, "Chad can't tell me what to do. Who does he think he is?" She and her boyfriend had broken up for the hundredth time, but that night Hayley looked excited. It was almost as if all the heartbreak had sloughed off her body, like some kind of heavy cocoon, leaving her raw and fresh and new. She and Bri had thrown themselves into the mass of dancing bodies, and for a while, the thrumming bass cleared all thoughts from Bri's head. She lost track of time, the number of drinks she threw back—and her friends.

Now Bri remembered seeing Leah doing lines of coke off an antique coffee table, holding her long honey-colored hair off her neck as she bent over. She remembered hands running up her hips, a slurring male voice telling her she'd be really hot if she grew her hair out. She remembered seeing flashes of Hayley, leaning up to whisper in the ear of a boy in a perfectly cut white suit, his eyes long lashed and sultry, his lips pouting playfully.

Beyond that everything was a blur. She'd woken up the next morning in a lawn chair by the motel pool, shivering in the early morning chill, her purse tucked under her head. She had no idea how she'd gotten home.

"Did you see her leave the party with someone?" Bri looked at her friends. Both shook their heads slowly.

"I'm sure she's fine," Melanie said hesitantly. "She's probably with some guy she met at the party. She'll come up for air sooner or later."

"But we promised we'd check in with each other at least once a day. We *promised*." Bri's voice was shriller than she'd meant for it to sound. They'd made a pact on the way down that no matter what they were up to, no matter how much fun they were having, they'd look out for one another. The dark, empty feeling in her gut yawned even wider. She opened her text window and typed a new message.

> Where are you? Come meet us for
> breakfast. Text back ASAP.

All they had to do was wait. Melanie was probably right—Hayley had lost track of time, just like they all had. She was somewhere out there having the time of her life. Still, when Leah and Melanie got up to go to breakfast, Bri shook her head no, her phone clenched in her hand. She sat alone in the motel room, shivering but too tired to change her clothes. She texted Hayley again. And again.

Stop being SELFISH and respond, Hayley.

Everyone's worried about you.
TEXT ME.

That's it—if we don't hear from you in ten minutes we're calling the cops. Totally serious.

Please answer.

Please.

CHAPTER ONE

"And what about this one?"

Veronica Mars sat in a hard plastic chair in the neurologist's office, one leg crossed over the other, her motorcycle boot jogging up and down as she listened to her father's exam. Keith Mars sat at a small table across from his doctor, watching as she flipped flash cards one by one with careful, deliberate movements.

"Wheelbarrow," he said without hesitation. Dr. Subramanian didn't nod or shake her head but, poker-faced, set the card down to her left.

The neurologist's office was cool and dim, lit by the cozy glow of floor lamps instead of the usual harsh overhead fluorescents of most medical offices. It always felt like early evening in here. Veronica pretended to be interested in a four-month-old *Redbook*, her eyes skating over a feature titled "Twenty Hostess Gifts for Under Twenty Dollars."

"And this?"

"Alligator."

Veronica glanced at her father and the titanium cane that leaned against his leg. It had been two months since the car crash that almost killed him. Keith had been meeting with Deputy Jerry Sacks about corruption within the Sheriff's Department when a van had broadsided them—then doubled back to hit them once more. Sacks had died, and Keith escaped only because Logan Echolls managed to pull him from the car before it exploded.

The official story—or at least, the one Sheriff Dan Lamb had fed to the media—was that Sacks had been on the take from a local meth dealer named Danny Sweet, and the van had been sent to kill Sacks after the deputy allowed three of Sweet's soldiers to get taken in on trafficking charges. It was crap, but the local news outlets didn't seem inclined to look any deeper.

Veronica had been trying to get her father to talk about the crash since the night it happened, but Keith was maddeningly cagey about the details, saying it was "my case, not yours." It had almost become a game between them. Every time she'd try to draw him out, guessing at who might have been behind the wheel—Lamb? Another deputy? Someone else entirely?—he'd casually bat her guess away. All he'd tell her was that the murderer had been after Sacks, not after him, and to let it go.

"Candle. Ring. Umbrella," Keith said loudly. Veronica examined her father. The violent purple bruises that had blossomed across his body had faded. But the real injuries— the broken ribs, the cracked pelvis, the torn liver—were still mending. He'd suffered a fractured skull, a subdural hematoma, and a mild cerebral contusion, and for a few weeks after the accident his reaction times had been slow. In the first days after he'd stabilized, he'd had trouble with word retrieval, sometimes floundering for a few seconds before he could speak. Now he answered most of Dr. Subramanian's questions quickly and firmly. Word by word, Veronica saw him sit up straighter, like he was actually healing himself by getting the flash cards right.

"Very good, Mr. Mars." The doctor's Oxford-accented voice was clipped but pleased. She offered a rare smile, straightening the edges on her flash cards.

Veronica put down the magazine.

"So what's the verdict, Doc? Is he good as new? Can we take him out for a test drive?"

Dr. Subramanian turned to give her a stern look over the tops of her wire-framed glasses. She wore her gray-streaked hair in a bun and sported a shade of lipstick Veronica had to believe was called No Nonsense. Veronica liked her.

"'Good as new' is not the phrase I'd use. But I'm pleased with his progress. How's your reaction time, Mr. Mars?"

"Lightning fast," Keith said, feigning a quick draw from his pocket.

"Any mood swings, strange behaviors, non sequiturs?" She turned toward Veronica.

"No more than usual." Veronica smiled at her father.

"Hmm." Dr. Subramanian looked down at the file folder in her hand. "How's everything else healing up? It looks like you met with your internist earlier this week."

"He says I'm not about to run any marathons, but I could probably sit quietly at a desk organizing paper clips. I'd like to get back to work as soon as possible," Keith said, straightening his jacket. Every day since he'd gotten out of the hospital, he'd made a point of getting dressed in a crisp-pressed shirt and tie as if he were going to the office.

"Hmm." The doctor slid open a manila envelope and

pulled out several grainy MRI images, which she pinned up to a light box. Then she snapped on the light and grabbed a laser pointer attached to a set of keys. "Well, the brain scans came back looking much improved. The swelling is almost completely gone, as you can see here . . ."

Relief blurred Veronica's vision, the image of her father's healing brain disappearing into a myopic smear. She dabbed surreptitiously at her eyes. It was only now that he was so definitively on the mend that she understood how terrified she'd been at the idea that her father could be taken from her that easily. He was all the family she had. Each morning she woke up with an ache in the pit of her stomach, waiting for things to get back to normal.

Because normal's the watchword, isn't it? She smiled a little to herself. Nothing in her life had been normal since she'd come back to Neptune after nine long and quiet and *normal* years away. As a teenager she'd wanted only to get away, to flee the confines of a town run by the moneyed and the corrupt—to flee the scars of her youth. And she'd done it, for a while at least. She'd left, first to Stanford, and then to Columbia Law. The life she'd put together for herself had looked pretty good. Hole-in-the-wall Brooklyn apartment in spitting distance of Prospect Park; a job offer from Truman-Mann, where she'd have a chance to learn from some of the fiercest lawyers in New York. Cute, talented, even-keeled boyfriend named Piz.

But she'd left it all behind. It had taken only one call to pull her back to Neptune. When Logan, her high school boy-friend, had been wrongly accused of his ex-girlfriend's mur-der, Veronica had dropped her entire life and rushed home to prove his innocence. She'd discovered the real murderer—

and reclaimed a part of her that she'd lost, the piece that knew she was meant to be a private investigator, not a lawyer.

And she'd also found Logan again. Now he was her . . . what? *New-old boyfriend? Lover? Skype buddy? Pen pal with benefits?* Whatever his title, his e-mails filled her inbox. Sometimes he sent five a day, short and quipping. Other times he sent longer, more serious ones. She kept her tone light when she replied. That'd always been her MO—a joke, a jab. A way to deflect from what she was really feeling. A way to keep the nonstop ache of missing him from becoming too painful to survive. And honestly, what was there to say that would come close to what she felt?

The moments they'd spent together before he'd shipped out on his latest naval tour had been the most peaceful she could remember—even with her anxiety about her dad. It'd been the first time she'd felt complete in a long time. And then, just like that, he was gone again.

". . . so I would like you to give it maybe two more weeks, just to be extra sure. And then yes, as long as you commit to starting slow, you can start light duty at work." Dr. Subramanian's voice came floating back to her. "But, Ms. Mars, I'm putting you in charge of making sure he does not overextend himself. If he makes a sudden move toward anything too strenuous, you have my permission to send him home."

"You hear that?" Veronica pointed at Keith. "Mars Investigations just got itself a brand-new low-paid intern. Copies, coffee, and mail, my friend."

He clasped his hands together. "I've been training for this moment all my life."

She forced a smile. Despite their banter, a vague sense

of unease tightened in Veronica's chest. Of course she was relieved that her father would be able to get back to work soon—she knew how important his job was to him. Back when she was in high school, she'd worked at his private investigation firm, Mars Investigations. Officially, she'd been his receptionist. Unofficially, she'd taken all the cases he hadn't had time for.

But now she had to wonder what it would be like when they had to go in to the office together. Would they run tape down the middle of the room à la *I Love Lucy*? Would they even be able to wedge another desk in there? She imagined a toy-size pink plastic desk next to his, a sticker reading FISHER PRICE'S MY FIRST OFFICE FURNITURE stuck to one corner. Her sitting with her knees to her chest, typing furiously on a pretend computer while her father looked fondly on.

It was ridiculous—they had worked together before, after all, but he was none too happy about her decision to forgo a lucrative career with a law firm for a life following philanderers with a zoom lens. For the past two months he'd been able to pretend she was there to help him in his convalescence, but more and more she sensed him rankle at the mention of her work. If she told him she'd be out late on a stakeout, or brought up something funny or strange she'd noticed in a case, he became quiet and looked away quickly. Like she'd just embarrassed herself and he was embarrassed too.

He couldn't understand why she'd come back. Some days, she didn't understand it either. Neptune was still the same glittering, dirty seaside town, like a tarnished bronze angel looking out over a graveyard. But the moment she'd started working Logan's case, she'd felt her desire to investigate, to discover the truth in a tangle of lies, pulling at her. Like an undertow.

A few minutes later they stepped out into the mild sunshine together. For a moment she watched him from the corner of her eye, noticing the way his mouth tightened as they went down the three steps to the parking lot. Keith Mars was a short, stocky man, mostly bald, his dark hair a low wreath around the sides of his head. His heavy jaw was usually in danger of five o'clock shadow by noon. He looked like a cop, she thought, smiling a little. It'd been eight years since he'd last worn the uniform, but he'd always look like a cop to her.

"How does it feel to be one step closer to prime fighting condition?"

He tapped the pavement ironically with his cane. "Getting there, one limping, minuscule step at a time."

"Hey." She nudged him gently. "Play your cards right and I'll even let you clean the fish tank."

Logan's sleek midnight-blue BMW convertible stood out in a parking lot chock-full of midsize sedans. He'd insisted on loaning it to her during his deployment. "I'm going to be stuck on a giant tin can in the Persian Gulf for the next six months. What good's it gonna do me?" She'd tried to protest—it cost more than she could expect to make in the next few years—but sliding into the car always gave her a little thrill. And it wasn't just that the dashboard looked like that of a spaceship and the leather interior was soft as a cherub's backside. A faint smell, warm and woodsy, lingered in the driver's seat—the distant notes of Logan's aftershave. And when she curled her fingers around the steering wheel she could almost feel his hands there, under hers.

You're losing your edge, Mars, she told herself as Keith

buckled in. *You don't have the luxury of acting like some love-struck teenager anymore.*

Besides, they were already two and a half months in—only one hundred and twelve days to go, and Logan would be back.

CHAPTER TWO

Traffic was already a nightmare by the time Veronica dropped her dad off at home and headed back out toward Mars Investigations. Spring break had descended on Neptune in all its bacchanalian glory, and even though the worst of it choked the beaches and boardwalks, the party had spread inland, creeping up through the commercial districts and the historic downtown blocks. The drunk and disoriented glutted the bars, restaurants, and shops all over town, even at noon on a Monday. It'd already been going on for more than a week, and it wouldn't slow up until mid-April—there were hundreds of colleges within driving distance, each with its own spring break dates.

Veronica glanced in her rearview mirror. Traffic stretched as far as she could see, motionless in the sun. The sidewalks were crawling with undergrads, shouting at their friends, lifting glass bottles in impromptu toasts. Apparently Neptune's public consumption laws were being selectively enforced. But that was par for the course during the three-week spring break season—money talked in Neptune, and no one heard it louder or clearer than Sheriff Dan Lamb. He spent most of the year chasing "undesirables" (translation: anyone flirting with the poverty line) off the streets, only to turn a blind eye to binge-drinking eighteen-year-olds descending en masse.

Someone laid on his horn. A girl with feather hair extensions leaned down into the gutter to vomit, then straightened up and kept walking as if nothing had happened. A cluster of bikini-clad girls on roller skates tripped laughing across the road while several boys stood on the sidewalk filming them with their cell phones. She sighed and fiddled with the radio dial. She'd let Keith man the stations on the way home and now Blue Öyster Cult blared from the speakers, the cowbell ringing loud and proud. *Five hundred stations on this thing and he went straight to 1976. There's no help for some people.* She played idly with the controls, looking for something to pass the time.

"I can tell you one thing: I wouldn't let *my* daughter go to Neptune for spring break."

Veronica paused. She knew that voice right away: Trish Turley, big, blond, and Texan, sounded like an avenging fury cutting across the airwaves. Her TV show ran daily on CNN, and Neptune's local talk radio streamed the audio.

"I mean, the place is just a pressure cooker of hormones, drugs, and alcohol. Kids these days aren't taught to respect their own limits. And have you seen the way these girls act?" You could practically see Trish Turley shaking her head in approbation. "All you have to do is look up Neptune in your World Wide Web and you'll find video upon video of them showing their breasts for free beer. And then we're shocked when someone gets hurt."

Ah, the twin pillars of outrage journalism: slut shaming and victim blaming. Trish Turley liked to call herself a "victim's rights" advocate, but anytime she could turn an eye on the general decay of society (as witnessed through WASP-colored glasses), she made sure to cover all the bases. The corruption of youth? Check. Amoral decadence? Check. Missing white girl? Yahtzee.

But even Veronica had to admit that it was disturbing how little difference eighteen-year-old Hayley Dewalt's disappearance had made to the festivities. The news had hit that weekend: Hayley, down with friends from UC Berkeley, had been missing for almost a week. But you'd never have guessed it from the air of celebration hanging over the town. The bass pounded on and the beer still flowed freely. She wasn't sure what the reaction to one of their own vanishing into thin air should be, but the spring breakers' blind and blissful determination to carry on as if nothing bad could happen to them surprised even her. She wasn't sure she'd ever had that invincible, indestructible air, even when she'd been younger.

"And then there's this Keystone Kop sheriff."

That caught her attention. She turned the radio up a little.

"This Dan Lamb character? What a joker. Who goes on national TV in the post–Natalee Holloway world to say we shouldn't worry about a missing teenaged girl? I hope that the Dewalt family has a good lawyer on the books. A lawsuit might just get Lamb's attention."

A slow smile spread over Veronica's face. *Trish, Trish, Trish. We have so little in common, and yet suddenly I have a powerful urge to kiss you.* She'd been watching Lamb for the past few months, waiting for any opportunity to nail him to the wall—but if he kept this up, he'd do it himself.

The video Veronica had sent to TMZ had started the

ball rolling, of course. She'd caught Lamb on tape talking about the Bonnie DeVille murder case, saying, "I don't care if Logan Echolls ain't the guy. America thinks he's guilty and that's good enough for me." That little snippet had hit the airwaves hard. Lamb had an election in eight months, and for the first time his reelection was a less-than-sure bet. The town's wealthiest residents still supported him—Lamb looked after their interests, after all—but his approval ratings had taken a nosedive in the past few months.

"Let's listen to this guy's statement when the press finally cornered him Friday afternoon," Turley continued.

The sound quality changed—wind crackled against a cheap recorder. Sheriff Dan Lamb's voice was calm, but there was no mistaking the hint of impatience.

"We are definitely on the lookout for Miss Dewalt, but as far as we can tell there's no evidence of foul play. At this time we are not conducting a criminal investigation, nor are we conducting a missing person search. Look," he said, his voice rising over the sudden murmur of a crowd. "This happens every year. Kids get separated from their friends. They overindulge, they forget to check in, and everyone panics. Then they turn up a few days later, safe and sound. There's absolutely no safety problem here in Neptune."

Some part of Lamb must have realized it was a bad idea to answer questions off the cuff about a missing girl, but he had a pathological inability to turn down media attention. It clearly ran in the family. His brother, Don—who'd been the sheriff when Veronica had been in high school—had been cut from the same cloth. And now Lamb's sound bites had been playing on repeat through the weekend, making

Neptune's Sheriff's Department look cavalier and incompetent.

The traffic started to move again. Veronica eased the car forward, narrowly missing two girls who stopped in the middle of the street to light each other's cigarettes. They both held up their middle fingers in perfect unison. Veronica cheerfully flipped them off in return, then took a right toward Neptune's Warehouse District.

The redbrick building that housed Mars Investigations had been a brewery at the turn of the twentieth century, but in the past decade it'd been subdivided into lofts and offices. Veronica was still getting used to it—back when she'd worked as her dad's receptionist in high school, the office had been in a modest commercial district, surrounded by bookstores and Chinese takeout joints. But when the '09er, an exclusive new nightclub, opened just down the street from their old location, rent had shot through the roof, effectively gentrifying her dad's one-man operation right out of the neighborhood. Rent here was more manageable.

Though if she didn't land a good case soon, it still wouldn't be manageable enough.

The Mars Investigations logo—a modified Eye of Providence with horizontal lines across the triangle—hung over the door to the walk-up, etched in glass. Veronica climbed the creaking stairs. The place had an old-building smell, dry and dusty and warm. At the top of the landing she pushed through the double doors to the outer office.

The room was neat but shabby. Light streamed through the blinds, falling in long bars across the floor. The walls were a deep taupe shade that took on a brooding tone in the shadows—the color had been picked for its cheapness rather than aesthetic qualities. A thrift-store sofa sat beneath the hallway windows, a dusty rubber plant in the corner. Across from their color copier, a fish tank burbled quietly.

Cindy Mackenzie sat at the reception desk, watching Trish Turley on the biggest of the three monitors on her desk. Mac's short shock of brown hair fell over one eye, and a slouchy gray sweater hung off one narrow shoulder. Veronica and Mac had been friends since their junior year at Neptune High. They'd been drawn together by Mac's hacking skills, but it was their mutual misanthropy that had sealed the deal.

Mac looked up as Veronica shrugged out of her leather jacket, hanging it on a coat rack by the door. "Morning, boss."

"Boss?" Veronica widened her eyes. "Did I start *paying* you?"

"No," Mac said, her eyes darting back to her screen. "But it's also not really morning."

"I think thousands of spring breakers would disagree with you," Veronica said.

"Touché."

A few months earlier, Mac had left a secure job at Kane Software to work with Veronica at Mars Investigations. The pay at Kane had been great, but the job itself was a little too bland for a self-proclaimed digital outlaw. Finding new and creative ways to dig up dirt for Veronica's clients was much more her speed. The title they'd been tossing around had been "technical analyst," but at this point it seemed mostly philosophical—the caseload had been dry for weeks, and the few gigs they'd had had been completely lowbrow. Cheating spouses, fraudulent insurance claims, due-diligence investigations. Things Veronica could easily have managed by herself.

"Did you see Neptune made the news?" Mac nodded at her monitor and turned up the volume. Turley's enormous hair filled the better part of the screen, a stiff blond bouffant that didn't budge when she moved. The woman's eyes blazed as she spoke, enunciating every word with righteous indignation.

"I'd like to encourage anyone who can to donate to the Find Hayley Fund. If this sheriff's not going to find her, it's up to us, viewers."

"The fund is up to nearly four hundred thousand dollars, and it's only been open a few days," Mac said.

Veronica whistled. "Well, Trish Turley may be an opportunistic parasite thriving off our broken criminal justice system. But she sure can throw a booster sale."

She sank down into the threadbare couch and rested her head back against the wall. "Next year, let's go somewhere for spring break, Mac. Anywhere college kids aren't puking. Someplace with no booze."

"Next year, spring break in Tehran. I'm booking it now," Mac said, not even looking up from her computer. "How's your dad?"

"Good. The doc says just a few more weeks and he can do some light-duty work. He can't wait to get back in here."

"Catastrophic injuries are wasted on some people." Mac shook her head. "If I'd ruptured every single one of my organs, I'd be milking it for everything it was worth."

Veronica stared at a long crack that zigzagged like a constellation across the ceiling. She distantly realized she'd have to call the landlord about it. But talking to Sven about the shitty roof would necessitate talking to Sven about the rent, which was three days late. She exhaled loudly and closed her eyes.

"You may have noticed that another Friday has come and gone, and your bank balance is nonetheless unchanged," she started.

Mac cut her off. "It's okay, Veronica. I know things have been tight."

Veronica opened her eyes and smiled weakly. "Mac, I'm so sorry. This isn't how I imagined any of this."

"Hey," Mac said chidingly. "We both knew there was a chance it wouldn't work. Look, I've already started looking around for another paying gig. Just to cover my bills, you know? And I can still come in as, like, a consultant next time you need me." She gave a lopsided grin. "Of course, my prices are double for consulting."

"Of course." Veronica smiled, but inside she was cringing. It wasn't just that she was letting Mac down, but on top of that she worried there'd never be another case complicated enough to require Mac's technical savvy. She'd worked for her dad long enough to know the truth about the PI game—for every high-profile case, for every Sherlock-level puzzle, there were a hundred boring, petty cases. And she was barely scoring the latter.

Was this really what she'd chosen? Over New York, over a corporate law job where she'd be pulling in six figures— *before* bonus time? Well, at this rate it wouldn't last much longer. Unless something changed, she'd bring Mars Investigations—and all her father's work—crashing down around her.

As if on cue, the door swung open. In walked a woman

with chestnut curls flaring out from high cheekbones and a light wool suit tailored to fit her ample curves. Her stiletto heels rang sharply against the floor as she strode forward. She moved with heavy, almost sultry grace. Her dark, velvety eyes made a circuit of the room before finally coming to rest on the couch where Veronica sat.

"I'm looking for Keith Mars," she said. "I need his help."

CHAPTER THREE

Veronica struggled to her feet, mentally swearing at the sagging couch—there was no way to stand gracefully. She ended up doing an undignified little hop to catch her balance.

"Mr. Mars is actually on a leave of absence right now. I'm covering his caseload." She held out her hand, and the woman hesitated for a moment before shaking it. "I'm Veronica Mars."

"Petra Landros." Her voice was low and musical, with the faintest trace of an accent. Veronica sized her up quickly, a detached, calculating part of her brain rapidly punching numbers. Armani suit, Jimmy Choos, diamonds in the earlobes, diamonds on the fingers. Crow's-feet just starting to crease the corners of her eyes, but a body that was clearly the result of dark magic, Pilates, or severely restrictive undergarments. She looked vaguely familiar. Most important, she looked wealthy, like an opportunity to keep the lights on another week. Especially with Veronica's special sliding-scale rich-bitch rates.

Petra frowned. "I'm sorry, how long did you say Mr. Mars would be out of the office?"

"He'll be gone for the next few months." Well, he wouldn't be in any shape to go peeping through windows before then, so it wasn't a complete lie. "But let me reassure you that we are committed to delivering the same excellent service that we've always provided to our clients, even in his absence."

"And by 'we,' you mean . . . *you*, right?" Landros gave her a skeptical look.

Veronica had seen that look before—especially from female clients. It usually meant she was about to lose a job. Back when she'd been an amateur, the fact that she didn't look the part had been an asset. It kept people off their guard, gave her freedom of movement. But now that she was the face of the operation, it was rapidly becoming clear that her petite frame and blond hair didn't exactly win the confidence of her clients.

A sudden flare of irritation shot through her. Before she could stop herself she gestured at the window. "You see the sign that says 'Mars Investigations'? Well, that's me. I'm Mars. So yes. I mean me."

Behind Landros, Veronica caught a glimpse of Mac pretending to hit her head on the desk. *Maybe we need to hire a people person,* she thought, her heart sinking slightly. But when she turned back, the woman looked amused.

"I know who you are, Ms. Mars. You're the woman who brought Bonnie DeVille's killer to justice. *And* you humiliated the sheriff on national television."

Veronica shrugged. "Lamb humiliated himself. I just made sure he got airtime."

Landros gave her a wry smile. "Yes, well, that's the attitude that makes me wish your father were available. From what I've heard, he's more . . . discreet. But the situation being what it is . . ."

Then a business card was in Veronica's hand, and she

had to fight to keep her jaw from dropping. Embossed along the left of the card was the red-and-gold logo of the Neptune Grand Hotel. Typed under Petra Landros's name it read, simply: OWNER. And that was when she realized why the woman was so familiar. Petra Landros, the one-time underwear model who'd married the premier boutique hotelier in Southern California. Veronica remembered seeing her pictured in the glossy magazines she and her high school best friend Lilly Kane once pored over by the pool, pouting in a diamond-studded demi-bra. For a few years she'd been the trophy wife Veronica had assumed her to be—until her husband had died in a tragic skiing accident at the age of forty-six. And then, to everyone's surprise, she'd taken over the company. At first the whole thing was treated like a bad local joke. But if Landros's feelings were hurt, she was crying her way to the bank. She'd not only increased the Grand's profits, she'd bought up a good chunk of the boardwalk and started construction on two new restaurants. Plus she'd elbowed her deceased husband's own brother off the board with a ruthlessness that would make Leona Helmsley blush.

In other words, Veronica's rates had just gone up dramatically.

"Why don't you step into my office?" Veronica gestured to the open door.

Veronica's office—*Keith's* office—was brighter than the outer room, with two large windows facing east and south. The walls had been painted a sunny yellow, and her father's model ships rested along the windowsills and on top of the filing cabinets. Landros walked ahead of Veronica, sitting down in one of the low chairs and crossing her long legs.

Veronica had just enough time to exchange baffled glances with Mac before shutting the door behind her.

"So, what can I do for you?" Veronica walked around the desk to sit in her father's low leather chair. Sunlight streamed through the big window behind the desk, catching every diamond Landros wore so that she glittered with each gesture.

"I'm actually here on behalf of Neptune's Chamber of Commerce. You may have seen the news this weekend." The woman pursed her full lips. "Our beloved sheriff has created something of a PR nightmare."

"You're talking about Hayley Dewalt's disappearance?"

Landros sighed. "Of course. We asked Lamb to keep everyone calm. Instead he managed to make us look like a town of callous sociopaths. And now Trish Turley has her teeth in the story, telling parents not to let their kids go to Neptune for spring break."

Veronica's eyebrows shot upward. "I see. So you wanted Lamb to downplay Hayley's disappearance, but not in a way that made it look like you care more about tourism dollars than, say, a teenage girl's life."

"You're really not a saleswoman, are you?" Landros raised one perfectly groomed eyebrow. Her chair creaked slightly as she shifted her weight. "Look, I won't bullshit you, Ms. Mars. My hotel and the tourism industry here in Neptune make almost forty percent of their total annual income during spring break. It's not a piece of the pie we can afford to lose. So yes, we want this disappearance handled with some delicacy. But that doesn't mean we don't also want to find Hayley."

Veronica leaned back in her chair, glancing out the window. Even from the comparative quiet of the office, she could hear the thrumming of car radios, the peals of shrill laughter, and sounds of breaking glass from the commercial streets a few blocks away. "It doesn't sound like you're losing too much business."

"A few city blocks of teenagers do not a spring break make," Landros said calmly. "This crowd is nothing compared to last year. We've had hundreds of cancellations over the weekend alone. That's not just hundreds of canceled rooms, but hundreds of drinks that won't be ordered. Hundreds of meals that won't be eaten. Hundreds of swimsuits and flip-flops that won't be purchased. Hundreds of scuba masks and kayaks and scooters that won't be rented. And every day Turley is out there telling parents that Neptune is unsafe, telling them their daughters will be kidnapped or raped or murdered if they set foot in the city limits."

"So you want me to . . . ?"

"Find Hayley Dewalt."

Veronica gave her a long, flat look. "Isn't that what the sheriff's office should be doing?"

Petra leaned forward, looking Veronica hard in the eye. "Do you honestly think Lamb will be the one to find her?"

"Does this mean the Chamber of Commerce is retracting their endorsement of Sheriff Lamb?" Veronica asked sweetly.

Landros pursed her lips. Veronica read the answer in the woman's face. Lamb, inept as he was, was just too handy for the COC to cast away. He looked after their interests too well. They'd fund his campaign even while hiring Veronica to do the real police work. To them, it was worth the expense.

"Will you do it?" Landros asked, avoiding the question.

Veronica listened to the roar of the crowd. Somewhere at the back of her mind, she could see Hayley Dewalt—the clean-scrubbed brunette whose face had been on every TV station since last week—and felt a sharp pang. She hadn't known Hayley Dewalt, but she'd known girls like her.

"My rate is two hundred an hour, plus expenses. I'll need a daily retainer of seven hundred for the duration of the case. If I find Hayley, I keep all associated reward money, in addition to my fee." Veronica's voice was hard and flat. She laced her fingers together in front of her chin.

She didn't have the luxury of examining her motivations too closely. If there was that much money at stake, the Chamber would pay. And if she could find a missing girl in the process of keeping her father's business open, even better.

They eyed each other across the desk for a moment. The light from the window caught on Landros's left earring, and for a moment it was so overwhelmingly bright Veronica had to blink. Finally Landros nodded.

"Not a saleswoman, but certainly a businesswoman." She smiled. "All right, Ms. Mars. You have a deal."

Veronica pulled a pen from the barrel-shaped holder on the desk. "What do you know about the case? Where was Hayley last seen?"

"At a party up on Manzanita Drive. None of the girls she was with seems to know whose house it was, but according to Lamb it belongs to a rental agency. He's supposed to be looking into who had it rented." She brushed a lock of hair behind her ear with a careless hand. "I've donated the main conference room of the Neptune Grand for the search efforts. We've also set up a website for tips and donations to help fund the search—you've probably heard Trish Turley talking about it. It's pulled in nearly a half million in three days, and it doesn't show signs of slowing down. We've siphoned off ten thousand dollars as reward money, so if you do find Hayley, there's an extra incentive for you."

"Where's her family staying?"

"I have them in one of the business suites. They can put you in touch with the friends who were with Hayley at the time."

"Have there been any tips yet? Anything credible?"

Landros snorted. "The usual disgusting pranks. If I had any particular faith in humanity, the messages I've seen come in from anonymous 'tipsters' would have shaken it. So far we've at least kept her parents from seeing them—we have volunteers filtering through the inbox." She adjusted a delicate bracelet on her wrist. "I've set up a meeting with Sheriff Lamb this afternoon. I'd like you to come."

Veronica tapped her pen lightly on the desk. "I'm not exactly his favorite person."

"Neither am I." Her smile was a tight, humorless curve on her face. "But you're technically working in tandem on this case, and I want to make sure it goes as smoothly as possible. Besides, he can bring you up to speed on the details better than I can."

She stood up. For a moment, Veronica could picture what she must have been like on a runway, hips pivoting to the beat of a cranked-up techno soundtrack, feather wings strapped to her back in a pure white spray. She fought a smile. This was a woman who'd figured out how to be fearless, even standing in her underwear.

Landros smoothed her skirt. "I need to get back to work.

Have your girl e-mail me the contract and I'll have it in your inbox by the end of the day."

"Of course." Veronica followed Landros to the front door and opened it for her. The woman paused for a moment, then turned to face her.

"Do me a favor, though, Ms. Mars. Please do try to keep a low profile on this. We want answers. Not theater."

Veronica smiled. "Understood."

They shook hands once more. Then Petra Landros was gone.

Veronica pivoted slowly around. Mac sat at her desk, her mouth hanging slack. Their eyes met, and Veronica couldn't help it. She grinned.

"Feel like working for Mars Investigations a little longer?"

Mac's cheeks flushed with dawning excitement. "We've got a case?"

"A big one." She strode across the room and leaned down on Mac's desk to look at her, face to face. "I'm going to need background checks on Hayley Dewalt's immediate family members, along with Hayley's phone records and e-mails for the past few months. But first things first. Where are we ordering lunch from today? Because I'm starving . . . and Neptune is buying."

CHAPTER FOUR

Later that afternoon, Veronica pulled up in front of the regal brick-and-sandstone entrance of the Neptune Grand. She handed the BMW's keys to a valet in a pillbox hat and pushed through the enormous revolving door.

The lobby glinted with brass and brocade, the low trill of a jazz piano wafting from the speakers overhead. The Neptune Grand had undergone some changes in the past few years—Petra Landros had built a gleaming tower on the north side of the courtyard, ten stories higher than the original structure, with a glass-sided elevator looking down over the luxurious gardens below. But here, in the "Old Grand," the lobby looked the same as it ever had, with cream-colored walls and marble surfaces. Veronica had spent the better part of her senior year in this place, first visiting her old boyfriend Duncan Kane in his penthouse suite and, later, Logan.

Reception wasn't nearly as busy as she would have expected for the Monday of spring break. A few girls with silk caftans draped over their swimsuits bounced out of the elevators, and a bored-looking boy wearing Gucci shades and a UCLA sweatshirt leaned against the reception desk, waiting for his key. The Neptune Grand wasn't generally spring break central—only the trust-funded would be able to afford a room there during peak season—but true to Petra's word, it felt strangely quiet.

Veronica took the elevator to the ninth floor, then followed the red-and-gold chevron-print carpet to room 902 and knocked softly. From the other side of the door she could just make out a female voice, low and muffled. After a moment the door swung open, and a woman stood in the doorway.

She was short and plump, wearing a UC Berkeley sweatshirt that was two sizes too big. Her hair had been dyed a brassy blond, but the roots—dull brown with a few threads of gray—were starting to peek out. Ruddy bags were stamped underneath her eyes, and her face had the moist, crumpled look of someone who had been crying too much. She gave Veronica a weak, tentative smile as she stepped back from the door.

"You're the private investigator?" Her voice was high-pitched, a little bit girlish. "I'm Margie, Hayley's mom."

"Yes. Veronica Mars. I'm so sorry for all you're going through, Mrs. Dewalt." Veronica stuck out her hand.

Margie looked at Veronica's fingers with a distant, wondering expression. Veronica was just about to let her hand fall awkwardly back to her side when Hayley's mother grasped it and shook her head. "I'm so sorry. I'm exhausted. Come on in."

The suite was laid out like a small luxury apartment, decorated in tones of gray and red. The central room was a combination living room and kitchenette, separated by a small round dining table. A tall, bearded man in a flannel shirt sat at the table, nursing a cup of coffee. He barely looked up when Margie led Veronica into the room, his eyes distant and red rimmed. Veronica recognized him as Mike Dewalt, Hayley's dad, from the press conference they'd held last week.

A young man, maybe twenty-two or twenty-three, slouched on the scarlet sofa staring at a plasma screen TV on the wall. He was thickset, with wide, muscular shoulders and the beginnings of a beer gut, his premature jowls bristling with unshaven growth. He held the remote against one knee but seemed engrossed in a nature program where a wiry British man stood hip deep in a muddy river describing the way a tigerfish stripped its prey of flesh. On the other side of the couch sat a gangly-limbed teenager, her mousy brown hair long and limp around her face. She seemed intent on a hole in the knee of her blue jeans, probing it carefully with her fingertips.

"The investigator is here," Margie said. Only her husband looked up and nodded briefly at her. "Miss . . . March, did you say?"

"Mars." Veronica stood next to the kitchenette island, taking in the room. "But please, call me Veronica."

She noticed a large digital picture frame plugged in at one end of the island. It cycled slowly through a number of pictures, one fading into the next. Small Hayley Dewalt, riding a pink bike up a driveway. A preteen version with braces on her teeth and greasy bangs flattened across her forehead. One of her playing flute in what looked like a church. Another of her, older, in a cap and gown for graduation. She'd turned into a pretty girl, with dark hair and a sunny, easy smile that struck Veronica as unguarded, vulnerable. *You've got to put up your dukes, kid,* she thought, though she wasn't sure if the advice was for Hayley—or herself.

"The investigator is here," Margie repeated more loudly. The girl looked up from the couch, then back down at her jeans. The young man on the couch didn't respond.

"Turn off the goddamn TV!" Mike Dewalt exploded, his voice furious and booming.

Silently, slowly, the boy lifted the remote and turned off the TV just as the nature program cut to a clip of muscular fish thrashing around in a feeding frenzy. The screen went dark.

For a moment the silence in the room had weight. Margie covered her face with her hands. Veronica noticed that her fingernails were painted Easter-egg blue, the polish chipped and cracked. Veronica pegged her as a classic, self-proclaimed "fun" mom, the kind who thinks of herself as her daughter's best friend. *Just like dear old Mom.* Veronica's alcoholic mother, Lianne, had been the same way before she walked out on their family.

When Margie pulled her hands away from her face, she seemed calmer, her breath slow and careful. She pointed to the couch. "That's Ella—she's Hayley's little sister—and my stepson, Crane."

Ella pulled her knees up to her chin. Crane straightened up and looked at Veronica, his dark hazel eyes taking her in.

Veronica placed her bag on the floor and sat on a small upholstered armchair facing both of them. "How are you guys holding up?"

"You know. We're worried about our sister." Crane's eyes darted toward Margie as she sat down in another chair catty-corner from Veronica. It might just have been his way of dealing with stress, but Crane's body was taut with pent-up energy. His knee jiggled up and down, and while he clasped his hands politely in his lap, the knuckles were white. "Well, she's only my half sister," he continued, "but I'm just as upset as everyone else."

Veronica pulled her notebook out of her purse and flipped it to a blank page. She clicked her pen a few times and then wrote: *If you have to say it out loud . . .*

She didn't really need to take notes—she had a memory for details that was at best useful·and at worst obsessive—but the little notebook was a good smoke screen during an interview. Too much direct eye contact made people nervous, cagey. This way they didn't feel overly scrutinized, which loosened up their tongues. Now she glanced up and tapped the tip of her pen on her pad.

"What can you tell me about Hayley? Anything you can share about her habits, her plans, and her personality might be helpful. I'm going to try to retrace her steps in the next few days, so the more I know about her, the easier that will be."

Margie Dewalt rubbed her arms as if to warm them, though the room was actually quite stuffy.

"She . . . she's a sweet girl." A small, fluttering smile lit her mouth and then was gone. "Friendly. Really social—she makes friends everywhere she goes. She's always been so easygoing, especially compared with her siblings." She glanced at Ella with a look that was more sad than accusatory. "Ella won't go to the mall with me anymore, says only losers do that." Ella drew in her breath audibly but didn't otherwise move.

Veronica jotted *out of touch* in her notebook. "Did she have a lot of friends?"

"Oh, yes. In high school she did. In college, I think she's

had a harder time." She pressed her lips together. "I've met a few of the so-called friends that she came down here with. Two of them are always hovering around the conference room pretending they're torn up about Hayley. But they didn't even realize she was gone until two days after they'd last seen her. If those were the best friends she had . . ." She shook her head.

"Do you have their contact info? I'd like to talk to them," Veronica said.

She nodded. "I'll get it for you."

"What about a boyfriend? Was she seeing anyone?"

Margie frowned a little. "I know she was dating—she sort of hinted at it. I don't think there was anyone serious, though. I mean, she would have told me if she were hearing wedding bells, you know?"

Would she though? Veronica looked up from her notepad. "Did you know she was planning to come down for spring break?"

The woman nodded. "Of course. I wanted her to come back to Billings for the week. I thought it'd be nice—she could see her old friends, spend some time with the family. But she wanted to come down here." She wiped at her eyes. "Well, I understand. She's eighteen. I can't expect her to come home every chance she gets. I sent her a little money. Told her to send me a postcard." She stared blankly into space for a moment. "I wonder if she did."

"Did any of you speak to her last week?"

"She texted Ella Monday night," Mrs. Dewalt said, looking quickly at her daughter. "Right, honey?"

Ella nodded but didn't look up. "She sent me a picture of her drink. It was one of those tall ones, with an umbrella."

She shrugged awkwardly. "We used to send each other random pictures of our food. It started as a joke, because she hated the food at Berkeley. I kept sending her pictures of Mom's cooking. She'd send me back pictures of whatever disgusting thing she had to eat."

"Did she say anything else?" Veronica asked gently. Ella just shook her head. Veronica cleared her throat awkwardly. "Was it like Hayley to go out a lot? Was she a . . . heavy partier?"

"Well, it's obvious from that picture that she was drinking," Crane pointed out. "She was probably drunk the whole time she was here."

"That's not Hayley, Crane." Mrs. Dewalt gave him a pale and wounded look.

"Oh yeah? You really think Hayley came down to drink Shirley Temples at Chili's and get to bed by ten p.m.? You've seen how the girls act down here. Wasted. Entitled. Stupid," he said bitterly. His nostrils flared.

Congratulations, Crane. You've just received the one-of-these-things-is-not-like-the-others award. The prize: a full background search and my undivided attention.

Margie's gaze shot toward him. "What difference does that make? What, are you saying she deserved to be . . . to go missing?"

"No, of course not," he said quickly, holding up calloused, stubby hands. He took a deep breath, his voice calmer. "But look, Veronica said she needs to get a complete picture so she can retrace Hayley's steps, right? I'm just trying to help."

"Hayley's a good girl." Margie sounded almost pleading. She looked on the verge of tears again.

Veronica set her notebook on her knee and glanced between them.

Crane seemed to hesitate, then leaned toward his stepmom. "If we want to find Hayley we need to tell Veronica everything we can about her. The truth is, Hayley's changed."

"She has not!" Margie whispered, but Crane continued as if he hadn't heard her.

"She came home at Christmas and she was like a different person. She was moody, you know? Coming in at weird hours, ignoring the rest of us, hiding out in her room. I don't know what was up with her, but she sure didn't seem to be happy." His voice was neutral, but Veronica thought she saw a vindictive gleam in his eye as he spoke.

Veronica glanced at Margie. Tears started down her face. She half expected Mike or Ella to go to her, to comfort her, but no one moved. "Did you notice anything different about her behavior, Mrs. Dewalt?"

For a moment Margie looked like she wanted to argue. Then she gave a helpless shrug.

"I don't know anymore," she said miserably. She put her hands over her mouth and closed her eyes, sobs rolling through her body like waves.

Veronica glanced around the room. Every few moments Mike would lift his coffee to his lips and take an absent sip. Ella looked like a creature huddled in a shell, hard and pensive. Crane kept jiggling his knee up and down. Behind them, on the counter, the digital frame showed a photo of Hayley at twelve or thirteen, her dark hair streaming from beneath her hat. She wore a softball uniform and stood with her arm hooked around her mother's neck. Margie flashed a peace sign at the camera, her hair cut with the same bangs as her daughter's.

A personality change at college? Not such a strange thing. Wasn't that what was supposed to happen? You left home and tried out new identities. Jocks suddenly took up clove cigarettes and went to art history lectures, buttoned-down valedictorians traded in books for bongs, until everyone got bored and tried something else. Then again, a lot of psychological disorders showed up in the late teens. Depression, bipolar disorder, schizophrenia. A real shift in behavior could have been a warning sign.

"Did she say anything specific that might lead you to think she was unhappy?"

Crane shook his head. "Not to me."

"And she didn't mention anything about her life in Berkeley that might explain it? Anything about school—teachers giving her a hard time, classes that were overwhelming?"

"That's what I assumed it was," Margie said, her voice choked. "But she wouldn't talk to me about it."

Veronica sat for another moment, pretending to write in her notebook. She wanted to give them another few beats to think about anything they'd seen, anything they'd heard. But nobody spoke. The only sounds were Margie's soft sniffles, and the air-conditioning kicking on. Finally Veronica closed the notebook and slid it into her bag.

"All right—Mrs. Dewalt, if you can get me those phone numbers I think I have enough to get started with. I'll leave you my card. You can call day or night if you think of anything that might be helpful."

Margie rummaged through her enormous quilted purse, emptying its contents on the counter while Veronica waited by the door. Crane had turned the TV back on. The host of the nature show was now describing how a canoe full of schoolchildren had capsized when a monstrous fish rammed against the hull. "There were no survivors," he said soberly.

Suddenly, Mike Dewalt looked up from his coffee. His eyes, nestled in swollen pouches of flesh, were light blue and surprisingly warm.

"Be careful out there." He took a shaky breath. "I don't care what that sheriff says. Someone in this town took my baby. And whoever did it is still out there."

He held her gaze for another moment, then looked down. Veronica's heart gave a lurch as Margie shoved a scrap of paper into her hand. A phone number was scrawled on one side.

"That's the cell number one of them left me. I don't know which one."

"Thanks." Veronica slid it into her wallet. "Hang in there. I'll be in touch."

Outside the room, she took a deep breath and glanced at her cell phone. It was nearly two, coming up on time for her meeting with Lamb. She was almost at the elevators when she heard footsteps behind her. She turned to see Ella Dewalt hurtling determinedly after her.

The girl didn't speak until she'd caught up with Veronica. Panting slightly, she jerked her head toward the terrace beyond the glass doors. "I only have a minute. Mom thinks I went down to get something from the vending machine."

Wordlessly, Veronica followed her.

The air on the terrace was warm and dusty, the tile beneath their feet sun baked. A glittering blue pool twinkled in a courtyard below, a handful of spring breakers floating on rafts. Ella pulled a pack of Camels out of her back pocket and lit a cigarette with shaking fingers. When she noticed Veronica watching her, she offered her the pack.

"Hasn't anyone ever told you those aren't good for you?" Veronica said, waving her off.

"Yeah, well." She took a quick drag and exhaled. "Neither is living in a two-bedroom hotel suite with your family."

"Has it been like this the whole time?"

"It's always like this." The girl leaned on the balustrade like it was too much effort to hold herself upright.

Veronica didn't say anything. Ella Dewalt looked brittle, nervous. She didn't want to push her.

She smoked in silence for a moment, carefully blowing her smoke away from Veronica. When she spoke, her voice came in a rapid tumble of words.

"Crane can be an asshole, but he's not exactly wrong." She exhaled loudly through her lips like a horse. "Hayley *was* weird when she came home at Christmas."

"Can you be a little more specific?"

The girl shrugged with a quick jerk of her shoulders. "She didn't tell me anything. She always treated me like . . ." She trailed off, and Veronica could hear the unspoken *like a child*. "I don't know. She didn't go out with any of her high school friends the whole time she was there. She just holed up in her room. And she pretended to be sick when it was time to go to my grandma's for Christmas dinner. Not that I blame her— that meal always blows." Ella made a face. "I overheard her fighting with her boyfriend on the phone a few times."

Veronica raised a brow. "So she *does* have a boyfriend?"

"Yeah, my mom means well, but she doesn't know half of what goes on in Hayley's life."

"Do you know her boyfriend's name?"

"Chad Cohan," Ella said promptly. "I've never met him. He goes to Stanford. I thought he looked like a tool in his Facebook pictures."

Veronica nodded slowly. "So what's the story with Crane?"

A cagey, uncomfortable look suddenly flashed across the girl's face. She glanced down at her hands as she spoke.

"I don't know," she said softly. "He was mad when Mom and Dad sent Hayley to school. She got a really good scholarship, but they're still spending a ton of money on it."

"Why does that make him mad?"

"He's been unemployed for ages." Ella scuffed her sneakers along the ground. "Last summer he asked them for money to start a T-shirt printing business. They said no. Since then he's been pissed. He thinks they're playing favorites, paying for her school and not his screen-printing stuff."

"Sibling rivalry is not pretty."

"Fucking tell me about it." She stabbed her cigarette out viciously against the bottom of her shoe, then pocketed the butt.

"Look, I have to ask. Is there any way Hayley would disappear like this on her own steam?"

The girl hesitated, then shook her head.

"I kind of wish there were. I wish she'd just show up and say, 'Sorry, guys, didn't mean to make you worry!' But there's no way. Not with Mom sending her panicked texts every single day. Not with . . ." Her voice faltered a little, but she steadied herself. "Not with me sending pictures of every single meal I've had in this suck-ass town. Mom's right. Even if she made some kind of mistake, she wouldn't do that to us."

She shoved her hands in her pockets and took a deep

breath. "I guess I'd better go back. Mom freaks out if I'm out of her sight for more than ten minutes."

She looked at Veronica for a moment. Her eyes were fierce and apprehensive at the same time.

"Are you going to find her?"

It was almost unconscious, the way Veronica's jaw tightened. The way her shoulders squared off, her fingers curling into fists. She hadn't realized it before that moment—before meeting Ella's eyes. But now she was sure.

"I won't stop until I do."

CHAPTER FIVE

The Balboa County Courthouse occupied a large sandstone building in downtown Neptune, fifteen or so blocks from the Grand. Its front steps were smooth and worn, power-washed daily to keep the city's grime at bay, though these days the Sheriff's Department was as dirty as they came.

She'd spent half her life haunting the Sheriff's Department. Her father had started as a deputy, and when she was nine, he'd been elected sheriff. She and her mom used to visit him on lunch breaks and, in later years, she did her homework in an empty interrogation room while eavesdropping on the dispatch. After Lilly Kane's murder, when a recall election had ousted Keith from office, when she should never have had to set foot in that cesspool again, some invisible path always seemed to lead her back. Visiting Logan or her friend Weevil Navarro in lockup. Prying information out of the too-adorable-for-words Deputy Leo D'Amato, now a detective down in San Diego.

Reporting her own rape, and then being laughed out of Don Lamb's office, humiliated and aching.

But that was ancient history, right?

She made her way down the familiar hallway, decorated in shades of terra-cotta and gold, and turned into the Sheriff's Department. No one manned the tall wooden reception desk. Three or four officers sat at their desks working on computers or talking on the phone. She didn't recognize any faces. Her father had told her that when Dan Lamb took over, the handful of worthwhile cops left on the force had taken early retirement or transferred elsewhere—along with Inga, the kind-hearted woman who'd been the office manager since Veronica was a little girl.

She stood at the desk and waited. No one appeared to notice her—or maybe they just didn't care. One guy seemed to be swiveling his chair away from her as he talked on the phone. No surprise there—she was persona non grata around the Sheriff's Department. The first thing she'd done when she'd gotten back to town was solve Bonnie DeVille's murder right out from under the sheriff's nose.

Dan Lamb wasn't the type to forgive and forget. Then again, neither was she.

She caught sight of a tall man in departmental khaki, walking past with his arms full of files. "Excuse me. Sir? I have an appointment with the sheriff."

When the officer turned to face her, Veronica blinked.

"Norris Clayton?" Veronica's voice was breathless, shocked.

The man's warm brown eyes flickered over her face and his lips curved up. "Veronica Mars. I was wondering when I'd run into you."

For a moment they eyed each other warily. In middle school Norris had been suspended nearly every other week for fighting. By high school, he'd donned the trench coat and combat boots required for discontented youths—and had a weapons collection to make his scowl this side of terrifying.

For a while, he'd been suspected of calling in bomb threats to the school, but Veronica had been able to prove his innocence. Beneath his trench coat and fuck-the-man attitude, Norris was just a regular misfit with a Japanese weapons obsession—and, as it turned out, a crush on Veronica.

Now he was barely recognizable, muscular and clean-cut in his crisp khaki uniform. But something in his eyes was just the same—brittle, both wary and resigned. Like the world was just bullshit, all the way down. Veronica couldn't imagine that working at the Neptune Sheriff's Department would help that feeling.

Norris set his paperwork down on the desk and rested his hands on top. "You still working for your dad?"

"Kind of. More like tentatively with. Or perhaps in spite of?"

Norris's lips curled up into a smirk. "Yeah, well, my dad is just glad I have a job."

Veronica could only imagine. Norris's dad was a law-abiding programmer at Kane Software. He'd once bribed his son with a trip to Japan if he'd stay out of trouble and keep his grades up. "I have to admit I never quite imagined you as an upholder of the peace."

Norris gave a quick snort of laughter. "Yeah, well, we all have to grow up sometime, right?" Then he shrugged, suddenly serious. "I was pissed off about everything for so long. I guess I found a place to put my fight. Anyway, what are you doing here? You out here working a case?"

Veronica gathered herself. "Kind of. I have an appointment with Lamb."

"Lucky you."

They looked at each other for a moment, and then, at the same time, both broke into grins.

"This way." Norris opened the little gate next to the desk and jerked his head back toward Lamb's office.

In the hallway outside the sheriff's office, her eyes darted unconsciously at the Fallen Heroes wall. That was where they hung the photos of all the cops who'd been killed in the line of duty. Down at the bottom was the most recent—Deputy Jerry Sacks, his mustache glossy and perfect in immortality. His picture was hung next to Don Lamb's. She stared at both for a moment, complicated feelings fighting inside her. Lamb had made her life a living hell in high school, but she'd also come to suspect that he'd grown up in an abusive home. It was that same old vicious cycle: the Lamb boys were bullied; they became bullies. And while she'd never thought of Sacks as anything but Lamb's gofer, his desire to help her dad investigate the Sheriff's Department is what got him killed in the end. Now Lamb and Sacks were both gone, and something oddly like grief twisted in her gut.

"What's *she* doing here?"

She turned to see Sheriff Dan Lamb staring at her through his half-open door. Petra Landros sat across from him, her long legs crossed, an impatient grimace on her face. Veronica exchanged glances with Norris, then stepped inside. Lamb's office was dim and wood paneled, with a map of the states on one wall and an American flag in the corner.

She smiled sweetly. "Nice press appearance last week. Your hair looked *great*."

They stared at each other across the desk. Logan had once told Veronica she didn't have any flight—just way too much fight for her own good. Now she felt her hackles rising as she looked at Lamb. At his smug leer; at the way he leaned back in his chair like a toad on a choice lily pad, just waiting for nice fat flies to fall in his mouth. He was in his early forties, tall and fit, with the mildly fussy air of a man vain about his looks. His face was boyish, with a wide, sullen mouth and round cheeks, and he wore his hair in a sleek mane around his ears. Most unsettling were his eyes—the same bright blue as his dead younger brother's.

Don Lamb had been lazy and inept, a bureaucratic tool, and Dan wasn't much better. He allied himself with the powerful and preyed upon the weak. She had reason to believe he was strategically redistributing evidence—just two months earlier a Glock 9 mm had been planted on her friend Weevil Navarro's unconscious body after Duncan's mom, Celeste, shot him, and while she couldn't prove it yet, she was almost certain the sheriff—or one of his cronies—had planted it on him. And according to public defender Cliff McCormack, Weevil wasn't alone. If there was a dollar to be made, the Sheriff's Department happily bent the law for the highest bidder.

"Close the door, please, Ms. Mars." Petra Landros gestured for her to come in. Veronica shut the door and sat down at a second chair across from Lamb. His eyes tracked her closely. She kept her movements casual, almost dismissive, but she felt the tension in her arms and legs, like bent springs poised to snap.

Petra turned to look at Lamb. "The Chamber of Commerce has decided to hire Ms. Mars to work the Hayley Dewalt case. I'd like for you to catch her up on any details you have so she can get started."

"You have got to be kidding me." An ugly flush swept through his cheeks. "Ms. Landros, there's no need—"

"I've already made up my mind on this, Lamb." Petra's face was cool, her voice firm. Her smile widened slightly.

"Come on, Dan. With the upcoming election, don't you think you've got your hands full enough already? The Chamber is invested in another Lamb administration in the Sheriff's Department. We need you to focus on doing what you do best—keeping the town clean and the riffraff off the streets."

The subtext was so obvious even Lamb couldn't miss it. *If you want to keep your funding and your endorsement, you'll play nice.* Veronica wished she had a camera to capture the particular shade of violet Lamb's cheeks were turning.

His eyes flashed toward Veronica with unadulterated loathing, his mouth twisting wildly as if he was fighting to keep it shut. After a long moment, he grabbed a thin manila file folder and thrust it across the desk at her.

"Let's get one thing straight," Lamb said as she opened the file. "You're here to assist in an investigation. Not to run it. You're in my house now, Mars. I set the rules."

She flipped through the folder. There was nothing other than the initial missing person's report filed by Hayley's friends two days after the party. No notes, no transcripts, no records.

She looked up with a raised eyebrow. "This is it? Is one of your rules to *not* interview people?"

Lamb gave her a condescending sneer. "What else do you want, a *Family Circus*–style map retracing her steps? We took her friends' statement and logged it in the system. There wasn't anything else *to* do. There's absolutely no evidence that anyone took Hayley anywhere against her will. If there were, we would have followed it."

"Did you check out the house she disappeared from?"

Lamb flicked his hair back. "First of all, just because that was the last place her friends saw her doesn't mean she disappeared from that house."

She stared at him incredulously. "So your argument for not checking the last place she was seen is that it's just the last place she was *seen*? Nice. Very thorough."

Something flitted across Lamb's face and was gone. Then he shrugged. "My people are already spread thin. I've got most of my guys down by the boardwalks making sure kids don't drown in their own puke. We don't have the manpower to look under rocks for drunken sorority girls."

Veronica gave him a withering look but didn't say anything. She could ask for more—for the rental agreement for the house where Hayley went missing, for information on the owners, for the deed—but it'd be just as easy for Mac to access that. Not to mention faster, and one less time she'd have to talk to Lamb. All kinds of wins.

"Anything else we need to discuss?" she asked, looking at Petra. The hotelier was already on her feet, threading her arm through her purse strap.

"I don't think so," she said. "I realize you don't have much to work with. Please call my office if you need anything at all—my assistant has been instructed to put you right through." She gave Lamb an icy smile. "I want Hayley Dewalt *found*, Lamb, and I expect you to assist Ms. Mars in any way she requires." With that, she strode out the door.

Lamb looked up at Veronica, the color fading from his cheeks, his eyes narrowed to slits. She looked back at him steadily, unflinching, waiting for him to speak first. Watching the sheriff take his medicine from Landros had been fun—but she knew a humiliated Lamb was a dangerous Lamb.

After a long moment, he leaned back in his chair again, but this time without his former swollen smugness. He jabbed his index finger toward her. "I want to hear everything you find out. You don't take a fucking step without reporting it to me, you understand?"

"So, the work is beneath you . . . until you want to take credit for it. Is that it?" Veronica shot him a contemptuous look and stood up. "Look for me under a rock if you're curious. I'll let you know when I find Hayley Dewalt." And with that, she slammed his office door and left the station.

CHAPTER SIX

The number on the scrap of paper Margie Dewalt had thrust at Veronica turned out to belong to a girl named Bri Lafond, one of the three girlfriends who'd taken the bus down with Hayley from Berkeley. Veronica called her from the courthouse parking lot to ask if she could meet that evening. The eager, anxious voice on the other end told her that one of them—Leah Hart—had been taken home by her parents the week before. "She was really upset," she said. "But Melanie and I are still here. We'll tell you anything we can."

They were staying in the Camelot Motel. The sun-bleached building was surrounded by pawn shops, storefront churches, and bars so divey even the spring breakers didn't bother—which meant it was one of the only places the girls could afford after their spring break reservations ran out. Veronica had spent more caffeine-fueled nights outside the motel than she liked to recall—it was a favorite for the kind of trysts that resulted in shattered prenups, messy divorces, and broken hearts. Read: a home away from home for an enterprising young PI.

At just after seven, she knocked on the door to their room. From the other side of the blinds she saw the reddish glow of a table lamp.

The girl who answered the door was short and muscular and luridly sunburned. Her strawberry blond hair hung in an uncombed tangle around her face, and a small silver stud winked from one nostril. She peered out around the edge of the door with startled woodland eyes.

"Hi," Veronica said gently. "I'm Veronica Mars. Are you Bri?"

The girl hesitated, as if she had to think about her answer, then nodded. "Hi. Yeah. Come on in."

Veronica stepped into the drab, cramped little room. Two full-size beds were shoved against opposite walls, the faded floral coverlets made from the same material as the curtains. The décor was thrift shop Americana: a painting of ducks taking flight from a lake hung adjacent to one of a small cabin releasing puffs of smoke into a wintery sky. Clothes covered the floor, and an unwashed, sweaty odor mingled with the smell of old takeout.

A second girl sat on the far bed, but she stood up when she saw Veronica. Her long dark hair was looped through the hole in the back of a beat-up Dodgers cap. She wore a hoodie and a pair of denim cutoffs, but her curves were obvious even under the baggy clothing.

"Hi. I'm Melanie." Her voice was husky but even. She held out a hand for Veronica to shake. She glanced around the room, then gestured wryly to the bed. "Sorry we don't have a chair to offer you."

"No problem." Veronica sat down on the edge of the bed. Bri locked the door and leaned against the chipboard dresser. She chewed on the corner of a fingernail. Melanie sat cross-legged on the other bed, leaning toward Veronica, an intense, focused look on her face. Both girls were a stark contrast to the bright, careless spring breakers on the beaches—they looked ragged edged and tired, more like kids who'd just finished finals than like kids at the end of a vacation.

"So you guys stayed in town to help with the search?" Veronica flipped her notebook to a fresh page and jotted down the date and their names.

They both nodded. Melanie twirled a lock of brown hair around a finger, coiling it so tight the tip of her finger was bone white. "Yeah. We've been handing out flyers at the boardwalk." She took a piece of green paper from a stack on the nightstand and held it up. Hayley's senior portrait beamed out from it.

"No one even cares, though." Bri's voice was so soft Veronica had to strain to hear it. Her lower lip trembled a little. "We hand them out to people and they take them. Then they just crumple them up and throw them on the ground a few feet away. No one cares that she's missing."

The words swiped at Veronica, and she flinched. She suddenly realized that this was Bri Lafond's first lesson that people sucked. Veronica remembered that letdown, the way the world suddenly seemed stripped of bright colors, your beliefs toppled like dominoes. She'd learned it when she was sixteen, after Lilly was murdered and Keith, sniffing out the cover-up but not the truth, had gone after Lilly Kane's rich, handsome father. Keith was recalled as sheriff, and suddenly she'd found herself not only friendless but a pariah. Her friends circled their wagons around the Kane family, and Veronica spent the better part of the year scraping spray-painted expletives off her locker and replacing her slashed tires. And for a while, no one had raised a finger to stand up for her.

That had changed, of course. She'd made peace with some of her old friends—Duncan. Meg. Logan. And she'd found new, fierce ones in Wallace, Mac, and Weevil. She'd come out of it stronger, smarter.

But that didn't mean it hadn't hurt.

"Do you think Hayley's okay?" Melanie asked, bringing her back to the messy little room.

"I don't know." Veronica took a deep breath. "The last thing I want is to give anyone false hope. I'm going to do everything I can to find your friend, but I need your help. Can you walk me through the last night you were with her?"

The girls glanced at each other, and then Melanie spoke.

"I was on a sailing trip with a bunch of other Berkeley kids, but we got a text from Hayley at seven that she'd heard about some party up the coast. We all met up at the motel—we were at the Sea Nymph last week, closer to the beach—and got ready together. It was a black-and-white party, so you had to wear—"

"Black or white to get in." Veronica nodded. "Sure. Somewhere Truman Capote is spinning in his grave."

"Who?" Bri cocked her head like a curious spaniel.

Veronica shook her head. "Never mind. Where were you that afternoon, Bri?"

She bit her lip. "Me and Hayley and Leah lay out on the beach for a while, but Hayley got bored and told us she wanted to wander around. We weren't in the mood, so she went off on her own. A few hours later she texted us about the party."

"How'd she seem that night while you guys were getting ready?"

"She was fine," Melanie said, picking at the pilled fabric

of the bedspread beneath her. "Normal. She told us some guy had invited her and said she could bring as many girls as she wanted if they were as cute as her." She rolled her eyes. "She always eats lines like that up."

"Did she say anything else about this guy? Did you bump into him at the party?"

Again, that subtle exchanged glance.

"She didn't say anything else about him. And the party was kind of . . . *crazy*. If Hayley bumped into him, we didn't see it. We were sort of out of it." Bri took a deep, shuddering breath.

"Okay. Let's talk about the party." Veronica looked down at her notebook, where she'd jotted the address from the police report. "The address you gave the police was 2201 Manzanita Drive. Is that right?"

"Yeah," Melanie said. "It's a huge place, right down on the beach. A mansion. We showed up around ten. They had security guards at the gate doing pat downs and bag searches—it was kind of intense."

Veronica frowned. Plenty of Neptune's wealthier families had security precautions—cameras, alarms, the works—and it made sense for someone planning a Gatsby-esque blowout involving crowds of unknown people to hire some extra guards. But what kind of person required a pat down for a party?

"Did you meet the host?" Veronica asked.

"Well, no one ever came up to us and introduced themselves." Melanie shook her head. "It wasn't that kind of party. The place was packed. I mean, there were bartenders and waiters going around with drinks, and more security guards inside, but no one who was, like, obviously in charge or anything."

"From what we heard, there's a party at the house every night during spring break," Bri said. "A couple kids we talked to had been a few times already."

"Okay. So what did you do once you got there?"

"We . . . I mean, we partied." Melanie's eyes, so eager and so intense just a moment ago, darted away toward the window. "I danced for a while. There was a bonfire on the beach. I played a little pool. You know. Party stuff."

Veronica glanced from one to the other, then set down her notebook on her thigh. "Okay, I get that some of the 'party stuff' might not be the kind of thing you want to write Grandma about. But the more I know about what happened that night, the better my chances of finding Hayley. I promise, I'm not here to bust you. I just want to help your friend."

Bri's cheeks were an even deeper pink than before, clashing horribly with her hair. She stared at the ground, eyelashes drooping with shame. But Melanie turned her gaze suddenly and firmly back to Veronica. She was blushing too, but her expression was steady, determined.

"Look," she said. "The thing is, neither one of us remembers a whole lot about that night. We were both pretty wasted. We don't even remember how the hell we got home. And before you tell us it was stupid and selfish to get that fucked up, trust us. We already fucking know."

"Sheriff Lamb didn't believe that Hayley was missing," Bri said, her voice barely more than a whisper. "We thought if we admitted we were drunk and high it'd be worse."

Veronica crossed her legs. "Okay. Why don't we focus on what you *do* remember. What was Hayley like that night? Was she as drunk as you guys were? Was she talking to anyone specific?"

Bri grabbed a rhinestone-encrusted iPhone from the top of the dresser and started swiping her thumb over the screen. After a moment, she held the phone out to Veronica. "She spent a lot of time with *this* guy," she said.

The picture on the phone was of a buxom, scantily clad brunette draped across a boy's lap—a far cry from the clean-cut photo of Hayley on the missing person flyers.

Veronica held it up to see it more clearly. Hayley was in a short white dress with a plunging neckline, one spaghetti strap sliding down her shoulder. Her eyes were heavily made up, making her look older than she had in her senior portrait, and a delicate pendant in the shape of a birdcage hung in the shadow of her cleavage. She looked up at the boy through heavy lashes, a small, sensual smile turning up the corners of her lips.

The boy was college age, dark haired, his posture the image of casual grace. His angular, sculpted face ended in a gently cleft chin, a lazy smile hovering around his mouth. One hand rested lightly on Hayley's hip, and he watched her with undisguised hunger.

"You get a name?" Veronica looked up at Hayley's friends. Both of them shook their heads.

"No. But Hayley spent the whole night all over him. There are more pictures," Bri said.

Veronica scrolled through. One showed the two of them pressed tight together on the dance floor, Hayley's legs between the unknown boy's. Another showed her whispering in his ear, one hand on his chest.

"You took these?" she asked Bri. Bri's already pink cheeks darkened.

"She asked me to," she said, shrugging. "I took them with her phone, actually. You're looking at her Facebook page.

She put them up that night." Bri fidgeted with a gold bangle bracelet at her wrist. "I mean, she seemed to be having a really good time. We were happy she was on the rebound."

"On the rebound?"

"Yeah," Melanie broke in. "She and her boyfriend, Chad, broke up the week before spring break. She almost didn't come with us. She'd been in her room crying her eyes out for a couple days."

Veronica sat up a little straighter, the words jabbing sharp and sudden into her brain. "Why'd they break up?"

"They got in a huge fight over the phone when she told him she was coming to Neptune for spring break," Melanie explained. "He goes to Stanford and his spring break is two weeks past ours—he didn't want her running off to Neptune unsupervised. Whatever, they've broken up about five times this year. We were all hoping it'd take this time, but none of us had much faith."

"Not a fan of Chad?" Veronica raised an eyebrow. Melanie just rolled her eyes.

"We told her time and time again she should get rid of the guy. He's a creep. Controlling, patronizing. He'd tell her what classes to take and didn't want her to party without him. He didn't like her hanging out with us. He thinks we're trashy," Melanie said.

"We *are* kind of trashy," Bri cut in. Melanie flipped her off. A beat later, both girls laughed. It sounded too high pitched, right on the edge of hysteria, but when they'd settled down they both looked a little calmer.

"Anyway," Melanie said, taking a deep breath. "We were all kind of rooting for this guy at the party. He was the anti-Chad."

"But if he had something to do with her going missing . . ." Bri's voice trembled. "I mean, if he was the one who . . . who took her, or whatever . . ."

"Did you see them leave together at any point?" Veronica asked. Both girls shook their heads.

"But like I told you," Melanie said, "that night is pretty hazy."

Veronica looked at the phone again. The photos had been uploaded to Hayley's Facebook at 11:57 p.m. on the night of the party. If what Ella said was true and Hayley and Chad's relationship had been mercurial at the best of times, it seemed likely that in the wake of their breakup Hayley was making damn sure Chad saw just how much fun she was having.

Veronica pulled up an e-mail Mac had sent her an hour ago with Hayley's phone records. Throughout the day there were a bunch of texts to her friends and one to her sister. Then at 12:13 a.m., she'd received a phone call from a number registered to Chad Cohan that lasted exactly fifty-three seconds. There was no activity after that.

"Has anyone spoken to Chad since Hayley went missing? Did anyone call him to let him know?"

Melanie gave a humorless bark of laughter. "Oh, he called me. Told me it was my fault Hayley was missing because I was the one who lured her down to Neptune. I told him if he was so worried he should come down, help us look. You know what he said?" She adopted a lilting, smug voice. "'She's not my responsibility anymore, Melanie. She made that abundantly clear.'" For a moment, she looked angry; then all at once her face crumpled. Her eyes went shiny with tears, and her lower lip started to shudder. "But he's kind of right. I mean, we were supposed to look out for each other.

We talked about checking in twice a day on the way down. And we just . . . *lost* her."

Bri hurried to the bed, sliding an arm around the other girl's shoulders. Melanie twitched beneath shallow sobs.

A motorcycle growled on the street outside. From the room next door Veronica could just make out the murmur of a television. She leaned across the gap between the beds, resting her forearms on her knees.

"Melanie, if someone did hurt Hayley—they're the *only* ones responsible." Veronica's voice was low and urgent. "And if that's what happened, I'm going to find them. And I'm going to make them pay."

Melanie looked up at her from under her baseball cap, eyes wet with tears.

Veronica stood up and handed the phone back to Bri. "Do me a favor and send me copies. None of the pictures on the flyers show what she looked like the night she disappeared. It might be useful to circulate them." She shouldered her bag. "I'm going to ask around about our Mystery Man. In the meantime—if you two remember anything else about that night, call me right away."

The girls nodded. Melanie hesitated, then carefully disentangled herself from Bri and got to her feet. She straightened her cap, then held out her hand to shake Veronica's.

"We will. We promise." She opened the door, wiping fiercely at her eyes with her free hand. "Thanks, Veronica."

In the parking lot, Veronica dialed Mac.

"How hard do you think it'd be to hack into the databases of a major research university?"

Mac hesitated. "Since you're asking me on a cell phone, in front of God and the NSA—impossible."

"Okay, fair enough. Look, I need to go home and check on Dad, but do you think I could come by your place later? I've got some, uh, overtime work for you. It might be a long night."

"OT, huh?" There was no mistaking the excitement in Mac's voice. It'd been a while since she'd had an excuse to take her skill set out to play. "Sounds fun."

"In the meantime, can you get me on a flight to San Jose tomorrow morning? And I'll need a car. Something sensible." She thought about it for a moment. "Not too sensible, though. I need to represent the Neptune Chamber of Commerce in style."

"Give a girl a BMW for a few weeks and suddenly she's got standards."

"See you tonight."

The moon crested the skyline as she pulled the car out of the parking lot. It'd been a week to the day since Hayley's disappearance. Now hundreds of innocent kids like Hayley were pouring out into the streets for another night of drinking and debauchery, oblivious to just how cruel the world could be.

CHAPTER SEVEN

An hour later, Veronica sat in front of the computer in her bedroom, fingers flying over the keys. Logan's face grinned crookedly from the corner of his most recent e-mail—it was the picture she'd set as his contact photo, taken right before he'd deployed.

I wish you could have seen Lamb's face when she told him I had the case. He looked like he'd just swallowed a bug, she typed. *It would have made your day.*

Keith hadn't been there when she arrived home at the little blue bungalow. He was most likely out for a walk. The muscles in his leg needed to be strengthened, so he'd taken to circling the block a few times a day, slowly, deliberately, his cane tapping lightly against the concrete. He was wearing away at his convalescence with the same patience, the same resolve that made him a good detective.

Veronica's room—until recently known as "the guest room"—was decorated with a mélange of high school artifacts and the odds and ends her father had shoved in there before she'd moved back. One of his model ships sat on the dresser, between old photos of her as a little girl. All of her old books—Salinger, Plath, Toole, the literature of choice for the brooding outcast—were lined on the small wooden bookshelf. It was a little surreal to be back under her father's roof after all this time—but maybe a little comforting too. With all the changes she'd made, all the things in her life that didn't make sense, she kind of liked the sight of her old panda alarm clock perched on her desk.

She'd just hit Send on her e-mail when the familiar Skype chime came singing out her speakers. She gave a little start.

It was Logan.

She clicked Accept, and his image filled the screen. She could tell her picture wasn't coming in clear for a moment—he stared blankly at the camera for a few beats. It was a strange thing, watching him without his knowing. His long, vulpine face had a stillness she didn't usually see in it, pensive and expectant. His hair was short and spiky—he shaved it himself rather than letting the company barber mangle it month after month—and he wore a blue crewneck T-shirt, his off-duty garb. Just a few inches behind him was a steel wall. She could just make out the corner of some kind of inspirational poster containing eagle feathers and a flag.

Then, all at once, a grin broke across his face.

"Hey," he said, his voice soft.

"Hey," she said, smiling. "This is a nice surprise." Usually they had to plan their Skype dates weeks in advance, and then there was still the chance he'd miss them.

"I saw that you were online. I figured I'd take my chance." His eyes didn't quite meet her eyes—his camera must be a little off center. She felt like he was staring at her ear.

"What time is it there?"

They always started like this—awkward, banal. And by the time they got over the strangeness, it was usually time for one or the other of them to leave.

"Almost eight." He glanced to his left, speaking to someone off screen. "Ten minutes. Come on, please?"

"Someone's got a timer out, huh?"

"Yeah, it's okay." He turned back to her ear, smiling, and she wondered what part of her he was really staring at. Her eyes? Her lips? For some reason the whole thing—the way they could never quite sync up right—made her indescribably sad. "So Petra Landros. In your office. I've had that fantasy a few times, but it usually didn't involve a missing person case."

"She's not nearly as sexy in real life. That beauty mark?" She leaned in and lowered her voice. "It's really just a mole."

"Don't tell me that. Right now the 2004 Victoria's Secret Christmas catalogue is all I've got keeping me warm at night."

"Really? That thing must have seen some mileage by now."

"The seaman's life is one of privation," he said soberly. She smirked.

"How's the sinus infection? You still grounded?"

"For another few days. The flight doc says he'll clear me by the end of the week."

"I hate that news," she said softly. "You sneezing is you not on missions."

"This is the life I chose, Veronica." He said it simply, without irritation or anger. And she knew he was right. He'd joined the navy because he wanted to fly, because he wanted to do something that might stand a chance of helping someone. She of all people had to understand that.

He looked to his left again and sighed. "Yeah, okay. Sorry, man." Then he turned back to face Veronica. "I gotta go.

Hughes's wife just had a baby—he's got to be online at oh-eight hundred to talk to them."

"Okay. Tell him congratulations."

"I will." He looked at her for another long moment, his honey-brown eyes warm and sad. "You free this Thursday? Three thirty your time?"

"I can be for you."

He smiled. "It's a date."

She watched him for another half second, and then his screen went black.

For a few more minutes, she swiveled back and forth in her office chair. She tried to imagine the aircraft carrier—tried to picture Logan walking down the narrow halls, beneath pallid fluorescent lights. Tried to imagine him in the gym or the mess, surrounded all the time by hundreds of people in those cramped quarters. It was almost impossible. She closed her eyes. She preferred to see him on the beach in the early morning, his hair thick with salt, his board tucked under his arm as he trudged up the sand to meet her.

She heard the front door swing shut. *Dad.* Quickly she shook off her reverie and went out front to meet him.

He knelt by the door unlacing his sneakers, wearing track pants and a T-shirt.

"You're home! I've got news. But it can wait—I want to tell you over dinner. Say . . . steaks at O'Mally's? My treat?" She nudged him gently.

He shook his head. "No can do, honey. Wallace is coming over with a pizza. March Madness is under way." He walked toward the kitchen, cane thudding dully on the hardwood. She followed.

"Ah, yes, March Madness. The rumspringa of college hoops fans." She smiled. "Just don't strain anything yelling at the TV."

"I make no promises. San Diego State's playing Michigan. There's gonna be some yelling." He pulled a glass down from the cupboard, then paused to look at her. "So what happened today? It *must* have been crazy if you can suddenly afford a T-bone."

For a moment she hesitated. He'd been resisting talking about work since she moved back in, as if even acknowledging that she'd taken up the family business was tantamount to encouraging her. But there was a difference between crummy infidelity cases and the opportunity to find a missing girl. This was something he could be proud of.

"You know the Hayley Dewalt case? Missing girl, totally ignored by Lamb, current obsession of Trish Turley? Well, guess who's been hired to find her? Me! I'm heading to Stanford tomorrow to talk to Hayley's ex-boyfriend." She leaned back against the cabinets. "I met with her family today. They're pretty intense—I mean, they're obviously scared about Hayley, but there's also just something off about them. Especially her brother. He strikes me as kind of creepy."

Keith poured a glass of iced tea and replaced the pitcher in the fridge. "Oh yeah?"

She nodded, buoyed by his question. "Apparently she went missing from some party, but get this: no one seems to know whose party it was. The house is up on Manzanita. I mean, it's not like those are low-profile houses up there, so we should be able to figure out who was hosting and ask them some questions, right? I think Lamb knows something he's not telling me. He was doing that weird hair-slicking thing he does when he thinks he's hiding something. Oh, and her friends have pictures of Hayley the night she went missing, hanging all over this guy. No name, no information about him, but they look pretty cozy, and that was just hours before she was last seen. I'm trying to decide if I should ask around about him, or if I should keep that information close to my chest. I mean, I don't want to give him the chance to go underground if he gets spooked." She paused. "So what do you think?"

For a few seconds he stared sullenly out the kitchen window, his glass half raised to his lips. A frantic, scrabbling feeling filled her chest as he set the glass down with a firm clink on the countertop.

"Honestly?" His voice came a moment later, low and tight. "I think you're wasting your talent, your brains, and your entire life, Veronica. I think you should get on the next plane to New York and take the bar exam."

The words hit her like shards of glass from a breaking window.

"How can you call it a waste? We *help* people." She strode over to him, bracing herself against the island and staring him full in the face. "This is who we are. It's in our blood."

"You're treating it like something you have no control over, like you just can't help yourself." Keith's cheeks were flushed, his hand shaking. "But that's just an excuse for giving up on a chance at something better. It's childish, Veronica."

"Why don't you want me to be like you?" The desperate eagerness of a moment ago curdled in her stomach, pure and righteous anger replacing it. "Why is that such a shameful thing?"

"Because you could be safe!" he shouted. "Do you know what it does to me to think of you, out there, every day?"

She inhaled sharply. "Of course I do. How many times have I almost lost *you*? But for some strange reason, you keep going right back in. Like you *just can't help yourself.*"

The doorbell rang. Both Veronica and Keith froze where they were, faces tight with anger. She could feel her pulse, heavy as a drumbeat in her temples.

"That'll be Wallace," Keith said. His jaw was still rigid, but his voice was soft, almost sad. Veronica turned away.

"I'll let him in."

She could see her old friend through the glass door as she approached, a lean-muscled man in jeans and a San Diego State hoodie, an extra-large pizza box in both hands. He grinned when he saw her, that same easy, comfortable smile that had buoyed her in even her most bitter moods. She took a few quick breaths as she opened the door, trying to calm herself, but Wallace was not fooled.

"You all right?" he asked, the grin fading.

"Are you kidding me? A fine-looking man just brought me a pizza and I didn't even have to tip him. All's right with the world."

He tilted his head back to size her up, looking skeptical. Wallace Fennel had been her best friend since their junior year at Neptune High. He'd been the first person besides her dad she'd been able to trust after Lilly Kane's death. And he'd been able to see right through her bullshit from day one. But before she could say anything else her dad came in from the kitchen. "Wallace!" He pretended to waft the scent of the pizza toward himself. "And pizza!"

"Half Canadian bacon and pineapple, half Carnivore's Delight—pepperoni, hamburger, sausage, ham, and bacon." Wallace cracked the box open just a little and inhaled. "Topped with Mr. Cho's special recipe marinara and three kinds of artisan cheeses. And a side order of salad, because we're watching our figures."

"What do I owe you?"

"This time's my turn. You got the wings last time, remember?"

Veronica stepped back to let him in. "You guys have this whole hunting and gathering thing down pat, don't you?"

"Men gotta *eat*." Wallace nudged her playfully. "You watching the game with us tonight?"

"Um . . . no, I have to get over to Mac's. We're working late tonight."

His face lit up. "New case, huh? Anything good?"

She glanced furtively at Keith. He'd turned away and was already making his way back to the kitchen. "Um . . . yeah. The Chamber of Commerce hired me to find Hayley Dewalt."

Wallace did a double take, eyes widening. "Damn, that is a step up. So what's the problem then?"

She cleared her throat a little, glancing toward the door her father had just disappeared through. She heard plates clatter loudly in the kitchen. "We're not exactly on the same page."

Understanding dawned in his eyes. Wallace balanced the pizza box on one arm and wrapped an arm around her shoulders. "Yeah, well, he'll come around."

She didn't answer, but she leaned against him for a moment, feeling the vise around her chest start to loosen a little.

"Would you mind stopping by tomorrow, just to check in on him?" she whispered. "I'll be at Stanford until late. He should be fine, but . . ."

"Yeah, no problem." He squeezed her shoulder and then let go. "Say hi to Mac for me. I hope she gets to hack something good. Or . . . you know, whatever it is nerds do for fun."

"I think it involves pwnage." She grabbed her bag. For a moment she thought about going into the kitchen to try to make some kind of peace with Keith before she left. But what would she say? How could she apologize for who she was?

CHAPTER EIGHT

Veronica arrived on the Stanford campus just after noon the next day. The sky was cloudless, the blue a perfect contrast to the dark red tile roofs. College kids shot around on bikes or ambled past in little groups. A few sat on picnic blankets with books piled around them, taking advantage of the mild spring weather. The air smelled like grass clippings and earth, and she could hear the distant hum of landscaping equipment as the grounds crew made their rounds.

It was surreal to be back on the farm—she instantly snapped back into her old grooves, taking familiar routes through the corridors of the Mission Revival buildings that, for a while, had been her home. It almost felt as though she'd been gone for a very long summer break and returned to a newer, younger student body.

She glanced around, scanning the crowd in case she caught a glimpse of Chad Cohan's crop of reddish-blond hair. She hadn't called him ahead of time to set up a meeting; she wanted to surprise him. If he was as controlling and jealous as Hayley's friends described, she wanted to find out what she could about him before he had a chance to put his guard up.

Veronica and Mac had stayed up until 2:00 a.m. the

night before dredging up anything they could about him—his schedule, his grades, his extracurriculars. Anything that might give them an idea what they were dealing with. What they'd found had been a portrait of a high-achieving student, a clever, talented boy with plenty of advantages—according to his file his mom was the CEO of an outdoor clothing company in Seattle—and a fierce, focused drive. He was the star attacker of the lacrosse team. His grades were in the top 5 percent of his class. He'd just declared his major as political science, and he was in the process of applying for internships in Washington, D.C.

And, as luck would have it, he was taking a small social psychology seminar with Dr. Will Hague, Veronica's one-time academic advisor.

Hague's office was in Jordan Hall, a large sandstone building on the main quad. She felt another rush of nostalgia as she pushed her way through the double doors, the familiar dusty scent burning in her nostrils. She'd spent so much time in this building as an undergrad. In addition to fulfilling her prelaw requirements, she'd gravitated to psychology—it was comforting to crunch numbers from clinical studies and analyze data. It was a way to solve puzzles without all the mess and drama.

Hague's office was on the second floor. It looked the same as ever—copies of scholarly articles were tacked to the bulletin board outside, along with a hodgepodge of *New Yorker* cartoons, art postcards, and a single dry red maple leaf, broad and crumbling beneath the pin. The door was closed, and no light shone underneath. But Hague had a notorious habit of hiding from his students during office hours. She rapped softly on the door.

Silence answered. She stood there uncertain, waiting. Then she saw a shadow moving under the door. A knowing smile spread over her lips.

Gotcha.

"Dr. Hague?" she called softly. "It's Veronica Mars, one of your old students. I was wondering if I could speak to you."

For a long moment nothing happened. She started to wonder if she'd miscalculated. Maybe he wouldn't even remember her. The thought sent a surprising ache through her chest.

Then the door jerked inward, and Dr. Hague filled the entryway.

The first thing anyone noticed about Will Hague was his height, a perfectly ludicrous six foot six. He was beanpole thin, a series of jutting angles strung together with tweed like some academic scarecrow. An overgrown goatee hung from his chin, gray shot through with a few lingering strands of red. A startled, pleased expression lit his eyes when he saw her.

"Well, well," he said. "Veronica Mars."

"Hi, Dr. Hague." She smiled up at him. The top of her head was more or less level with his armpit. "Sorry to drop in like this. How are you?"

He checked his watch and grimaced. "I'd be fine if not for the faculty meeting this afternoon. If I have to sit for another hour listening to Hobbes drone on about the budget . . ."

Veronica grinned. In her time as his research assistant and occasional administrative aide, she'd helped Dr. Hague dodge more meetings than he made. "Tell them you've got food poisoning. Or . . . have you tried conjunctivitis?"

"Alas, Zhang threatened to send security to my office with manacles next time." He pushed his glasses up his nose with one finger. "But I have a few minutes before I have to slink my way over there. Come in."

He walked behind his desk and pulled open the blinds, allowing sunlight to fill the little office. Heavy books lined his floor-to-ceiling shelves. A blue-and-gold Rothko poster hung on one wall, his thirty-year-old Schwinn parked beneath. On the desk was a small pile of dark blue yarn. Hague was a compulsive knitter, sometimes even knitting straight through a meeting. He claimed it helped him think, and perhaps it did—he was one of the foremost research psychologists in his field. All Veronica knew for certain was that he was patently terrible at the knitting itself, the evidence clear in the misshapen sweaters and lumpy scarves he wore daily.

He sat down in his chair, pivoting back and forth a little. "So what brings you back to our beloved institution, Veronica? Last I heard, you were still in New York. You must be done with law school by now, yes?"

"Um, yes. I am." She sat down across from him.

"So, how's life as a big-time lawyer?" His voice dropped. "Or are you in Quantico now? I always suspected you'd end up with the Bureau, especially after the work you did with me on risk aversion in antisocial personalities. You've got exactly the kind of mind they need there."

Veronica gave a weak smile. "Well . . . I'm still working with antisocial personalities." She cleared her throat. "I'm actually working as a private investigator now. In Neptune."

Dr. Hague's surprise writhed around his face before settling into a confused smile. Veronica stifled a sigh. Why did every man in her life have to look at her like she was a personal disappointment?

"A private . . . well, that's interesting." He took off his glasses and made a show of cleaning them on the edge of his shirt. She could almost hear the gears turning in his head. Hague's background was in deviant behavior and psychopathology. Throw away a $150,000 education in order to track down deadbeat dads, bail jumpers, and philanderers? Didn't get any more deviant than that.

"Very interesting," he repeated, putting his glasses back on. "Are you . . . are you enjoying that, then?"

"I'm actually here on a job, Dr. Hague. And I was hoping to ask you a few questions about one of your students. Chad Cohan?" Veronica held up a photo she'd found of him online.

He blinked. "Chad Cohan? He's in my social psych class Tuesdays and Thursdays. A lacrosse player, right? He's the one who misses half my classes for away games." He snorted. "I'm supposed to pass him anyway. Apparently he's a big deal on the field."

"I take it you're not impressed?"

"Oh, he's clever enough. He does good work when he's in class—just turned in a strong paper on social cognition."

"But?" she prodded.

He hesitated. "What exactly is this about, Veronica? What do you think he did?"

She pressed her lips together for a moment, measuring her answer.

"I'd rather not say, Dr. Hague. I don't want to color your findings."

His face lit up in a sudden, brilliant grin. "Perhaps you

are in the right line of work after all." He picked up his knitting absently, winding the yarn around the needles. "Well, I don't know how much help I'll be. I only see him twice a week, at most. He's smart, a little full of himself. Frequently seems to have an entourage. His work is competent—he's making an A. He wouldn't be if I were allowed to dock him points for missing class, but . . ." He shrugged.

Veronica leaned forward a little. "Do you happen to remember if he was on time for your class on the eleventh of March? It was last Tuesday."

"My TA keeps a roster." Hague leaned over and picked up a canvas satchel that was propped next to his desk. He pulled out a jumble of paperwork, shuffling through until he found what he was looking for. "The eleventh? That was the day I asked everyone to hand in their lab reports. Yes, he was there." He held up the attendance roster to show her the neat little checkmark by Cohan's name.

"Did anything strike you as out of the ordinary that morning? Did he seem strained, or tired, or distracted?"

Hague frowned a little, trying to recall. Then he shook his head. "I honestly didn't notice anything like that. I'm sorry."

"No, that's okay. This is helpful." She smiled earnestly at him.

He cast a quick glance at his watch and made a face. "I hate to run, but I do have to get to this meeting or they'll release the hounds."

She shot to her feet. "Of course. Thanks so much for your time, Dr. Hague." She stuck out her hand, and he shook it warmly.

"Give me a call the next time you're in town. I'd love to catch up more."

"I will."

Back out in the balmy afternoon air, she took a deep breath, Hague's words ringing in her ears. Not what he'd said about Chad Cohan—but what he'd said about her. *Perhaps you* are *in the right line of work after all.* She hadn't realized how desperate she was to hear that from someone. The gratitude, and relief, she felt at his words was almost embarrassing.

But she didn't have time to dwell on that now.

It was time to track down Chad Cohan.

CHAPTER NINE

Veronica found Chad as he left his three o'clock international relations class. She recognized him from his Facebook pictures—a tall, wiry boy with light hair, a sharply defined jaw, and wide, sensual lips. He walked for a ways in a small cluster of other students, all talking animatedly. Veronica wasn't close enough to make out what they were saying; she hung back, walking slowly but keeping Cohan in sight.

He broke off from his group as they passed the library. Veronica followed him through Canfield Court, where groundskeepers were blowing leaves off the walk, and then up another narrow street. In front of the New Guinea Sculpture Garden he paused to talk to a slender girl in a knit beanie before turning up the walk to his dormitory and disappearing through its wide double doors. Veronica found a spot on a bench outside and sat down, pulling out her phone and pretending to text. She wanted to give him a few minutes to get to his room and start to feel safe. Cohan liked to be in control. If she caught him off guard, he might reveal something he hadn't intended.

After about ten minutes, she stood up. She followed two girls holding hands up to the double doors; they swiped their passcard, and then, assuming she was a student too, held the door open for her.

"Thanks!" she chirped.

Mac had gotten Cohan's dorm number out of the Stanford databases—he was on the first floor, at the end of a dimly lit hallway. Veronica walked slowly down the corridor. A few doors were propped open with concrete blocks. Inside kids sprawled across their beds highlighting passages in enormous books or hunched at their computers, playing games. Music floated through the dorm from a dozen different places, Kanye West, Vampire Weekend, and the Indigo Girls weaving together a clumsy mashup. No one seemed to notice Veronica, or if they did they gave her brief, distracted nods.

Chad Cohan's door was decorated with clippings of his lacrosse wins. A few articles had pictures of him in his red and white uniform, hurling the ball toward the net, face obscured by his helmet. The whiteboard on his door was covered in doodles, well-wishes, and enigmatic bro-speak.

Good luck Chad-Chad! ☺

SPANK THE DUCKS
THIS WEEKEND!!

Where are you? ☹

Veronica took a deep breath and knocked softly.

A few seconds passed, and the door opened. Chad Cohan stood in the doorway, looking politely startled. His pale blue eyes flitted over her face, his brow furrowed.

"Hi, Chad." She offered up a disarmingly bright smile. "Sorry to bother you. My name's Veronica Mars. I'm assisting in the search for Hayley Dewalt, and I was hoping you could answer a few questions for me."

He blinked rapidly three, four times. Then he seemed to shake himself into action. "Of course." He opened his door a little wider to let her in.

The room was fastidiously neat. The bedspread was smooth and tight against the mattress, and the shelves were devoid of clutter—no toys or tchotchkes, no mementoes. A few framed nature prints in black and white hung on the walls, perfectly centered.

"Are you a police officer?" he asked, turning to face her. "I talked to the sheriff on the phone the other day. I already told him everything I know, which unfortunately isn't much."

"No, I'm actually a private investigator. I've been hired to assist with the case."

His face remained almost still, a mask of civil curiosity, but she thought she caught a flicker of skepticism as he looked her over.

Fine. Let him underestimate me. I can work with that.

"Do you have any new information about what may have happened to Hayley? I still can't get over that she's missing," he said, closing the door.

"Not yet." She moved slowly around the room, looking at the books on his shelves, the few framed photos perched on top of the dresser and desk. They showed Chad, smiling with friends and family in fancy restaurants, on the steps of Mayan ruins, outside the Paris Opera House. There was one of Hayley, sitting on a boulder and looking out over the ocean, her hair whipping in the breeze. Veronica picked it up. Chad stiffened almost imperceptibly, as if having a stranger handle his belongings physically pained him.

"Did you take this?" She held it up, baiting him. "It's great work. I'm something of an amateur photographer myself."

"Um, yeah." He moved closer to her, gently taking the picture from her hands and setting it back on the shelf exactly where it'd been, just as she suspected he might. "I did. Hayley was a great subject."

"She's a pretty girl." Veronica smiled as he gave the photo one more minute adjustment. *Textbook control freak with a side of OCD.*

He sat down on the edge of his desk. His long, slender fingers tapped a quick syncopated rhythm against the top. "Look, I want to help find Hayley, but I'm not sure what I can tell you. We actually kind of broke up before she went to Neptune."

Veronica gave him a wistful, sympathetic smile. Between the smiley faces and loopy handwriting on his whiteboard and the way Hayley's friends had described him, she guessed that Chad was used to solicitous female attention. "That's what I heard. And I'm sorry if this is painful for you. I didn't come to open up any wounds—I'm just trying to get a better sense of who Hayley was, what she was like. I was hoping you could help me fill in a few of those blanks."

He hesitated, then nodded. "Sure. Sure, if it'll help you find her. I'll tell you anything I can."

"Thanks." She held his gaze for a moment, then took her notebook from her purse, flipping to a blank page. "How long were you and Hayley together?"

"Five months, on and off." He glanced at the photo on the dresser, as if checking with Hayley's image to affirm this was right. "We met at a Hey Marseilles concert. I saw her across the room during 'Heart Beats.' I knew I had to be with her the second I laid eyes on her."

Veronica gave an *awwww, so sweet* smile, jotting down

romantic lead in his own imaginary movie in her notebook. "How often did you see each other? Berkeley's almost an hour away—I'd imagine it's not an easy trip to make when you're busy with school."

"She came down on the weekends. Sometimes during the week, if we weren't too busy, but weekdays we mostly talked on the phone."

"And when you got together, what kind of stuff did you do?"

He leaned back a little. His collar gaped, and for the first time she noticed a long scratch along his neck. It looked like the skin had been broken, but it was mostly healed now. *Interesting. Lacrosse injury . . . or something else?*

"We went to movies, to parties. She came to my games. We studied together sometimes. I was trying to help her decide what she wanted to major in—she kept talking about nutritional science but I thought she should take a wider focus, do biology or chemistry. I mean, why settle for nutritionist when you could aim for doctor?" He shrugged. "She had a tendency to sell herself short."

"Hayley's friends told me you guys fought a lot."

"Hayley's friends need to mind their own business." Color rose in his cheeks, his body tensing. "Look, we had ups and downs, obviously. But Hayley's friends were always trying to convince her to dump me. They caused a lot of problems between us—they'd put things in her head, give her crazy ideas about me. They told her I was trying to control her. Like they weren't?" He rolled his eyes. "Hayley can be really . . . innocent. She trusts people too easily. I worried about her a lot. She'd call me to tell me she was on her way to some frat party or some club, and I'd spend the whole night imagining . . . awful things."

"Is that why you broke up?"

His eyes didn't move from Veronica's. He hesitated for a moment, as if reading something in her face. After a moment, he nodded.

"I asked her not to go to Neptune. I tried to tell her what the scene's like—crazy. Depraved. *Dangerous*. She wouldn't listen to me." His eyes narrowed slightly.

"I take it you've been there yourself?" Veronica said wryly.

He shrugged. "I've been. Don't get me wrong, I like a good party as much as anyone, but that place gets wild as hell. I didn't like the idea of her down there. And I hate to say it, but I was right. She shouldn't have gone."

Veronica didn't let her expression change. She glanced down at her notebook as if reading from a list of questions, so he wouldn't realize how his words and body language guided the conversation. "According to Hayley's phone records, you called her the night she disappeared at twelve thirteen a.m. That was the first time you'd called her in five days, but prior to that you guys talked at least twice a day—and often as many as six times—every day for months. Can I ask what you talked about?"

His pupils flared, ever so slightly. When he spoke, his voice was even and simple.

"I wanted her back. Look, the night we fought, things got kind of . . . heated. I said some things I wasn't proud of. I'm sure she did too. After that I couldn't think about any-thing else for days. I was . . . mad, and ashamed, and just exhausted." The intensity of his gaze was unsettling. "Have you ever had a relationship that you knew wasn't working, couldn't work, would never work? But you just couldn't help yourself, because the way it didn't work was so damn good? That was me and Hayley. That was what we had."

Veronica looked down at her notebook to hide her uneasiness. His words needled her, working their way under her skin. Yes—she'd had that relationship. She'd had that relationship over and over and over. She'd broken a lot of things for that relationship—and now here she was, back in it again.

Chad paused for half a beat, then continued.

"Anyway, I'm assuming you've seen what she posted on Facebook that night. I freaked out when I saw the pictures of her with that other guy. So I called her. We talked for a few minutes. I told her I was sorry, that I'd do better. I asked her for another chance. She told me in no uncertain terms she wasn't interested." He raked his hand through his hair, the front pieces standing up in short spikes.

Veronica frowned. "You didn't happen to get a name, did you? Did she tell you who the guy was?"

He looked away. "She didn't say. She was more interested in telling me what a great kisser he was," he said bitterly.

Veronica sat for a moment, her mind sifting through the information, moving it from one column to the next. Sure—Chad Cohan might be a run-of-the-mill disgruntled ex, still reeling from the Sturm und Drang of a complicated relationship. Maybe it was worse than that—maybe he was as controlling and demanding as Bri and Melanie claimed. As controlling and demanding as Veronica read him to be now. That didn't necessarily mean he was involved in whatever had happened to Hayley. But something about him raised the hair on the back of Veronica's neck. She asked her next question in a carefully neutral voice.

"Where were you the night you talked to Hayley?"

He looked up quickly. She kept her expression unreadable. "It was midterms so I was in the library, working on a paper, until around twelve thirty. Then I went home."

"Did anyone see you there?"

A sudden cold smile broke across his face. It changed his looks with the rapidity of a flash flood—the blandly helpful demeanor vanished, replaced with an air of contempt.

"After ten p.m. you have to use your student ID to get in and out of the library. You can probably get those records from the school. I don't remember seeing anyone in the dorm when I got home I went straight to bed. But I was in an eleven a.m. class the next morning. Plenty of people saw me there." His words were matter-of-fact, derisive. "So unless you think I can teleport—no. I didn't drive overnight to Neptune to abduct Hayley. Sorry, this time the boyfriend didn't do it."

"Ex-boyfriend," Veronica said pleasantly. "Right?"

His smile didn't falter. "If I were you, I'd focus on tracking down the guy in the picture. Plenty of people saw him with Hayley. The whole *Internet* saw him with Hayley."

"That must have really made you mad, Chad," she said, trying one last time to goad him.

He leaned forward, his eyes boring into hers.

"No," he said simply. "It broke my fucking heart."

CHAPTER TEN

"So his alibi checked out?" Mac asked on Wednesday morning.

Veronica was back in the office, leaning against the color printer as it churned out copies. Mac sat on the edge of her desk a few feet away, her slender legs crossed at the ankles, her short hair falling over her forehead. Her coffee mug was printed in running lines of binary. Veronica was willing to stake a day's pay on the fact that it read something like "Hackers do it better" in code.

"Completely. According to the surveillance cameras he left the library at twelve twenty-six, and Professor Hague said he was on time for his eleven a.m. class the next day. There's no way he could have made it from Stanford to Neptune and back in that window, even if he was driving like a bat out of hell." She sighed. "Did you dig anything else up?"

Mac shook her head. "He didn't use any of his credit cards that night or the next day. And he didn't fly—or if he did, the FAA didn't know about it."

Veronica stared over Mac's head at the window. Outside, the bricks of the warehouses looked a brilliant red in the afternoon light. The truth was, she'd *wanted* it to be Chad. Between what Hayley's friends had told her about him and her own investigative Spidey-sense, he'd looked like a perfect suspect. She'd spent the whole evening at Stanford, questioning security guards and professors about him. She'd even talked to a few of his friends. One hulking boy with a nose that had obviously caught more than its share of lacrosse balls said he'd always told Chad not to "tie himself down" with Hayley. "He gets all caught up trying to imagine what she's doing. I'm like, man, the point of having a girlfriend on the other side of the bay is so *she* doesn't know what *you're* doing. Why are you making such a thing of it? Let the girl have her fun and just make sure you're getting yours." Another one of Chad's teammates told her it was obvious that Chad had been head over heels in love. "She was all he talked about. He sent her flowers every week. He took her on a couple crazy shopping sprees for new clothes and jewelry. I mean, I've never seen him lose his head over a girl like this."

Ah, true love. Who ever went wrong measuring it in dollar signs? But there wasn't any evidence pointing her toward Hayley's ex, and his alibi was airtight. There were no recent charges on his credit card, except for the aforementioned shopping sprees and athletic socks from the campus bookstore. It didn't matter what she thought of what sounded like a very Stella-and-Stanley relationship if it didn't get her closer to the truth.

"Well, I got some interesting returns on the background checks you asked for." Mac set down her cup and rummaged around on her cluttered desk for a minute before finding a plain manila folder that read DEWALT on the tab. She handed it to Veronica. "The first search didn't pull anything up, but I did a little creative digging."

Veronica flipped through the pages. "Crane Dewalt has a record?"

"It's a juvenile record, so it took a little extra work to find. The Montana Department of Corrections seals them when the offender turns eighteen. But their databases are, um, not that secure." Mac looked innocently out the window, and Veronica grinned.

"Underage intoxication. Shoplifting. Possession," she read. "All kid stuff. Until . . . oh, wow. Aggravated assault?" She flipped through the documents. At sixteen Crane Dewalt had attacked another kid with a bike chain wrapped around his fist. The victim lost two teeth—and the use of his left eye. Crane was sentenced to nine months in juvie.

"He's been clean since then. But he definitely has a temper. I've been going through his employment history. Looks like he was let go from a Kinko's after getting in a shouting match with a customer. He's been doing odd jobs for more than a year now."

"Interesting." Veronica closed the folder. "Anything in his recent history that might place him in Neptune the night Hayley disappeared? Credit cards, phone calls, flight records?"

Mac shook her head. "He has six credit cards, all in default. No savings. Twelve dollars and sixty cents in his checking account. So not a lot of traceable activity."

"If he works under the table, he might have a wad of cash, though. And freeing up some of his parents' income from Berkeley's tuition fees would be motive," mused Veronica.

Mac's eyes widened. "Motive? So are you saying . . . he killed her?"

"No, and that's the problem." Veronica frowned. "I don't even know what crime I'm investigating yet. And I won't until I piece together what really happened that night." She met Mac's eyes again. "What did you pull up on the party house?"

"Not a lot. It's a rental. Owned by a company called Sun and Surf, Inc." Mac frowned. "I'm still digging, but as far as I can tell that particular address wasn't rented out to anyone the night in question. According to their records, every single property they have is rented through the month of March. Every single property except that one."

Veronica was about to respond when loud voices on the stairwell interrupted her thoughts. She and Mac both looked up to see Wallace Fennel herding two teenage boys through the office doors. Neither one looked happy.

"This is blackmail," said one. He was a tall, dark-skinned boy with long, gangly limbs, a Lakers cap perched at a jaunty angle over his forehead. The other boy was shorter, with carroty red hair and a light smattering of acne over his pale face. He stared around the room in mutinous silence.

"You can't do this to us," the first boy said.

"Excellent," said Veronica, pushing up off the copy machine. "My assistants have arrived."

Mac looked at Veronica, one eyebrow raised. "Your what?"

"This one tried to bolt while we were coming up the stairs," Wallace said, jerking his head toward the first boy. "You'll have to keep an eye on him. Hey, Mac."

"Hi, Wallace. Why are you delivering urchins to our door?"

"Because I'm a helpful guy. Veronica Mars says she needs boots on the ground, I find her some boots." Wallace gave a lopsided grin, running a hand over the stubble of his goatee. "See, Coach Fennel knows all and sees all. I caught two of my best players in the Cabo Cantina with the worst excuses for fake IDs I've ever seen. In exchange for my clemency they're gonna help you out this afternoon."

The kid in the hat turned around to scowl at Wallace. "It's no fair. You can't give us detention for something that happened during spring break. We weren't even at school, Coach!"

Wallace gave him a pleasant smile. "You're right, T.J. I can't give you detention. But I *can* bench you for the rest of the season. Or—now, here's an idea—I could call your mom." A look of horror flitted over the kid's face. Wallace pretended to pick up a phone. "Ring ring. Well, hello, Mrs. Wiggins. I just wanted to make sure that T.J.'s allowed to drink three-foot piña coladas, right?" Wallace dropped his hand. "But see, I want to keep my point guard *alive*. So instead, I'm giving you the option of a few hours' work to pay your debt to society. Sound fair?"

The kid nodded, eyes wide.

"How about you, Quinton?" He turned to the redhead, who nodded too.

Veronica grabbed the stack of flyers off the copier and held one up. She'd arranged two pictures of Hayley on the page, both of them from the night Hayley went missing. One showed her on the dance floor, her hair suspended in midair as she moved. The other showed her curled up on a couch with the handsome stranger. Instead of the tip line, she'd put the number of one of Mars Investigations' dedicated phone lines across the flyer.

"I need you guys to hit the pavement for me. Put these up on lampposts, hand them out on the boardwalk, see if you can get them in shop windows. Especially in places where there are lots of spring breakers."

They both took stacks of flyers from her, their eyes darting over the pictures. They exchanged glances, and then T.J. looked up with an earnest and helpful expression on his face.

"Do you need us to interview people too? We can ask around, see if anyone wants to talk to us. You know, on the beach?"

Veronica gave him a piercing look before she answered. "You have my permission to talk to any bikini babe you want, as long as you get the flyers circulating."

"And as long as you are perfect gentlemen who do not make your coach or your team look bad," interjected Wallace pointedly. "Because your next not-detention isn't going to be this easy. Got it?"

T.J. looked insulted. "Hey, I don't need lessons on how to respect the ladies. I respect *all* the ladies. Skinny ones, medium ones—"

"Boys." Veronica clapped her hands. "Let's focus here. I need these to get out as quickly as possible. As an added incentive, if I *do* find Hayley, I'll give you a hundred bucks."

Both boys looked suddenly alert.

"Each?" asked T.J.

"Each," said Veronica. "So make sure you get these flyers posted in as many places as you can. This will only work if they get seen."

T.J. and Quinton turned to each other, strategizing in low voices—deciding where they could get the most flyers seen by the most people, versus where the hottest and least-dressed girls hung out. It seemed to be mostly T.J. doing the strategizing, with Quinton muttering "Yeah, yeah" every few seconds. Veronica turned to Wallace.

"Thanks," she said, handing him another pile. "You're a lifesaver."

"Can't say I planned to spend my spring break supervising teenagers," he said under his breath. "You owe me, Mars."

"Just add it to my tab."

He grinned. "So what are you guys doing tonight? Want to go get a few beers?"

"Tempting," Mac said. "But I thought I'd stab my eyes out with a spoon instead."

"Come on, it's not nearly as crazy out there as it was last year." He looked from her to Veronica. "If I'm going to be wrangling these kids all day, I'm going to need a little R and R, you know what I mean?"

An idea suddenly came to Veronica. A slow, thoughtful smile spread over her face. Wallace's eyes widened, and he leaned back a little.

"It scares me when you smile like that."

"Scares you? Wallace, come on. Don't you trust me?"

"Are you looking for the honest answer or the one where we stay on speaking terms?"

"All right, fine." She lifted up her hands in mock surrender. "I thought you were looking for some R and R, but if you don't want an invite to the party of the season, I can't make you go with me."

He gave her a wary look. "Party of the season?"

"Party of the century, if the stories are to be believed."

"Uh-huh. Veronica Mars, social butterfly? No one's buying it. So what's the catch?"

"No catch." She looped her arm through his. "But if we're lucky, we may just score some information on what happened to Hayley Dewalt."

CHAPTER ELEVEN

Manzanita Drive was a winding road that ran parallel to Neptune's northern coastline, surrounded on both sides by the dense foliage that cloaked the hideaways of the super-rich. A lot of the houses were vacation homes for movie stars, diplomats, and CEOs, though a few were permanently occupied—Logan's friend Dick Casablancas lived on the Drive, in a Cape Cod overlooking the Pacific.

Veronica had passed his gates earlier that night, when she'd gone to check out the house Hayley's friends had told her about. They'd said there were theme parties there every night, and from the aloha shirts and flower leis she saw as she drove by the crowd of waiting guests, it looked like tonight was a tiki party.

She'd run home after, hoping against hope there was something trashy and tropical at the back of her closet. When she emerged an hour later, she was wearing a skin-tight red sarong dress, purchased more than a decade earlier for the pep squad's annual luau-themed fund-raiser. She'd curled her hair in bouncy Marilyn ringlets and, as an after-thought, picked one of her dad's plumeria blossoms and pinned it behind her ear. When her father caught sight of her he did a double take.

"Hot date at the Tonga Room, dear?" Keith sat on the sofa, a battered paperback copy of *Get Shorty* in one hand. Veronica kissed him on the forehead.

"Don't wait up," she said, looping her arm through the straw tote bag she'd traded for her studded leather purse, then leaving to pick up Wallace.

Now they were waiting in the house's gated driveway behind a RAV4 full of college kids. Beyond the gate, through a copse of palm trees, she could make out the pulsing glow of a mansion. Laughter, shrieks, and the steady thump of bass reverberated in the cool night air. She angled the rearview mirror toward her and reapplied her lipstick.

"Think I can pass for a coed?" she asked, blowing a red kiss at Wallace.

"Do you really want me to answer that?" He was wearing an aloha shirt that belonged to Keith, procured on a Maui vacation a few years earlier. It hung off him, two sizes too big. He caught her grinning and narrowed his eyes. "I *know* you're just marveling that I can look this good in a Don Ho shirt."

"Hell yeah, I am," she said, rolling the car forward as the line moved up.

She could now see a cluster of dump-truck-size security guards standing in front of the open gate. Veronica watched as one by one the occupants of each car stepped out. One guard appraised the guests and decided if they were going in or not. If they got the nod, a second guard—or maybe just an incredibly muscular valet—would step up and take the wheel of their car while a third guard patted the guests down.

"What kind of party is this again?" Wallace stared at

the enormous security guards ahead of them, brows arched skeptically.

"That's what we're here to find out."

It was all very organized for a spring break rager, which led Veronica to believe that either the parties were some kind of marketing campaign—maybe put on by a party promoter who had a special deal with Sun and Surf, Inc., or an alcohol distributor launching a new product. Or, perhaps, the owner of the mansion had some very good reason to keep security tight.

A guard waved Veronica forward, and her heart sped up as she pulled up to the gatehouse.

"Evening. Can you both get out of the car for me?" He was polite and no-nonsense. *A professional, for sure. Maybe even ex-military?*

"Sure!" Her voice was immediately up a half octave from usual, with a buoyant, eager tone. She opened the car door and stepped out on her towering wedges, looking around wide-eyed. "This is so ah-MA-zing. Is this, like, a movie star's mansion or something? Oh. My. Gosh. Tell me it's Robert Pattinson's, because if it is I think I might die. No, wait, *don't* tell me."

The guard was a hulking man with buzzed hair and a squashed-looking nose. The buttons on his aloha shirt strained to contain his bulk. If he hadn't looked so exhausted, he might have been terrifying. His expression— long-suffering but patient—didn't move as he listened to her prattle.

One of the guards back by the gatehouse muttered something in Spanish she couldn't quite hear, his eyes traveling over her. The others laughed. Veronica waited, her eyes ingénue wide. All of them were packing heat—she could see the telltale bulges of their holsters under their clothes, the way they all angled their bodies gun side away. She felt a prick of unease in the pit of her stomach. She hadn't brought her Taser, a staple when she was on a job; after her drive-by earlier, she'd anticipated being searched. More than the thin, flimsy cotton dress that barely covered her torso, its absence made her feel strangely naked.

"So is there like some kind of cover charge? Do I have to buy a cup, or . . ." She trailed off, cocking her head at the guard. He was watching her with an unmoving expression, almost as if waiting out her monologue. On the other side of the car, Wallace gave her a nervous glance over the hood, his arms held stiffly out while another guard patted him down.

The two guards looked at each other. The one patting down Veronica took her keys right out of her hand and gave her a small red ticket.

"Okay, ma'am, here's your claim ticket for the car. When you're ready to get out of here just bring it back, we'll get it for you."

Veronica staggered to Wallace's side and looped her arm through his. "Thanks so much, guys! Come on, Wallace, let's *party!*" She let out a wild whoop, tugging him along up the drive.

He looked behind them. "Man, these guys are organized."

Organized, and armed. Her nerves felt white-hot and electric as they walked up the driveway. A full moon had come up over the bluffs and cast deep shadows across the lawn.

The house itself was lit like a beacon, every window

shining in the darkness. It was a sprawling modern structure of slate and glass, set right on the beach. She passed a few clusters of stray partygoers on her way to the door. A girl in a grass skirt and faux coconut-shell bikini top staggered across the lawn after her friend, yelling, "Come on, Heather, don't be like that!" Her coconuts had gotten knocked askew, but she seemed to be too drunk to realize she was flashing half the party.

The closer they got to the house, the more kids there were, laughing and sharing bottles of tequila, or passed out under palm trees. They stopped to make sure one boy, facedown in the grass, was still breathing, then rolled him on his side and left him there.

"Another sacrifice to the party gods," Veronica muttered.

At the porch they paused. She checked her watch. It was just after ten. "All right, time to go in. We'll cover more ground if we split up, but let's meet out front in, say, two hours. Text me if anything gets crazy, though, all right?"

"Sure, sure." He watched a couple of girls in Uggs and bikinis tumble out the door, laughing hysterically. He shook his head. "You know, I remember the girls being my own age at spring break. I don't want to be the creepy old guy. Remember Lucky Dohanic? 'Where's the party this weekend, guys?'"

"Just relax." She smiled, straightening his collar. "Try to have a little fun. And keep your eyes peeled for anything *weird*."

They pushed through the wide oak doors.

The entryway was a marble cavern, a crush of bared limbs and gyrating hips filling the space from wall to wall. Instantly, the mingled smell of boozy sweat and a hundred pungent colognes assaulted Veronica's nostrils. Girls in grass skirts and bikini tops pressed up against bare-chested boys in open aloha shirts. From the second-floor landing a DJ draped in koa bead necklaces played exotica lounge music, remixed with a heavy bass. A sudden spray of liquid flecked her exposed skin as someone popped a cork and dumped champagne over the crowd. A cheer went up.

She glanced at Wallace one last time. He shrugged, then joined in the cheering, throwing his hands over his head and pushing into the crowd.

Veronica turned and staggered toward the hallway as if drunk. She marked three surveillance cameras in the upper angles of the room, aimed down at the crowd.

Wonder if those come standard with all Sun and Surf's rental homes, or if they're special for this one?

The house was mind-blowingly lavish, even for Neptune. She passed through a music room painted in an eye-burning crimson. Guitars hung off the walls Fenders and Gibsons and Yamahas, in a dozen glossy shades of wood and polymer. A muscular boy in Bermuda shorts played Lady Gaga's "Born This Way" on a gleaming grand piano. A few doors down was a billiard room, cigar smoke hovering over the red felt tables as a crowd gathered to watch a long-limbed girl in tight jeans and a lei aim her shot. Then there was a small theater where *Spring Breakers* was showing. Popcorn and empty bottles covered the floor, and beneath the sound of the movie she could make out low moans from amorous couples.

Tiki torches burned on the back terrace. A luau-style spread was laid out across several buffet tables, including a whole pig with an apple in its mouth. A short flight of stairs

led down to an infinity-edge pool, choked with naked and
half-naked coeds. She watched as a boy with flapping blond
dreadlocks did a cannonball into the middle of a group of
girls. In the Jacuzzi, the traditional "Gone Wild" activities
were already commencing. Bikini tops were strewn across
the slate stones like so many dead fish.

All right, Veronica. Time to schmooze.

She got in line for the keg and filled a red Solo cup,
knowing she'd stick out without a drink. Then she staggered
a few lopsided steps right into the middle of a group of kids.

"Oh my gosh, I am so sorry!" She gripped the arm of
broad-shouldered guy wearing, of all things, a woman's muumuu and a Hawaiian straw hat. He steadied her, grinning up
at his friends.

"Hey, no problem. You okay?"

"Yeah," she said, slurring a little. "I've had so much to
drink!"

"Me too!" He lifted one fist to the sky. "Spring break!"

It was like some kind of hunting call. All over the patio
people stopped to lift their plastic cups or jump as high as
they could and yell "Spring break!" in response. She giggled
and held up her own cup, a half second too late. "Yeah, spring
break!" she shouted, leaning against the guy in the muumuu.

"So what's your name?" he asked.

"I'm Amber." She beamed.

The guy in the muumuu couldn't seem to track her very
well—he was almost as drunk as she was pretending to be.
"Where you from, Amber?"

"I'm down from UNLV," she chirped.

"UNLV?" he boomed. "Hey, Trang. Trang! You said you're
from UNLV, right? Do you know Amber?"

Trang, who'd done his hair in a Hawaiian Elvis pompadour and wore a crushed carnation lei, stared at her with red-veined eyes, swaying slightly on his feet. "Huh?"

"It's such a big school," Veronica cooed. "What's your major, Trang?"

"Undeclared," he mumbled. "Maybe econ."

"Oh, I'm in the history department." She stared around the little group, her hand still on the first guy's arm. "This is so *cray*. I've never seen a house this big in my life. Whose party is this anyway?"

They all shook their heads.

"Guy down at the boardwalk invited me," said Trang. "After I gave him some E."

"Yeah, I got the nod after the rap battle," said a skinny boy with plastic-framed glasses and a yachting cap. "Some kid with dreadlocks said I should come, that he liked my rhymes."

"So none of you know the host?" Veronica stared around the circle. "You just heard about it?"

"Yup," said the guy in the muumuu. "It's just, like, whoever throws the party sends a dude around looking for cool people. And if you're cool enough to be noticed, you get in."

"So awesome!" Veronica chirped. "But oh my gosh, you guys, did you hear about the girl who went missing last week? Someone in the pool room just told me she disappeared from *this* house. Isn't that scary?"

"Someone went missing?" The guy in the yachting cap looked startled. "I didn't hear that."

"Yeah, dude, her picture's on that billboard over by the Cabo Cantina? She's dead sexy," said the guy in the muumuu.

"She was at this party last Monday, and no one saw her after that," Veronica chimed in. "None of you guys were here that night, were you?" She gave an exaggerated shiver. "So scary!"

"Shit, no. Last Monday I was popping Adderall and studying statistics all night." He snorted. "Our spring break didn't start till Monday."

The feedback of a microphone interrupted their conversation. They all looked up to see a crowd gathered around a small dais on the lower deck, just to the left of the amoeba-shaped pool. A short, portly guy in a fedora and Hawaiian shirt stood on the dais. For a moment Veronica couldn't make out what he was saying over the crowd's catcalling. He held up his arms in a placating gesture, and the crowd noise died down.

"All right all right all right!" he shouted, pacing the length of the riser. "Let me hear you make some *noise!*"

Another cheer went up from the crowd. The guy grinned, pumping his fist in the air. "Spring break!"

"Spring break!" The call went up again, echoing up and down the terrace. "Spring break!"

"All right, we got a special treat for you all tonight. We've got five lovely ladies who are just dying to show you the tan lines they've gotten this week. And folks, you *know* how small some of these suits are." A round of hoots sounded from the crowd. "But first, let me introduce the judge. Here he is, your host tonight, Rico! Everyone give him a round of applause. Come on, now!"

The crowd screamed. Veronica stared. The man who'd just stepped on the dais was sharply handsome, with deep olive skin, dark hair, and a line of stubble along his jaw. He wore a pair of Bermuda shorts, and a lei draped across his sculpted chest.

It was the mystery guy from Hayley's pictures—the guy she'd been hanging all over the night she'd disappeared.

CHAPTER TWELVE

Veronica gripped the balustrade, staring at Rico. He grinned and waved at the crowd, his face lit up by the flickering tiki torches at each end of the stage.

Host of the party? He was young, college aged. Veronica had known plenty of superrich teenagers, so it wasn't a stretch that Rico was rolling deep enough to rent the place. But according to Mac's research, no one was renting. And there was no way this was an illicit squat—security was too tight, and apparently there were parties every night. Someone would have noticed by now. Did he *own* the rental company? Did his parents?

Up on the stage, Rico fanned ten crisp bills out with a snapping motion. He took the microphone from the emcee, a wolfish grin spreading across his face. "Just to show how dedicated we are to finding the best tan in Neptune, we've got a thousand bucks for our winner tonight. How do you like that?"

The crowd roared its approval. Rico gave the microphone back to the guy in the fedora and sat back in his chair like a spoiled prince on a throne.

The emcee paced back to center stage. "And now, if y'all are ready for it, we're gonna start the show. First up is

Aurora, from Tucson, Arizona. Aurora, why don't you show these people what you've got?"

An auburn-haired girl in a leopard-print bikini leapt lightly up on the dais and shouted a hello into the mic. Some burlesque-style music started up over invisible speakers, and she gyrated on stage, spinning in a slow circle. When her back was to the crowd, she shook her hips, looked over her shoulder, and suggestively pulled the waistband of her suit down, flashing her tanned backside at the audience. Then she untied her halter and spun back around, making the straps dance against her breasts. Tantalizingly, she lowered the triangles of her bikini top, revealing a pale patch of skin underneath. Rico whistled appreciatively and the crowd went wild.

"Take it off!"

"More!"

"Flash!"

"My cousin thinks he's a ladies' man."

The voice was deep and soft, close to Veronica's ear. She gave a little start and looked up into dark brown eyes, flecked through with greenish gold. The man was about twenty-six or twenty-seven, with dark, curly hair and broad, chiseled cheekbones. Unlike the other guys, dressed in loud floral shirts and flip-flops, he wore a perfectly tailored gray suit, no tie, and black loafers. Around his neck was a single lei made of purple and white orchids.

"Your cousin?" She smiled, cocking her head a little. From the suit, the smirk, the casual contempt for Rico's antics, she knew the drunken debutante voice wouldn't work with this guy.

"Rico." He nodded down toward the stage, where Rico

was on his feet now and dancing with the tan-line contestant. "Like a kid in a candy store."

"You don't approve?" she asked. She angled her body slightly toward him. Her heart beat fast, but she kept her movements composed.

"Oh, I don't mind at all. I love a good party as much as anyone. But Rico likes to play games, to make it a sport."

"And what do you like?"

"I just like to get what I want."

The way his eyes moved over her left no mystery as to what that was.

"I'm Eduardo," he said.

"I'm Amber." She glanced around the terrace, gesturing. "Is this your place? It's gorgeous."

"Thank you. I hope you're enjoying yourself."

"What's not to love?" She lifted her cup, then pretended to take a sip. "So what do you do, Eduardo? Besides throw amazing parties?"

"I'm a student myself. I'm doing my MBA at Hearst."

"Your MBA?" She laughed. "What do you need an MBA for? You already have everything an MBA could want."

He laughed too. "This? This is all inherited. I have to be able to stand on my own feet, to do my part. Otherwise it will all be wasted."

"That's . . . that's an interesting outlook." She frowned slightly. Not one she would have expected from someone who threw a high-end carnival every night of spring break.

"Family is important. This is how I honor mine."

Below, a fresh contestant was entertaining the audience with the stark white lines under her string bikini.

"What's your family's business?"

"Real estate, mostly. Some investments and the like." He waved his hand as if this was all too dull to speak of. "Tell me, Amber, would you be interested in walking down the beach with me? It's lovely this time of night—and we can speak a little more privately there than we can here." He drew closer to her. She could smell notes of sandalwood on his skin, as clean and expensive as everything else he wore.

Veronica smiled, calculating. Eduardo struck her as the type who might try even harder to get what he wanted if there was an obstacle in his way. "I don't think my boyfriend would appreciate that."

Eduardo looked around as if expecting to see this alleged boyfriend. "Oh, is he here with you? I didn't notice."

"He's inside, dancing," she said. "I came out to get some air."

Eduardo leaned closer, his breath warm on her neck. "You know, it's spring break. You're supposed to break the rules on spring break. And in my opinion, any man who'd pick a sweaty dance floor over your company probably doesn't deserve your attention."

She raised an eyebrow. "And it's *Rico* who thinks he's a ladies' man?"

He threw back his head and laughed. Below, on the dais, the women were lining up for the finale, posing like beauty pageant contestants. One suddenly whipped her halter off and shimmied, to the raucous approval of the audience.

From the depths of her bag, Veronica heard her phone chime.

"I'm so sorry, I have to check this," she said, rummaging in her purse.

"Of course," he murmured. She turned her back and took a few steps away, opening the message.

It was from Mac.

> URGENT. House belongs to Federico Gutiérrez Ortega and Eduardo Gutiérrez Costillo. Both students at Hearst. Both heirs to a Mexican drug cartel.

For a moment the shrieks and giggles around her seemed to mute, the colors to fade. She stared down at the phone.

Rico and Eduardo weren't just college playboys. They were cartel royalty.

"Amber? Is everything okay?"

All at once the world came rushing back. She looked up to see Eduardo, who'd moved in next to her arm. His eyes flitted down to her phone. She locked it and shoved it back into her bag.

She shook her head. "I'm sorry, Eduardo, I have to run. Something's come up."

He leveled his dark hazel eyes on her face. "I'm sorry to hear that. I hope everything's okay?"

"Yes, thank you." She smiled at him, her pulse throbbing in her temples. *Cocaine conspiracy. Human trafficking. Extortion. Kidnapping. Murder.* The words streaked through her mind. "Thank you for the party, Eduardo. It's been really fun."

She felt his hands close on hers again. His fingers were cool and slightly moist. He lifted her hand to his lips.

"I hope we meet again," he murmured.

Down below, Rico Gutiérrez Ortega danced with the girls on the stage. She gently retracted her hand from Eduardo's, then turned and half stumbled back through the double doors.

Wallace. She had to find Wallace. She called him, hands shaking, as she pressed her way through the crowd surrounding the snack-strewn kitchen island. The phone rang a few times and then went to voice mail. The party was probably loud enough that he couldn't hear it.

Where are you? she texted. She didn't wait for him to reply but started down the hallway in search of him. The crowd had gotten denser, more frenzied over the course of the night, and at five foot two she was at a disadvantage for seeing through it. She stood on her tiptoes, straining to see.

She passed a bathroom where a girl was crying in huge, racking sobs. In the billiard room three hulking guys were wrestling on the floor—she couldn't quite tell if it was in fun or not. There was no sign of Wallace. Her phone stayed maddeningly blank. She climbed the stairs to the second floor, where the hallway was slightly less crowded. Through an open bedroom door she saw a mass of writhing limbs on a king-size bed. In another, three kids sat around a lava lamp, jaws slack, while a fourth rocked herself on the bed.

Suddenly she felt a hand close around her wrist. She gave a little shriek and turned on her heel, her heart in her throat.

Wallace had come up right behind her. He jumped back just as she did, eyes wide.

"Breathe, woman!" He laughed, but he looked shaky. "It's just me."

People up and down the hall were looking at them. Most of them were partiers, but she caught sight of a tall, slender man in a Hawaiian shirt with a distinct lump beneath the armpit. Another, burlier and similarly armed, sat under a bay window, pretending to text on his phone. She caught his mouth tighten almost imperceptibly as he glanced at them.

"So much for a low profile," she muttered. She grabbed Wallace's arm. "Come on, we're getting out of here."

They wove their way through the crowd and to the door. It was just after midnight, and the party had reached critical mass. The acrid smell of spilled beer and sweat mingled throughout the house.

She gulped the cool night air as they stepped out onto the lawn. As soon as they were a few feet from the house, Wallace spoke in a low voice. "What happened?"

"I'll tell you in the car." She glanced into the bushes around the walk. "I'll drop you off before I head to Mac's. I think I'm working late tonight."

"I'll go with you." He looked over his shoulder. The house thrummed with light and noise behind them. "Veronica, those guards were armed. I saw one adjusting his piece. Whatever's going on in that house, it's serious . . . isn't it?"

She didn't answer, and he didn't seem to expect her to. They hurried the rest of the way across the lawn in silence.

CHAPTER THIRTEEN

"So, the guy was *right there* when you got my text?" Mac stared at Veronica in horror over the edge of her laptop.

It was an hour after they'd left the party, and Veronica and Wallace sat on the sofa in Mac's loft, describing what they'd seen.

Veronica nodded. "Yeah. I don't think he saw anything, but still." She sighed, taking a sip from her beer bottle and resting her head back against the couch.

Mac's apartment—rented in the salad days when she'd worked for Kane Software—was located in a sleek building just a few blocks away from Neptune's single art-house movie theater. It was sparely decorated: a dark red couch, covered in jacquard pillows, took up one wall, and a plasma-screen TV was mounted on the exposed brick opposite. Where most people would have put a dinner table, Mac had a high-tech ergonomic desk covered with monitors and computer equipment that changed height at the touch of a button. A half-dissected motherboard sat on the kitchen counter, surrounded by tools and chips.

Wallace frowned. "So these guys are, what, dealers?"

Veronica shook her head. "I don't think so. They're not soldiers—they're higher up."

"Way higher up." Mac sat in an overstuffed armchair, still wearing the flannel pajama bottoms and gray T-shirt in which she'd answered the door. Her face was pale and clean scrubbed but lit by an almost feverish glow. Mac was nothing if not an information junkie, and she'd spent her whole night digging further and further into the Gutiérrez family dynasty. *This* was what she'd been hired to do—not to man the phones or even to do the business's IT, but to dig. And no one was as good at it as she was.

"So here's what I've found so far. Both Eduardo and Federico were born in TJ. Eduardo's parents own an import/export firm. Federico's dad—he's a widower—owns some dude ranch in Rosarito, down on Baja." Mac frowned at her screen. "Looks like both cousins went to boarding school in Switzerland. Now they're at Hearst. They have clean records, in the States and abroad. They're listed as the owners of Sun and Surf, Inc.— they have a whole string of luxury vacation rentals along the coast. Their houses go for as much as ten thousand a night."

Wallace whistled. Veronica took another swig from her beer, the cold, bitter taste waking her up. "So other than blood ties, there's no obvious cartel connection."

"Well, I'm not an accountant, but there's a ton of money moving through the coffers. I don't know, maybe that's normal for this kind of business. But it seems a bit over the top."

"So it's a front?" Wallace asked.

"If it's a front, it's a good one," Mac said. "They have Yelp reviews and everything. And last year there was a blurb in *Condé Nast Traveler* calling the houses 'exquisite.'"

"There was a horse ranch in Oklahoma that got busted last year for the same kind of thing," said Veronica. "It looked totally legit. They trained racehorses, had a breeding program, and paid their taxes. They also happened to be funneling money through for the Zetas."

Wallace shuddered. "Man, I saw something about those guys on the news a couple months ago. Scared the hell out of me."

"Well, brace yourself," Mac said. "Eduardo and Federico's paternal uncle is Jorge Gutiérrez Trejo, aka El Oso, aka La Muerte Negro. Currently one of the DEA's most wanted. He's been in charge of the Milenio Cartel in Baja for almost twenty years. Again, I'm not an expert on these things, but twenty years is a long time. Most of the major cartels have gone through some kind of takeover or have splintered off into rival factions. Not the Milenios." She looked a little queasy. "And he hasn't stayed in charge by being a nice guy."

Veronica stood up and went behind Mac's chair, looking over her shoulder at the screen. What she saw sent her blood cold. Mac had pulled up a rap sheet detailing a list of El Oso's alleged crimes. In the last decade, as the cartel wars steadily escalated in scope and violence, his people had been connected with a spate of butchery across western Mexico—bodies of rivals had been hung from streetlights or bridges with warnings tacked to their chests. Known hangouts of other cartels had been shot up, bombed, even gassed. In September of last year, someone had left thirteen severed heads prominently in a bin of soccer balls in the Estadio Caliente, Tijuana's biggest soccer stadium. No one had been charged with the crime, but all of the victims were from the Sonora Cartel, which had been jockeying for position on the Milenios' turf.

And while the Milenios used the worst of their torture and bloodshed to send a message to their rivals, they weren't above using it to get what they wanted out of civilians who had nothing to do with the drug trade. Gutiérrez's men took anyone from poor farmers to wealthy college students for ransom, killing anyone who didn't pay up. There were stories too of women who'd been kidnapped from their homes and sold into slavery or prostitution.

"Well now," murmured Veronica. "I wonder if they expanded their trafficking operations to Neptune."

Mac looked up at her.

"You think they'd take an American citizen?" Wallace asked.

"Not likely. These guys aren't stupid. They wouldn't want to risk bringing the FBI down on their operations," Mac said.

Veronica started to pace. "You're right." She ran her hands through her hair. The curls had almost entirely fallen out by now, the flower bent and oozing a sickly sweet perfume. "Okay. What about this? What if Hayley saw something she wasn't supposed to at the party that night? What if she, I don't know, overheard a conversation about illegal activities? Or saw something that could be used against them in court? They might have thought they *had* to get rid of her."

"Get rid of her?" Wallace's forehead creased. "You think . . ."

"I don't know," she said grimly. "But if Hayley somehow made herself a liability, they might have decided killing her was worth the risk."

Silence descended on the room. Veronica went and stood by the window, looking out over the street. The traffic signal flashed red. A skinny cat wove its way between garbage cans. Otherwise, nothing moved. According to her watch it was almost two.

"We should go to Lamb with this." Mac's voice was slow and measured, but Veronica heard the strain in it. "We should tell him these guys are cartel connected, that Hayley was getting cozy with Federico."

Veronica thought back to her conversation with Lamb. He'd done his telltale hair flick and avoided her eyes when she'd asked about the house. "I'm pretty sure Lamb already knows they're cartel." Mac bit the corner of her lip; Wallace furrowed his brow. "I mean, he hasn't shut the party down yet—why is that? He has plenty of cause. The place is crawling with underage drinking, just for starters. But Lamb likes to be the biggest bully in the schoolyard. He wouldn't want to take on someone like the Milenios." She smirked. "He might even be in their pocket, for all we know."

"Then what are *we* going to do?" Mac asked, her voice tense. "Cartel stuff is kind of outside our skill set, Veronica. These guys are really dangerous."

She closed her eyes and saw Hayley there behind her lids—not as she'd been in the prim school photos on the billboards, and not as she'd been the night of her disappearance, sultry, sexy. Instead she saw her as she'd looked in the candid snapshots she'd seen in the Dewalts' hotel room: mild, friendly, perhaps a little ingenuous. A girl who could find herself deep in trouble without quite knowing how she'd gotten there.

"I don't know," she said. "There's got to be something I can do to draw them out. But I don't know what it is yet."

Mac laughed. The sound was shrill in the stillness.

"You'll figure it out, though," she said, and she sounded more scared than admiring. "It's what you do."

"Promise us you're not going to do anything crazy," Wallace said, looking nervous.

Veronica didn't answer, not wanting to make a promise she wasn't sure she could keep. There were answers in that house, and she might have to go back in to get them.

CHAPTER FOURTEEN

"Good morning, sunshine."

Keith Mars stood at the stove, moving eggs across a skillet with the edge of a spatula. He was dressed in a gray button-down shirt and slacks, a black apron tied around his waist. He smiled at Veronica as she padded into the kitchen, barefoot.

Veronica, head still fuzzy with exhaustion, poured herself a cup of coffee from the Krups. At the end of the counter, a small TV was on, set to mute and tuned to the news. Trish Turley's mouth moved silently, but the curl to her lips made clear she was upbraiding someone.

"You're cooking?"

"I woke up and felt like I could manage it. Got time for breakfast?" Keith held up a platter of bacon and wafted the smell toward her enticingly.

"Not really, but I'm going to have some anyway." She pulled out the bar stool at the island and sat. The wall clock read 10:45—she'd had five hours of restless sleep, disrupted by images of bodies hanging from bridges and the nagging of her own brain, fumbling at the details of the case even while she rested.

"So what'd you do last night?" Keith portioned the eggs

onto two plates that already held toast, cantaloupe, and bacon. He carried them to the kitchen island and set one in front of her.

She spread jam across her toast. "Well, we started out at Carlos and Charlie's for hurricanes, but after I lost the wet T-shirt contest we were like, *Forget this*, so we popped some mollies and headed to the '09er's foam party. I don't remember much, but I did get the digits for a really cute Delta Sig. His dad owns a Jaguar dealership!"

"I thought you already had a boyfriend with a fancy car," Keith said, taking a bite of bacon.

"You can *never* have too many fancy cars."

"Fair enough." He nodded. "So . . . how's the case going?"

"Oh, are we *talking* about that now?" She kept her voice airy, but her eyes darted to his face. He looked at her with mild brown eyes, his expression disarmingly bemused. It was a look she'd seen before—a look that had lured liars and cheaters into a false sense of security with a man they underestimated. Her eyes narrowed. It was then that she noticed the wooden box on the island, nestled between the salt and pepper shakers and the pitcher of orange juice.

"What's that?" she asked cautiously.

"I got you something," he said. There was a faint tension around his eyes that she couldn't read. She picked up the gift carefully with both hands, testing it. It was lighter than she expected. She unlatched the lid and opened it.

Nestled inside was a revolver so black it looked like a shadow against the red foam holding it in place. It was small, discreet, an investigator's gun. A gun that concealed easily. Carefully, deliberately, she shut the lid and latched it again and pushed it away, her heart racing in her chest.

"I asked for a pony. And year after year I'm disappointed."
He didn't flinch. "Veronica, listen to me—"

"Why would you think I'd want this?" She stood up. "Is this some kind of fucked-up scare tactic? 'Welcome to the business, Veronica. By the way, here's your piece. Try not to kill anyone.'"

"Veronica." His voice was louder now, but not angry. She shook her head, mute. But then she met his eyes and suddenly realized what that expression was. It was sadness.

She sat back down at the counter, as far from the box as possible.

"I've been thinking about what you said the other night." He took a deep breath. "Maybe you're right. Maybe you can't fight against this. God help me, maybe it's just who you are." For the first time in what seemed like forever, he looked away. His gaze rested on the wooden box. "It's my own fault. How were you supposed to see any other options, with me putting our family on the line time and time again over some case or other? With me letting you *help*?" His gaze snapped up to meet hers. "I accept that you're here. I accept that this is what you choose. But, Veronica, if this really is what you want, you have to take responsibility for your safety."

"That doesn't mean I have to carry a gun," she said. She realized she was humiliatingly close to tears and bit hard on the inside of her cheek. "Dad, this is ridiculous. Ninety percent of what we do is at a desk. I don't need this."

"This is what it costs." He shook his head. His fists were clenched, twisting a paper napkin to shreds between them. "Veronica, if you want to run with the grown-up PIs, this is what you have to do. You're going to get your permit, you're going to learn to use your weapon, you're going to practice with it, and you're going to use it if you have to."

They sat in tense silence for a moment. Veronica's hands clenched at her sides. She didn't even want to touch the box again. But a part of her, a part she didn't want to think about, kept whispering that he was right. She thought of the night two months earlier when Stu Cobbler had hunted her in her old classmate Gia Goodwin's loft. *I could have used it then.* But the thought sent a shiver up her spine. Did she imagine she would have shot him? *Killed* him?

Then she saw something that sent all thoughts of the gun out of her mind entirely.

She lunged across the island for the remote and unmuted the TV. A caption ran across the bottom of the screen: SECOND GIRL GOES MISSING IN NEPTUNE, CALIFORNIA. ". . . are saying the girl was last seen at a party Wednesday night between midnight and one a.m. Aurora Scott, age sixteen, was visiting a friend at Hearst College for spring break." Turley's lips were twisted into what looked like a furious sneer, but it was impossible to mistake the smug triumph in her voice. "No word out of the Balboa County Sheriff's Department yet; I'm guessing they're working out how to spin this after ignoring Hayley Dewalt's disappearance for more than a week."

A photo of a teenage girl appeared on screen. She had auburn hair with long side-swept bangs and catlike green eyes. Three or four silver hoops lined each earlobe, and the only makeup she wore was heavy black eyeliner. In spite of her hard-edged look, she smiled sweetly at the camera, a dimple in her left cheek.

"Oh my god," Veronica breathed, so soft she barely heard herself. She shook her head. "I've seen her."

"What? Where?" Her father turned to her, a hound dog glint in his eye. He'd seen the loose thread of a clue and couldn't help but grab at it.

"Last night, at the party." Veronica turned up the volume. Less than twelve hours earlier she'd seen Aurora Scott in a leopard-print bikini, looking older than her sixteen years by far. She'd been showing off her tan lines on a dais while the nephew of a drug lord leered at her—the same boy with whom Hayley Dewalt had last been seen.

"Sheriff Lamb!" Trish Turley stared directly into the camera with wide blue eyes. "It's time to wake up. You have a *predator on the loose* in Neptune, California. And until he's caught, every single girl who goes to Neptune for spring break will be at risk."

"It's getting harder to disagree with her," murmured Keith.

"We now go live to a press conference with the Scott family," Turley said. The camera cut to a podium where a middle-aged couple stood side by side. The man was thin and wiry with dun-brown hair tinged with gray. He had a kind of ravaged handsomeness, his face tan and craggy. But it was the tall, willowy blonde next to him who caught Veronica's attention.

Her hair was shorter than it used to be, bobbed around her ears. She'd gained a little weight too, and it suited her. Her large brown eyes pleaded with the camera. For a moment Veronica could not breathe. Her lungs knotted up inside her chest, clenched and useless.

Veronica dropped the remote.

"Holy shit," Keith swore, oblivious to his breakfast growing cold, his eyes glued to the screen.

"Please," said the woman, her voice faltering in the microphone. "Please, if you're watching this. All I want is to see my daughter again." She dissolved into tears, her hand fluttering up to rest on her mouth.

Veronica knew that voice as well as she knew her own. She still heard it sometimes, in her dreams.

It was Lianne Mars, her mother.

CHAPTER FIFTEEN

Lianne and her new husband were staying at a condo on the bluffs overlooking Neptune, nestled among the pines and palms on the hillside. Any cheaper accommodations were booked—the vacancies left by balking spring breakers were being snatched up by incoming reporters, cameramen, and producers as quick as they opened up. Petra Landros had put the Scotts in the modern marble and glass temple of the Apollo Heights Townhomes, courtesy of the Neptune Chamber of Commerce.

Veronica's mind was a staticky blank as she rang the doorbell to their unit. Sunlight wove through the trees, leaving dappled patterns across the beds of river stones and succulents lining the front walk. The birds chattered cacophonously overhead. Veronica noticed everything as if the information came from far away as she waited for her mom—or her new husband—to come to the door.

Landros had given her a quick spiel over the phone. Lianne and her husband, Tanner, lived in Tucson, Arizona. Tanner worked at the Home Depot. Lianne was a part-time receptionist in a dentist's office. They'd flown out that morning, as soon as they'd gotten the news. They were, of course, devastated.

Veronica didn't mention her connection to Lianne. She

probably should have; she now officially had a conflict of interest. Or, at least, she would if she had any intention of letting her feelings get in the way of solving the case. But she didn't. And given how she and Lianne had left things all those years ago, it all seemed too awkward, too personal to try to explain to Petra Landros. *So the client is my mother, but at this point it's more an honorary title than anything, as I haven't seen her in more than a decade. No big deal.*

Veronica gave a small start as the door latch scraped open. In the entryway stood a small boy with sandy blond hair. He was about six years old, in a Batman T-shirt and short pants. He had child-size bongos strapped across his chest.

He squinted up at her. "You don't look like the police."

She knelt down to his level. All at once the distant feeling disappeared, and she was terribly, intensely present. She looked into the boy's eyes. They were light brown, big in his small, serious face.

"Neither do you," she said, narrowing her eyes in mock suspicion. He didn't smile.

"The police are stupid. I'm Batman." With that he beat a little tattoo on his drums and ran back into the condo. "Mom! Someone's here!"

Mom. She watched the back of his head, getting slowly to her feet. Her skin prickled with adrenaline. *He called her Mom.*

For a moment she lingered on the threshold. Then she stepped through the door. A moment later, Lianne Mars— Lianne *Scott*—came in from the other room.

It'd been eleven years since she'd seen her mother. Eleven years since Veronica had looked Lianne in the face and told her to leave. Veronica had been seventeen years old, and it was one of the hardest things she'd ever done. But Lianne couldn't be trusted. All her best intentions—her love, her kindness, her good humor—had long since been drowned in the bottom of a bottle.

Now Lianne stood in the doorway, staring at her daughter. Her mouth was open, as if she'd been about to speak but had forgotten what to say.

The idea of saying anything at all was absurd. After such a long silence, after all that had happened in the long years between them—it was unthinkable. But they couldn't stand in the entryway forever. Veronica gave her mother an awkward smile.

"Hi, Mom."

Lianne shut her mouth. She took a few steps forward. Veronica realized that she was moving for a hug and took an instinctive step back. Lianne stopped in her tracks, her arms suddenly limp at her sides.

From the other room came a syncopated drumbeat, tapped haphazardly on the bongos.

Veronica cleared her throat. "Petra Landros sent me. I'm here to help you find Aurora."

Lianne laughed. It was a strange, shrill sound, like something breaking in her throat. "Of course. Of course you are. Of course it'd be you." She turned away. "Come in."

Veronica followed her mother into a plush, high-ceilinged room, where a sleek Danish living room set was arranged around a fireplace. Most of one wall was taken up by windows; outside, a wide balcony looked out over the Neptune skyline. The little boy sat on a thick-napped rug, still pounding on his bongo.

"Can I . . . can I get you anything?" Lianne's eyes kept

darting toward her and then away just as quickly. "Water? Coffee?"

"No, thank you." *She's just another client,* Veronica told herself. *Just another scared parent who's lost a child.* That thought made her want to laugh out loud, even as a humorless and hollow feeling opened like a chasm inside her.

Veronica stood awkwardly near a chair, waiting for the invitation to sit. Lianne squeezed her hands together like she was hoping to wring some comfort from them. She stared down at the little boy.

"Hunter, sweetheart. Can you go to your room and play alone for a little while? I need to talk to . . . to this lady."

Hunter stood up, picking up the bongos. He gave Veronica a long, inscrutable look. "Are you going to find Rory?"

"Rory?" She realized a beat too late that that must be Aurora's nickname. She sat down on the long edge of an L-shaped couch, just in front of him. "I'll do my very best."

A small crease formed between his eyes. He glanced up at Lianne, who watched fretfully from a few feet away.

"Mom, can't I stay?"

Lianne closed her eyes for a moment. "Please, sweetheart, do what I've asked. We just need a little privacy."

His little mouth turned down. He stood up and grabbed the end of his bongo drums, dragging them behind him as noisily as he could. He disappeared into the hallway, and a few minutes later the sound of a slamming door reverberated toward them.

Lianne slowly sank into a seat several feet away from Veronica. She stared down at her lap. "You must have questions—"

"We don't have to—" Veronica spoke at the same time,

her voice overlapping with her mother's. She pressed her lips tightly together in a rueful smile. "It's okay. I'm here to do a job. To help you find Aurora. You don't owe me any answers."

"I've been clean for seven years now. Seven years, three months, twelve days." It was like Lianne hadn't even heard. "Tanner and I met in recovery. He's Rory's dad. Hunter's dad too. I guess that's obvious. I'm sorry, I'm just . . . I'm nervous." She took a deep breath, and when she spoke her voice was calmer. Her eyes settled on Veronica's face. She looked almost frightened, her pupils wide and dark. "Hunter . . . Hunter's your little brother."

"Yeah," Veronica said softly. "I got that." She looked away, a strange knot twisting in her chest. She felt lost, disoriented—as if all the world's coordinates had suddenly rearranged themselves and she didn't have a compass. Anger had been her default for so long with her mother. And if it were just Lianne, she could have rallied that anger. She could have stoked it to protect herself, to keep her mother at arm's length. But a brother? She didn't know what to do with that.

"What is he, five? Six?" Veronica's voice was so soft it was almost swallowed by the enormous room. Lianne nodded.

"He's six." She smiled weakly. "He doesn't know about you. I . . . I've always wanted to tell him. But it's difficult to explain."

Veronica wondered if the little boy was in his room with his ear pressed to the door. She remembered being six. Keeping half an eye on the levels in the bottle, understanding even then that there was some mysterious relationship between that and her mother's behavior. Sometimes it'd been better than that—sometimes it'd been good. But that only made the bad times so much worse.

"Right now, with so much going on, I don't want to . . . to confuse him. He's already terrified. He loves Rory." Tears spilled down her cheek. She didn't try to wipe them away.

"It's fine, Mom." *There's no reason to change anything,* Veronica told herself. *I don't want you back in my life. I don't want your drama, your manipulations, your lies. I don't need you. I don't need this little kid whom I've never even met.* "We don't need to complicate things right now. We just need to focus on bringing Rory home."

Lianne nodded, chewing on the ragged edge of a nail. Her lips trembled slightly. She took a deep breath, her eyes settling on Veronica's. "When Ms. Landros said she was sending in a PI, I did . . . I had a moment where I wondered if it'd be your dad. I never thought it'd be you."

Veronica was spared having to answer by the sound of someone coming in the front door. Lianne shot to her feet. Veronica relaxed slightly—they wouldn't be *alone* together anymore. No more memory lane. No more risk of ripping open ancient wounds. A moment later, two men entered the room.

One was the lanky man Veronica had seen on TV hours earlier. Aurora's dad, Tanner Scott. He wore a denim jacket fraying at the wrists and carried two small white sacks that smelled of grease and salt. Behind him came a broad-shouldered boy in a gray cardigan and skinny jeans. He was maybe eighteen or nineteen, clean shaven and pale. He balanced a tray of fountain drinks in his hand. Something about him looked vaguely familiar to Veronica.

"We got lunch!" The first man held up the sacks. His eyes fell on Veronica.

"This is my husband, Tanner," Lianne said. "Tanner, this . . . this is Veronica. She's the PI Petra hired to help us find Aurora."

Tanner's pale blue eyes widened, and he did a double take, looking Veronica up and down. A sad, strained smile spread over his face. "Veronica, honey, I've heard so much about you over the years. It's great to finally meet you." His voice had a clipped Midwestern twang, the vowels hammered flat. Before she could do anything, he'd wrapped her in a quick, surprisingly strong hug, takeout bags still clutched in his hands. Veronica stood stiff and awkward in his embrace. When he let go, she stepped discreetly away.

"And this is Adrian Marks," Lianne said quickly, gesturing to the teenaged boy. "He's Rory's best friend; he practically lived at our house last year. He was with her the night she disappeared."

All at once, Veronica realized where she'd seen him. He'd been at the party—she'd seen him playing Lady Gaga on the grand piano. He nodded at her now. His mouth was small and sullen, his eyes dark and wounded. She felt a rush of sympathy—he had the same lost look she'd seen on Hayley Dewalt's friends. That same sense of some vital, careless, innocent thing ruined.

Paradise doesn't just get lost in Neptune. It gets razed to the ground.

Tanner set the food on the kitchen counter. "Do you mind us eating while we talk? I don't want the burgers to get cold."

"Not at all."

They took a few minutes, digging through the bags, opening the foil-wrapped burgers, and sorting out whose was whose. Lianne took a tray to Hunter in his bedroom. By the time she returned the others had gathered around a table topped with sea-green glass, burgers unwrapped, fries jutting from cardboard containers. There was extra food; Tanner had offered a burger to Veronica, but her stomach turned at the thought. She pulled out her notebook and a pen.

"Can you tell me a little about Aurora?" Veronica asked. "Her interests, her personality?"

Tanner stood halfway up so he could get his phone out of his pocket. He opened his picture albums app and handed the phone to Veronica.

"I made an album, to show the cops or the press or whoever," he said.

There were two or three dozen photos—the first was dated 2006, when Aurora would have been eight. Veronica started scrolling through.

The pictures showed first a whip-thin, wild-haired little girl. At eight, nine, ten, Aurora Scott had a coltish look, all hard angles and tensed muscles, like at any moment she was seconds from bolting. *A kid who ran and played,* she thought, looking at the skinned knee below a pair of shorts, the dirty arms and legs. She couldn't even hold still for Lianne and Tanner's wedding pictures—in almost every shot she was looking away from the camera or fidgeting with the bow in her hair, her flower-girl basket half crushed in one hand.

The girl grew up before Veronica's eyes. There were pictures of her in the Arizona desert, standing next to towering saguaro cacti. Pictures of her holding a two-year-old Hunter in her lap in front of a Christmas tree. One caught her in midair as she leapt from a diving board at the pool, arms and legs akimbo. In junior high she went through a lightning-quick girly phase—sequins and short skirts, bubblegum-pink lip gloss and long wavy hair. That look disappeared abruptly between snapshots, replaced with knit caps and baggy layers. Skater chic.

"She's spirited," Lianne said softly. "Funny, smart." Adrian nodded his agreement.

The last handful of photos—the ones taken in the past year—showed a girl with the casual, hard-edged style of a tomboy grown up to be beautiful. Black leather jacket, distressed jeans, stretched-out sweaters hanging off one shoulder. Her auburn hair was long and straight, and her eyes were green, catlike, and rimmed with black liner. She smirked and pouted, never quite smiling for the camera.

Veronica's chest tightened. Something in the tilt of the girl's head, the arch of her eyebrow, made Veronica think of Lilly Kane—brazen, fearless. And something else, maybe just a certain sharpness in Aurora's eyes, reminded her of herself. Sixteen, with a hair-trigger bullshit detector. Sixteen and looking for a fight.

She looked up at Lianne and Tanner. "Did you know Aurora was planning to come to Neptune for spring break?"

Tanner and Lianne exchanged glances.

"We did," Tanner said. "We drove her to the bus station. She came out to visit Adrian. We were nervous about letting her come, of course, but she really wanted to."

"This is Adrian's freshman year at Hearst," Lianne explained. She blinked, and Veronica saw tears forming in the corners of her eyes. Adrian's own eyes were downcast, heavy. "She begged us to let her come out and see him."

Because she "wanted to" is a strange reason to let your unaccompanied sixteen-year-old stay with a male friend in the combination drug den/orgy that is Neptune's spring break scene. Veronica tried to keep her expression neutral, but Lianne must have seen a flicker of judgment somewhere, because she shook her head.

"I know it sounds . . . negligent. But you have to understand. Rory doesn't . . . doesn't always make friends easily. She's been so lonely since Adrian moved to school. We thought it would do her some good."

Veronica shot a glance at Adrian. He picked at his french fries, his burger sitting untouched in front of him.

"How long have you and Aurora been friends, Adrian?"

His eyes darted up to meet hers. "Two years." His voice had a light, lilting tenor. "She was this little nothing freshman, no friends, no cachet. But she overheard some musclehead calling me a faggot the first week of class." He gave a sad little smile. "Our high school was hell on earth for a gay guy. She spray-painted 'homophobe' on the guy's Camaro in the parking lot—the security cameras caught her doing it, and she ended up in detention for a month afterward."

Ah. Well that explains the permission to stay with a male friend.

"That's our girl." Tanner patted Adrian roughly on the back. "Doesn't always know how to pick her battles. But goddamn it, she's got a good heart." His voice cracked a little.

Veronica smiled, handing the phone back to Tanner. "She seems like a great kid."

"Oh, she is." Tanner looked down at his phone and then set it next to his burger wrapper. "It hasn't always been easy for her. She's been through a lot over the years. Her mom left when she was little, and I . . . well, I was pretty much a useless drunk until I got clean." He said it matter-of-factly, but his lips twisted downward as he said it. "That sort of thing takes a toll on a child."

You don't say. Veronica looked at her notebook, just so she could look away from him for a moment. "Has she ever had any real behavior problems?"

There was a moment of silence. Lianne cupped her forehead in the palm of her hand, as if she had a headache.

"You know, she tests boundaries. She's made some mistakes." Veronica's mother smiled sadly. "For a while she was in trouble every week at school. Cheating on tests, talking back to teachers. A few fights. Last year she got busted with a bunch of fake IDs and an ounce of marijuana. She's been in counseling since then, and it's helped. We've seen a big difference at home."

"Has she ever done a disappearing act before?"

Lianne shook her head. "She's never gone missing like this. She's not always great about checking in, but she's never just disappeared."

Veronica nodded slowly. She looked at Adrian.

"You said you were with her the night she disappeared. Did you notice anything out of the ordinary that night?"

He bit the corner of his lip. "If anything, it was business as usual."

"What do you mean?"

Adrian glanced up at Lianne and Tanner nervously, then back at Veronica, idly picking a french fry apart between two fingers. "She's done it to me a hundred times. We go to a party together, she meets a guy, and then it's like I don't even exist."

"She's boy crazy, huh?"

"Girl, you don't even *know.*" He looked miserable. "So I told her before we even got there—if she ditched me I'd leave her, and she'd have to get her own ride home. She promised we'd stick together. But lo and behold, here comes some Rico Suave with a four-hundred-dollar haircut and she's on him like glue. So I hung out for a while and entertained myself. Then I left. It wasn't until this morning, when Tanner called saying he couldn't get hold of her, that I realized something was wrong. Then he called the police and here we are."

"You didn't happen to get any pictures, did you?"

"I did. And so did everyone else in the world." He tapped into his phone then passed it to Veronica.

He'd pulled up an inbox for the e-mail "findaurora@info blast.com." In the past two hours, more than fifty e-mails had come in, some with pictures attached. She scrolled through and read a few. *Just sent fifty bucks via PayPal—I will keep Aurora in my prayers!* read one. She opened another: *Recognized Aurora from the pictures I took last night—hope this helps.* Below was a photo of three white girls in bikinis making gang signs—and behind them, just out of focus but clearly recognizable, was Federico Gutiérrez Ortega, leaning close to whisper something to Aurora Scott.

"Ms. Landros set up the Find Aurora website this morning. I volunteered to sift through tips, so I'm getting some of the messages," he explained. He jabbed a finger at Rico. "This is the guy she was flirting with when I left last night. I took off just after midnight, and the latest time stamp on any of the pictures we've gotten is two twenty-seven a.m."

Veronica flipped through the photos. They weren't nearly as R rated as the ones showing Hayley Dewalt in the guy's lap, but they definitely showed Aurora looking flirty—and Rico looking interested.

She looked at her mother's pinched, pale face and Tanner's heavy frown. She didn't want to lie to them—but she didn't want to panic them either. Not yet, when there were still so many unanswered questions. If she told them Hayley Dewalt had been seen with the same boy, they'd be terrified. And if that information got back to the press, her quarry might go to ground.

Better to wait. To say nothing, until she had more information. If there was reason for them to panic, it wouldn't really matter when they started. She made a mental note to e-mail Petra for the passwords for the website so Mac could be cued in to what came through.

Veronica pulled out a few business cards and passed them around. "Please call me immediately, day or night, if anything changes, or if you think of anything that might be useful. I'll be in touch if I learn anything new." She stood up and grabbed her purse.

Lianne gave a startled little gasp. "Oh, I almost forgot. Wait there, Veronica, I'll be right back."

She hurried down the hallway. Veronica stood awkwardly next to the table. Tanner kept staring at her with a woeful, earnest expression. Adrian scooped his uneaten burger into one of the white bags, taking it into the kitchen and throwing it in the trash.

"I'm sorry to meet you like this, honey," Tanner said. He gave a strained little smile. "You know, your mama's my second chance at life. Well, truth be told, she's my fourth or fifth—but she's the one that stuck. We met in AA—I was fifteen months sober when she started. We kind of looked out for each other. Every day when I thank my creator for another sober day, I thank Him for bringing us together."

Veronica didn't know what to say. A pained smile pulled her lips tight. For a moment she was sure she caught Adrian casting a disparaging look over the kitchen island at Tanner. She suspected he'd heard the story before, more than once.

Lianne hurried back, a spiral-bound book clutched in her hand. It was covered with overlapping vinyl stickers— band decals, skateboarding logos, a bumper sticker that read "Cute but psycho: roll the dice if you dare."

She thrust it at Veronica. "It's her diary," she whispered. "I haven't read it. I don't . . . I don't want to invade her privacy. But it might be helpful."

Veronica swallowed, sliding the book into her bag. "Thanks. I'll take a look." She gave a faltering laugh and mimed zipping her lips. "I'll keep it confidential. I promise."

Lianne walked Veronica to the door. For one awful, sluggish second, Veronica was sure her mother was about to pull her into a hug. Then it passed, hugless, and she realized with a stab of irritation that a part of her was disappointed.

I don't want her hugs. I don't want her attention, her love. I don't want her.

Tears spilled down Lianne's cheeks.

"Please. Just help us find our little girl, okay?"

Veronica felt her fingers curl into fists. The muscles across her chest felt tight, like a carapace. Like armor.

"I'm going to do my best," she said. Then she opened the door and let herself out.

CHAPTER SIXTEEN

You'll never guess who showed up today.

Back in her office a few hours later, Veronica stared at her computer screen. The cursor blinked rhythmically, an ancient ode to the blank page. Even though there were hundreds—thousands—of things to say, she couldn't figure out what to write next.

She had work to do. There were lives at stake, careers on the line . . . and all she wanted to do was talk to one person. The one person she couldn't reach.

It was just after 4:00 p.m. in Neptune, California—which meant it was 0430 hours aboard the USS *Harry Truman*. They'd had a date to Skype a half hour ago, but he hadn't shown up. That happened sometimes; if he was called out on a mission, he didn't always have a chance to let her know. She tried not to let it bother her, but a part of her always thought, just for a split second: *He could be dead right now.*

It was stupid. But she couldn't help it.

Maybe you already saw the news—I don't know, do you get CNN on the Truman*? Trish Turley's been making a meal out of it. Another girl went missing, and because the cosmos hates me, she just so happens to be Lianne's stepdaughter.*

The late-afternoon sun filtered through the slats in her

blinds, sending shadows across her desk. She leaned back in her chair and stared at the plaster on the ceiling, her mind combing over everything that'd happened in the past few hours. It all seemed too complicated to try to describe in an e-mail—the strangeness of seeing her mom again, the confusion of feelings. The discovery that she had a little brother. She sighed.

I'll tell you all about it when we have a chance to Skype. Are you free Monday morning (my Sunday night?). Let me know and I'll be online.

She hit Send and snapped the laptop shut.

It was obvious that the disappearances were connected; Federico Gutiérrez Ortega was seen flirting with both girls the night before they went missing. But what had he *done* with them? What could possibly motivate him to kidnap or hurt two American girls when he had so much at stake? She knew the evidence had to be airtight before she made an accusation; the Milenios weren't stupid. If they caught a whiff of her poking around, they'd cover their tracks and then some.

Meanwhile, Hayley's fund had just hit $550,000 that morning; Aurora's was already up to $300,000 and climbing by the hour. As those figures rose, so did the number of cancellations rolling into Neptune's motels and hotels up and down the coastline. Trish Turley had rallied her fans, and the sudden drop in the number of spring breakers was becoming noticeable.

A door opened, and Veronica suddenly became aware of raised voices in the reception area.

"I know they came from this office. So unless you want to be charged with obstruction of justice, it's time to start talking."

She jumped up and ran to the door to see Sheriff Lamb leaning across Mac's desk. His stomach had knocked over a jar of pencils, and they rolled slowly toward the edge. He held a blue flyer under Mac's nose, shaking it back and forth with every word.

Mac sat with her chin propped on her hand, staring at him with flat, bored eyes. She didn't flinch as he shoved the paper toward her face.

"What's the problem with my flyers?" Veronica crossed her arms over her chest and leaned against the door frame. "Did the color not match Neptune's City Beautiful initiative?"

"Mars." Lamb turned away from Mac's desk, his lips curled in a sneer. Veronica could see Mac visibly relax behind him. "What do you think you're doing?"

She took the flyer from his hand and examined it. "It looks like I'm trying to find Hayley Dewalt. It's going to be hard to do if you keep taking my flyers down, though."

"How many times do I have to tell you to keep me informed about your activities?"

"Last I checked, you were busy ignoring my voice mails. And now that there's another girl missing—from the exact same house—it seems you might want to be printing up some new flyers right about now."

He stared at her with burning blue eyes, stepping closer until he was mere inches from her face. She could smell stale coffee on his breath. "There's no evidence the disappearances are linked," he said carefully.

"Isn't there?" She affected surprise. "Oh, I guess you wouldn't know, since you left the actual investigating for me to do. Well, buckle up, my friend, because I'm about to hand you actual clues to an actual crime, wrapped in a bow." She crooked her finger at him and went back into her office. A moment later, he followed.

"I don't have time for games, Mars."

"No doubt, what with all that graft and corruption filling your schedule."

Lamb smirked, one hand on the back of the low chair facing her desk. She grabbed her laptop, pulling up the photos she'd received from Hayley's friends and Adrian. Then she turned the computer around for him to see.

"Aurora Scott disappeared from the same house Hayley Dewalt did nearly two weeks ago. Both girls were talking to this guy right before their last sighting." She pointed at the picture of Federico. "He's who you want to be harassing. Not Mac."

Lamb's pupils dilated slightly, but otherwise his face was motionless. The bluster had gone out of him all at once, leaving a quiet, calculating intensity to his movements.

"I take it you know who this guy is?" he asked coolly.

She darted a glance at him. "Do you know something I don't?"

Lamb straightened up, tucking his thumb through his belt loop. "What I know is that you don't want to go slinging accusations at people like this. Not unless you're one hundred percent sure you can back them up."

And just like that, she was sure. He'd known all along that the house was owned by the Milenios, that the Gutiérrez cousins were laundering money for their family. He was just too lazy—or maybe too corrupt—to investigate. The taste of bile burned her tongue, but she swallowed it down.

"I thought you wanted my information, Lamb. I thought you wanted to find these girls."

He looked at the picture again, a conflicted expression flitting across his face. "Do you have any proof that this guy had any part in either disappearance?"

"No, but he was seen with both girls just before they went missing. That's enough to get him in for questioning."

"Is it? Suddenly you're some kind of legal scholar?"

"Uh, yeah." She smirked. "Suddenly I kind of am."

They glared at each other for a minute.

"Look," she said. "Cartels are a little out of my comfort zone."

He flinched at the word "cartel," but his gaze didn't shy away from hers. For a moment his eyes raked her face as he tried to gauge what she knew. She waited.

"This is a delicate situation," he said finally. "I'm not hauling anyone in without real evidence. So if you find something on them and bring it to me, I'll consider questioning them."

"So, let me get this straight." Veronica tapped her lips thoughtfully with her index finger. "You're going to let me do all the legwork, because it's not politically viable for you to look into wild, orgiastic parties thrown by the junior members of one of the most violent crime organizations in Mexico. I'll save you some trouble and just assume you're getting a kickback of some kind from the Milenios—maybe in one of their more legitimate guises." She cocked her head, feigning confusion. "But if I find actual evidence that they're, I don't know, using their parties as some kind of lure to kidnap pretty girls? Or worse? *That's* when you want me to hand it over to you."

"Sounds about right." Lamb gave her a smile that was all reptile. "The Sheriff's Department appreciates your assistance in this matter."

He gave her a little mock salute, and then he was sailing out the door, leaving the lingering notes of his Axe body spray in his wake.

She went to the reception area. Mac didn't even look up. Her fingers were flying over the keyboard. Veronica took in her friend's jutting chin, the jerkiness of her shoulders. She wasn't happy. Not for the first time she thought about how Mac had left a safe, quiet office—and a fat paycheck—for this. Now here she was, working as a glorified secretary, taking abuse from anyone whose toes Veronica stepped on.

"Are you okay?" She sat on the edge of Mac's desk.

"I'm fine." Mac looked up, her eyes bright and fierce, but a small smile flitted across her face. "One of these days, I'm going to find something on that guy that'll wipe the smile right off his face."

"You handled him like a pro."

"Luckily, my intimidated face looks remarkably like silent defiance." She exhaled loudly. "So is he trying to nab our collar?"

"Sure is. But only once I've got something on the Gutiér-rezes. He's scared of the big bad drug lords—doesn't want to take them on until we've got something solid."

"Well, shouldn't *we* be?" Mac raised an eyebrow. "Scared, I mean? Some of those stories . . ."

"Believe me, I am treating the ultraviolent gangsters with all the caution required. I'm not about to poke a rattlesnake nest if the snakes are all comfortably asleep. Did any of those background checks come in yet?"

Mac looked up at her, hesitating. Veronica rolled her eyes. "It's fine. Just tell me."

"Okay, well . . . Lianne Scott—I mean your mom—has a few misdemeanors on her record, none more recent than 2006. Public intoxication, shoplifting, and trespassing. Looks like she moved around a lot between 2004 and 2006. I've got her in Barstow, Reno, Scottsdale, and then finally Tucson." Mac's eyes flickered from her screen to Veronica and quickly back again. "Married Tanner Scott in January of 2007. Gave birth to Hunter Jacob Scott in December 2007. She started working for the dental office last year, after Hunter started school."

"And Tanner?"

Mac pursed her lips. "He's been kind of hard to track. Spotty employment history and no permanent address between 2000 and 2006."

"That's not too surprising. He told me he'd been in the bottle pretty hard before he met my mom."

"He was married to a woman named Rachel Novak in 1996; they divorced in 2000. Aurora was born 1998 in Albuquerque. Looks like he served ten months in jail for check fraud in 2005; Aurora was a ward of the state while he was away. After he got out he seemed to settle down. He got custody of Aurora and started working more steady jobs. Before Home Depot he was a janitor for the city for a few years." Mac looked up. "That's all that's coming up on the basic search. You want me to keep digging?"

Veronica shook her head. "No. I think I can fill in the gaps."

She knew the recidivism rates for petty crimes; no former criminal worked as a janitor for a few years unless he was determined to go straight. The idea of easy money became much too alluring after scrubbing toilets all night. Tanner Scott may have set off her bullshit detector, but it looked like he really had cleaned up.

She realized Mac was watching her closely, her forehead creased with concern.

"This has got to be weird for you," Mac said.

"It's not. It's fine."

"Veronica, look who you're talking to. If anyone has mom issues, it's me."

Veronica forced a smile. In high school, she'd been the one to uncover the fact that Mac had been switched at birth, that the family she'd never really fit in with wasn't really hers.

"Okay. It's completely weird. But I'm trying not to think about it. Right now I really just want to focus on finding Hayley and Aurora." She looked out the window over Mac's head. A seagull hung on the breeze outside, a pale streak against the sky. *Pretty, for an animal waiting for an unguarded Dumpster.* "Did you have a chance to look in on our other guys?"

"Yup. Chad Cohan is, as far as I can see, still snuggled up in Stanford. I've gotten into the Stanford security logs, and it looks like he's used his student ID to access the gym and the library in the past few days. No flight records, and no charges on his cards that would indicate travel."

"What about Crane?"

Mac shook her head. "I don't have much of an electronic trail for him. It doesn't seem likely that he'd be able to slip away from his family and hurt someone while they're the subject of so much media attention, though, right?"

"Unlikely, but not impossible. I'll check in with the Dewalts tomorrow. I should do that anyway." She put her hands over her eyes for a moment. A small headache was forming over her temples.

"What should we do next?" Mac's voice was quiet, almost tentative.

"The only thing we can do." Veronica drew her hands away from her eyes. Mac sat very still in front of her, waiting. "We keep going over the evidence, and we hope like hell that sooner or later, some part of it makes sense."

CHAPTER SEVENTEEN

"You know what I definitely don't miss about New York?"

Veronica swayed slightly in the hammock strung between two stolid oaks in Keith's backyard, a finger stuck between the pages where she'd been leafing through Aurora Scott's diary. It was just after dinner, and the last of the day's sun filtered gently through the leaves.

Keith looked up at her from where he crouched, yanking weeds from around the agapanthus. Their dirty dishes and the remainder of their lasagna sat on the little wooden table on the patio; they'd come out to enjoy the evening while they ate, a well-earned break.

"I've heard the sewer alligators are very intimidating," he said, wiping beads of sweat from his brow.

She leaned back in the canvas of the hammock, enjoying the sense of being supported.

"I don't miss crummy little apartments without yards or gardens or windows that open. I definitely don't miss that."

It was her favorite part of Keith's house—the yard. When she'd been in high school, after the recall election in which they'd lost everything, they'd made their home in an apartment, less crummy and less little than anywhere she'd lived in Manhattan, but definitely not anyone's picture of the good life. It'd been comfortable, though, and it'd been theirs, back when it was the two of them against the world. And at least there'd been a courtyard with a pool where she could sit and get some air.

But it was a true luxury to be able to sit in a little patch of garden while the light faded, to take charge of the weeds in the garden, to swing gently between oaks older than she was.

"Oh yeah? You might miss it more after cutting the grass every weekend for a few months." He glanced up at her from where he knelt, his mouth twisted wryly.

"Hm. I was thinking about adopting more of a supervisory position when it came to yard work. But I'll bring you lemonade between mowings."

He tugged a tough, sinewy weed from the soil. Its roots were dense and gnarled.

"What's that you're reading?"

She held up the little book. "Aurora's diary. Last entry is a little over a year ago, so it might not be the most up-to-date information. But it's somewhere to start."

The diary was actually a sketchbook, filled with line after line of wide, looping handwriting in multiple colors of ink. Sketches and doodles showed up throughout in pencil—a cartoon Frankenstein's monster shambling his way across the page, a perfectly shaded picture of a flower in a vase, an abstract doodle illuminating the margins. Aurora was a good artist. Sometimes the text ran in straightforward lines, but sometimes she'd turned the diary sideways or wrote in weird curlicues that spiraled around her drawings.

Can't stand another day around the dead-eyed
zombie hordes.

Every time Mrs. Nelson mispronounces the word
"chlamydia" in health class, an angel gets its wings.
Or maybe it just gets chlamydia?

Got a drug and alcohol lecture today from the
arch-hypocrite himself. Does AA make you retarded, or
did he kill all his fucking brain cells before that?

Aurora wasn't always so hostile—almost every page had a reference, sometimes punctuated by hearts or smiley faces, to "Barkley," who Veronica gathered was a family dog. And a full page of the journal was devoted to a sketch of Hunter, looking sober and skeptical, captioned with the words "The Boss." But the image of Aurora Scott that started to emerge somewhere between the lines was prickly and impatient. She was smart, creative, petulant, bored. Unlike Hayley Dewalt, she didn't seem eager to please anyone but herself.

"So how was your mom today?"

Veronica looked upward through the filigree of leaves. That morning, seeing Lianne on the small screen in the kitchen, neither of them had even said her name out loud. Veronica had watched the press conference open mouthed, lost in her own shocked horror, and it wasn't until the screen went back to Trish Turley that she thought to wonder what Keith was feeling. But there'd been no time to discuss it; Petra Landros had called, and she'd had to hurry to get dressed and out the door.

When she'd gotten home, Keith had dinner on the table, glasses of wine at the ready. They'd eaten in an almost polite silence. She had the feeling he was waiting for her to talk about it. She'd opened her mouth to speak once or twice and changed her mind. Maybe it was just habit that made it so difficult. She and Keith talked about almost everything— but Lianne was one of the few topics they'd always avoided.

Now she propped herself up on her elbow to look at him. "Devastated. She's terrified."

Keith nodded, not looking up. He jabbed a gardening fork into the tender earth, trying to pry out the deep and stringy roots of another weed. She watched him for a moment before going on.

"But besides that? She seems like she's doing well." She paused for a moment. "She has another kid. A little boy."

He nodded. "I saw that in one of the articles." He paused. "Did you meet him?"

"Yeah. He's cute." She just had to avoid saying the word "brother" and she'd be able to keep it together. "And Tanner's nice enough. I mean, he's a little sketchy. Mac turned up some old check forging charges from back before he married Mom. And he does that bullshitty, self-mythologizing thing addicts always seem to do. But it seems like he really does care about her. Since they've been together, he's been on the straight and narrow."

"I'm happy for them," Keith said simply. "I mean, not about what they're going through, obviously. But I'm happy they found each other."

She sat up in the hammock and swung her legs down. "What about you?"

"Me?"

"Yes, you. It's been a while. When are you going to get back on the horse?"

Keith grimaced. "I don't know if you've noticed, honey,

but I've currently got my hands full recovering from a cata-strophic injury or two. I'm not sure I could handle dating."

"Come on, ladies love vulnerability. You've just got to limp on out there and be yourself."

"Why, you know any MILFs in the market for a cripple?" He waggled his brows.

"Oh my god. Please never say MILF again as long as I live."

Her laughter was interrupted by the sound of her cell phone trilling in her pocket. She stood up out of the ham-mock and pulled it out.

"Veronica Mars."

For a minute all she heard was background noise—traffic, maybe, or the patter of a TV. Then there was a phlegmy cough. "I got this number off a flyer."

She froze, her senses going on alert. "I'm listening."

"I might have some information for you." Another cough. "You should probably come on by, 20111 Meadow View Road."

"I'll be there in forty minutes."

She drove down the stretch of smoke shops, free clinics, and pay-by-the-hour motels that ran along Meadow View. The address landed her in front of a small square building, a bright yellow banner hanging across the front that read WE BUY GOLD. A picture of a capering leprechaun was painted across one window. The iron bars over the glass made it look like he was in jail.

There was a bell on the door that jingled as she entered. A smell of burnt coffee and heavy-duty cleaner stung her nostrils. Inside was a waiting area, with a small vinyl chair adjacent to an empty water cooler. There was a service window in the wall, filled with warped Plexiglas like a bank-teller's station. To the left of that was a door, with a sign that read EMPLOYEES ONLY.

"Hello?"

A blurry shape appeared on the other side of the glass. Then a small window shot open, and a sagging, doughy face with bloodshot eyes and wiry gray hair appeared.

Veronica unfolded a copy of her flyer from her purse. "You called me. About the flyer?"

His expression didn't change, but a little glint came into his eyes. They were pale watery blue, veined like a cracked marble. "Is there some kinda reward?"

"Depends what you've got." She let her smile drop. "If you give me a lead I can use I have a crisp hundred dollar bill with your name on it. Actually, it's more like five crumpled twenties. But it spends the same."

"A hundred seems a little thin when there's a ten-K reward for finding the girl."

"Oh, does that mean you're going to bring her home?" Veronica mimed wiping her forehead. "That is a relief. Because I've been running all over town looking for information, but if you know where she is, that lets me off the hook."

"Hey, I just want to make sure my information is appraised at its proper value." He mournfully raised the straw of a Big Gulp to his lips and slurped loudly, eyes tracking her every move.

Veronica pressed her lips together. There might be other ways to get his information—but every second she stood here was another lost opportunity to find the girls.

"Okay. I have a hundred and fifty for you to tell me everything you know, right now. And if I find Hayley Dewalt, I'll come back and give you another fifty."

He suckled at his soda for a moment, slurping the dregs up from the bottom. Then he slammed the Plexiglas window shut.

For a moment she thought that was it—she was dismissed. Then the door in the wall swung open. The face was now a body, slouching and slow, in a wrinkled khaki-colored shirt the same miserable shade as the carpet and the walls. He beckoned for her to follow him to the back room.

His work space was cramped and cluttered, every surface covered with a hodgepodge of equipment—electronic probes and scanners, tweezers, scales, gauges. Small bins lined the shelves on the walls, dusty and full of odd parts. A broken watch lay in pieces across a counter. A small TV was perched precariously on the corner of his workstation, tuned to Fox News, the screen smeared with something greasy.

The shopkeeper leaned down and pulled a small basket from a shelf below his workstation. A label on one end read 3/12. Inside, Veronica could see a jumble of plastic baggies, each containing something different—a gold-link bracelet, an ugly old brooch. A few engagement rings. She wondered briefly if any of their owners had been her or her dad's clients.

"She's not wearing it in any of the pictures they're showing on the news," he muttered. "But I recognized it the second I saw that flyer. Never seen another one like it."

Veronica was about to ask him what he was talking about when he found what he was looking for. He ripped open the bag and poured a necklace out into one surprisingly fine-boned hand.

It was a pendant—a tiny gold birdcage, on a slender golden chain.

Veronica stared at the necklace in his hand. For a moment she didn't recognize what she was looking at. Then, all at once, she understood. She reached into her purse and pulled out one of her flyers. There it was, hanging from Hayley's neck on the night she disappeared. It dangled into her cleavage, the cage hitting the curve of a breast.

"This came in two days after that girl disappeared."

"It's pretty." Veronica shrugged, playing it cool. "Are you sure all the girls aren't wearing them? It's not being mass-produced for Urban Outfitters or anything? Birds are sort of 'in' these days."

"That's not mass-produced," he scoffed. "Whoever made it is a real craftsman. And look . . ." He opened the cage door on tiny hinges. "Her initials are engraved inside. I noticed 'em, but I didn't put it together until I saw your flyer."

Veronica held out her hand. The man reluctantly let the necklace slide into her palm. He was right—even she could see it, and she wasn't exactly a jewelry expert. The birdcage was skillfully cast, the bars on the cage delicate and glittering. A cluster of three small diamonds was set in the roof. And there, inside, were the initials HD.

"Most of the stuff I get I sell for scrap. This? This is special. I was going to try to resell it."

"Do you keep records on your clients? Who brought this in?"

He set his drink down on the counter and shuffled painfully over to the TV. A small stack of VHS tapes sat next to it. "It's lucky I saw your flyer when I did. I usually only keep 'em for a week and then tape over 'em." He selected the tape that said WEDNESDAY and pushed it into the built-in VCR.

There were a few tense moments as he fast-forwarded through the day's tape. It looked like he didn't get a lot of business until late evening—but by 9:00 p.m. the parade of despair commenced. Very young women with young children clinging to their legs; wobbly old men with unkempt beards; strung-out, bone-thin beings of indeterminate age. They filed in, one by one, the black-and-white cameras picking up their raw hope, and then their defeat when they realized how little time their treasures had bought them.

Then, at 10:05, a white guy with a sprout of pale dreadlocks came in. The shopkeeper hit Play.

"This is the guy," he said, pointing at the screen. His fingernail was lined with grime, but his hands were otherwise clean. "I've got his ID information on file too. William Murphy, twenty-four years old. He signed the paperwork 'Willie.' Real twitchy kid—I assumed he was jonesing. Talked non-fucking-stop."

"What'd he talk about?"

"Oh, he had a big long story about where he'd gotten it. His sister's best friend's cousin sent him to see what he could get for it, because she needed milk for her sick infant son or some crap like that. Basically didn't want me to think he'd stolen it."

"Which of course you believed, because buying and reselling stolen goods is a crime." Veronica gave a tight smile. The man gestured as if to say, *Sure, whatever.*

She leaned closer to the screen, trying to get a glimpse of his face. Something about Willie Murphy was familiar to her. She'd seen him somewhere around town—or maybe he was just one of the handful of trustafarians who came to Neptune for spring break. He *was* twitchy—there was no sound, but she could tell by the quick, birdlike movements of his hands that he was talking excitedly. He kept looking behind him, like he thought someone might be sneaking up on him.

When he turned to leave, stuffing the bills into his wallet, he looked up for a split second, right at the camera. "There. Can you rewind and pause it when he looks up?"

The shopkeeper did.

And that was when she recognized him.

He'd been in the background in one of the pictures Hayley's friends had given her, nursing a beer while Hayley Dewalt fed Rico Gutiérrez a strawberry. And he'd been at the party the night Aurora went missing—she'd seen him jumping into the pool.

She turned away from the shopkeeper, pulling her phone out of her purse. As she dialed, she put the necklace into her wallet.

"Hey, you gonna buy that?" the shopkeeper demanded.

She snorted, covering the microphone to reply.

"You mean this stolen necklace that you illegally purchased? I don't think so. This is evidence." She uncovered the microphone. "Hi, Mac, sorry about that. Yeah, I need you to run another background check for me and e-mail the results, ASAP."

"Sure," Mac answered. "What's the name?"

"William Murphy."

She paused. For a split second she thought about telling Mac what she was planning to do. But then she remembered how Mac and Wallace had looked at her that night in Mac's apartment, after they'd discovered just who owned the house on Manzanita.

Well, what they didn't know wouldn't hurt them. And if she wanted to find Willie Murphy, she didn't have a choice.

She was going to have to go back to the party.

CHAPTER EIGHTEEN

The theme that night was simple: bikinis. Only for girls, of course; the guys seemed to be perfectly happy in pop-collar polos and baggy jeans. But to get in with a pair of X chromosomes, you had to be showing some skin.

Veronica moved slowly through the crush, a beach bag tucked under her arm like a life preserver. She didn't have a lot of time for sunbathing these days, and she was painfully aware of the fish-belly white of her bared midriff. Still, she could feel eyes tracing the lines of her body beneath her pink string bikini, prying and eager.

As she made her way through the house, she kept her eyes peeled for any sign of Willie Murphy's dark blond dreadlocks. Mac's background check had yielded a portrait of a petty criminal: public intoxication, possession, disorderly conduct, trespassing. He'd been in and out of county lockup since he was seventeen years old, the longest stay a six-month stint for possession with intent to sell. His last known address was a grimy efficiency down the street from the Camelot, but he'd been evicted in January. Since then he'd had no known permanent address.

She'd considered calling Lamb, handing her new evidence straight to him—but she'd decided against it. Lamb wouldn't want to bust the party. He'd just put Murphy's picture all over the news and give him a chance to run. No, the only way she'd get answers was to talk to him before he knew he was being hunted.

Now she just had to find him.

The house was packed with sweaty, bared bodies, faces leering from every dark corner she passed. Tonight's celebration was, if anything, more frenzied than the party she'd seen the night before. It was nearing the end of spring break for most of these kids, and they seemed determined to push through the exhaustion, as if holding still would bring an end to this magical pretend world where everything felt good and you didn't have to do anything you didn't want to. Clouds of smoke billowed up from the crowd—she caught a whiff of tobacco and the sticky-sweet smell of pot, and something else, acrid and chemical, like the air in a cheap salon. Meth. She'd encountered the smell once before, tracking down a deadbeat dad in Riverside, finding him in a garbage-strewn apartment with a pipe in his hand.

She squeezed through the crowd, eyes sharp. A herd of beefy, shirtless boys stampeded past her in the hallway, chanting something she couldn't quite make out. In the kitchen a game of strip poker was under way, and a smooth-chested boy had already lost his shirt. A girl in an electric-blue bikini sat across his lap, wearing an incongruous silk necktie. In the music room an elfin boy sat on a gilt coffee table, a friend helping him secure a length of tubing around his upper arm.

Out on the patio she took a deep breath of clean air. She made her way down the stairs to the lower level, where the pool roiled with activity. No sign anywhere of Willie—or the Gutiérrez cousins. She craned her neck to scan the pool and the Jacuzzi and for a moment forgot to watch where she was going. She walked right into someone.

"Ow!"

"Oh my gosh, I'm so sorry . . ."

The words died on her lips. Standing in front of her, in board shorts and a puka shell necklace, was Dick Casablancas.

He did a double take. "Hey, Ronnie," he said. "You know, this is *not* where I expected to bump into you."

The cluster of girls he'd been standing with eyed Veronica with interest. She stood frozen to the spot, hoping against all hope that he wouldn't say anything too stupid.

She'd known Dick since high school for a while, after her father's fall from grace, he'd been one of her tormenters. After she started dating Logan—who just happened to be Dick's best friend—he'd eased up, and over time they'd made a kind of peace, though she wasn't sure she'd call him her friend. He was rich and careless and had the emotional depth of a chunk of concrete; the only real goals that registered for him were surfing, drinking, and screwing.

In other words, she really shouldn't have been so surprised to see him at a party run by the offspring of cartel kingpins a half mile down the beach from his own house.

"Hi!" she said, in her clipped, bright Amber-the-Coed voice. "Isn't this party *amazing?*"

He gave her a confused, blank look. "Um, yeah? That's kind of why I'm shocked to see you here." He turned back to his audience of bikini-clad girls. "We went to high school together. I guess you girls would have been in, like, fifth grade? Crazy."

She glanced at the girls—a few of them stared daggers at her, territorial aggression alight in their eyes.

"Anyway, Ronnie here's a private dick," he said loudly, gesturing at her. He leaned toward one of the girls, chortling and nudging her with his elbow. "I'm a not-so-private Dick, if you get what I'm saying." The girls giggled as he thrust his pelvis at them.

Veronica grabbed him by the arm and pulled him, staggering, a few feet away from the little entourage. She threw a big, shiny smile over her shoulder at the girls, then turned back to Dick.

"Whoa, whoa. I know Logan's been gone for, like, weeks, but I can't go all the way with you, no matter how lonely you are." He smirked affably. "Bros before hos, you know what I'm saying? Handies *only*."

"Shut up," she commanded. She kept a smile frozen on her face, her eyes darting over the patio. "I'm here to work, Dick."

His gaze moved up and down her body. "Nice uniform."

She punched him in the arm. From far away it might have looked playful. Dick clutched his bicep, groaning.

"Jeez, Double-O-Psycho, what's your problem?"

"Listen, just keep your voice down, okay?" They were walking back along the edge of the patio now. On their left, a set of stairs led down to the dark beach. The ocean glowed gently beyond, the tidal roar completely swallowed by the noise from the party. She rummaged in her straw beach bag and pulled out her phone. "I need your help. Have you seen this guy here tonight?"

He glanced at the picture on her screen, frowning. "That guy? Yeah, I've seen him. He's always hanging around Rico and Eduardo."

She blinked. "You know the Gutiérrez cousins?"

"Yeah, kind of. I've played squash with Eduardo a couple

times. He's a poor loser, so I stopped." He shrugged. "He's got a bad temper. Broke a two-hundred-dollar racquet last time I beat him. But dude knows how to throw a party."

"And Willie Murphy is a friend of his?"

Dick snorted. "Friend? No. I think he's, like, an errand boy or something. He rounds up people for the parties and stuff."

She stood for a moment, her mind processing all this. What if Willie was working for the Gutiérrez cousins? What if he'd gotten rid of Hayley and Aurora on their orders? Then, trying to cash in another time on the crime, he'd taken Hayley's necklace and sold it. Not exactly criminal mastermind behavior—but then again, Murphy wouldn't be the first guy to screw himself over that way.

"Have you seen him here tonight?"

"Sure." He pointed up toward the terrace. "Right over there."

She looked up to see a scrawny form in oversize patch work pants, his dark blond dreadlocks bobbing around his shoulders as he walked through the doors into the house.

She released Dick's arm. He rubbed it again, frowning. "Thanks, Dick. I've got to run." She walked a few quick steps away from him, then turned around. "And, Dick?"

"Yeah?" He frowned.

"If anyone asks, my name is Amber."

He blinked, then shrugged. "Whatever you say, Rons."

She turned and walked up the steps, as quickly as her heels—and her bikini's precarious arrangement with her anatomy—allowed. By the time she reached the door he'd vanished into the house.

She looked around the kitchen. The strip poker game had deteriorated, the boy who'd been shirtless just a few minutes ago now in nothing but boxers and a single white sock. The girl in the necktie had a rancid-smelling cigar clamped between her teeth. "Did you guys see a boy with dreadlocks come through here? Which way did he go?"

The girl gestured with the burning end of her cigar toward the hallway that led to the front of the house.

Veronica pushed into the hall, into the depths of the crowd. In the front entryway, kids gyrated and screamed like the world was about to end, climbing on top of one another. She couldn't see anything at her height—but looking up, she caught sight of Willie Murphy heading upstairs.

By the time she got to the second-floor landing, he was disappearing through a pair of wide double doors at the end of the long hall.

When she finally fought her way to the doors, they were locked.

She pressed her lips together, glancing around. The hall was filled with people, and while none of them seemed to be paying attention to her, she didn't want anyone to suddenly look up and see her trying to get access to a locked room. *Especially not those guys,* she thought, noticing that in the crowd there were a few granite-faced men with suspicious bulges beneath their armpits. More heavies, in case crowd control was needed.

She staggered back downstairs with a ditzy, drunken grin on her face. She paused for a moment on the lowest stair, pretending to clutch the banister for balance. There would be only one shot to make this work, and it was a long one. She had to pick her target carefully.

Then, before she could talk herself out of it, she plowed

into a bull-necked guy in a University of Washington football jersey as hard as she could.

The size discrepancy between them was vast, to say the least. Veronica barely came up to his armpit. But she threw her weight low in his center of gravity. He staggered forward a few steps, then turned to see who'd hit him. She could have sworn she saw steam coming from his nostrils.

She'd always been able to summon a few thin crocodile tears. Now her lip trembled, and she pointed at another man, a big guy with a ponytail and a shirt that barely buttoned over his massive chest. "That guy just threw me down," she whimpered. The football player's eyes narrowed. He chivalrously helped her to her feet. Then he strode over to the other guy and started shouting in his face.

She couldn't hear what they were saying over the sound of the music, but it was easy to piece together what was happening when the football player started to shove the other guy with sharp, taunting pushes. Ponytail didn't back down. His lip curled up in a savage sneer. Then he swung a punch.

It happened quickly. Everyone moved to the edges of the room, trying to get out of the way while still securing a spot to watch the fight. People coming in from other rooms craned their necks to see over the crowd. Johnny Football had a nasty uppercut and could take a punch like a pro— but it turned out Ponytail was some kind of mixed martial artist. His leg lashed out in a sweep beneath the football player's knees, and suddenly both men were on the floor, rolling around in a tangle of limbs. The music drowned out the dull, fleshy sound of punches landing. The crowd cheered.

A stampede of footsteps, and five enormous bodyguards came running down the stairs. Three of them worked to try to herd the crowd outside, away from the fight. Two moved in to try to get the guys off each other. Veronica didn't stick around to watch who won.

It was just as she'd hoped—the upstairs hallway was almost empty. She heard predictable sounds coming from some of the bedrooms—moans, shrieks of laughter, catcalls—but the double doors she'd seen Willie go through were unguarded. She pressed her ear to one side. Then she knocked. When she was sure there was no one there, she pulled the hairpin she always kept in her wallet and jammed it in the lock.

Interior locks were usually pretty easy to get into. She felt the pin moving at the end of the pick. Then the door swung inward. She slid the pin into her hair, stepped in, and locked the door again behind her.

She stood at the head of another long hallway, the walls painted peacock blue and wainscoted in dark, glossy wood. An end table beneath what looked like a signed and dated Picasso sketch held an enormous urn of roses in white and yellow, and stained glass sconces gave off a mild glow up and down the hall. From somewhere inside one of the rooms she could hear a low rumble of music. She froze for a moment, straining to hear where it was coming from. She couldn't tell.

Several doors stood open along the hallway. Moving as quietly as she could, she started to look around.

The first door led to a bathroom, lined with shining green tile and dark slate. The drawers beneath the sink were empty, but in the medicine cabinet there was a cornucopia of pill bottles—Dilaudid, Percocet, Oxy, and some others she didn't recognize—and an antique snuff case, full of loose white powder. She carefully put everything back where she'd found it and shut the cabinet.

Another door looked in on a small suite that could have come straight out of the Playboy Mansion. A huge round bed took up most of the room. Red and green neon lighting ran around the walls in abstract shapes, and a bar stood in one corner. In an adjoining room, a huge Jacuzzi-style tub sat bubbling quietly, already warmed up.

A set of wide French doors stood open to show a circular library beyond. Built-in wooden bookshelves lined the walls, filled with heavy leather tomes and fronted with glass. The books seemed to be actual collectors' items, carefully curated. She saw Aristotle, Erasmus, Machiavelli. Someone was a classicist—or had the money to look like one. A fire crackled in an enormous stone hearth, and the furniture was glossy and dark.

She moved quickly and quietly, her high heels dangling from one hand so they wouldn't make a noise on the hardwood. It wasn't until she turned the corner in the hall that she saw where the music was coming from. It streamed out of a partly open door, an ominous electronic thud. Veronica's heart hammered in her ears, asynchronous with the music's rhythm. She held her breath and crept toward the open door.

It led to a den. Framed movie posters—*Scarface*, *The Godfather*, *GoodFellas*—hung around the walls; track lighting generated a warm, indirect glow. A wide scarlet couch sat in front of a plasma-screen TV mounted on the wall. Two men were sitting on the couch, playing a video game, their backs to the hall. One had short, shiny dark hair.

The other sprouted with wild dirty-blond dreadlocks.

The dark-haired head bent down for a moment. The smell of pot suddenly filled the air. She could hear the gurgling sound of someone taking a deep, committed hit.

"I'm not complaining, man," said Willie Murphy. He talked quickly, in a lilting, urgent patter, never taking his eyes off the screen, where the burly army guy he was playing let loose a hail of bullets at an alien. "You guys are like family to me, you know? I mean, anything you want, anything I can do, I'll do."

She watched as Rico Gutiérrez Ortega tilted his head back and exhaled.

"Anyone ever tell you you talk too much?" he finally asked as his lungs cleared.

Pulse throbbing in her ears, Veronica took a few steps back from the door. She pulled out her phone with shaking fingers, and then, covering the speaker with her thumb to mute it, she dialed Lamb's cell.

It rang six times. She clutched the phone with white-knuckled hands, wondering if he'd seen her name on the caller ID and was screening her out. She didn't want to just call 911—there wasn't an emergency to report, and by the time she convinced dispatch that this was related to the missing girls, it might be too late.

Just as she was about to give up, he answered.

"What is it?" His voice was brusque and dismissive. She closed her eyes, mentally thanking whatever higher power had talked him into answering.

"Lamb, it's Veronica Mars. This afternoon I got a lead on a suspect who was caught on camera selling Hayley Dewalt's necklace two days after she disappeared. A small-time crook named William Murphy—Mac can get you the details. I'm at the Gutiérrez mansion on Manzanita, and he's here. He's in one of the back rooms playing video games with Federico."

For a moment there was silence on the other end of the line. Back in the den something exploded on screen; the boys both groaned loudly. Veronica waited.

"So you want me to bust into private property, without a warrant, because someone may or may not have stolen a necklace? You're out of your mind, Mars."

She gripped the phone tighter. "There's a huge party going on downstairs. I counted about fifty laws being broken. You have plenty of probable cause to get you in the door."

"How do you even know this guy got the necklace from Hayley? How do you know—"

"Lamb, this is your chance," she hissed, losing her temper. "I can prove that Willie Murphy had a missing girl's necklace. Do you want to let that slip right through your fingers? Or do you want to be the big damn hero that bags the bad guy? I don't know how long he'll be here. You have to *move*."

He was silent for another second.

"Okay, keep on him. We're coming."

Then he hung up.

She made her way back around the corner. Willie was still talking: ". . . you ever think we might all be some kind of livestock for aliens? Like maybe Earth is just a big wild game reserve and aliens come back from time to time to make sure we've got enough to eat and we're healthy enough to propagate, and to pick off a couple million of us for food? I saw a program on the Discovery Channel about people who think they've been, like, abducted and shit. But maybe the anal probe is, like, their version of a brand. You get the old double bar up the ass, and it's their way of marking you as theirs."

Rico laughed wildly. One of the soldiers on the screen exploded in a shower of blood, and half the screen went black, the words GAME OVER in red. Neither one set down his controller—both seemed to think they were playing the surviving character.

The minutes crept by. She stood at the door, hoping that in the middle of their stoner ramblings they'd say something about one of the girls. Any minute she expected to hear sirens, shouts through a bullhorn, the party being invaded. Willie and Rico kept jamming the buttons on their controllers, shouting whenever one of them died.

"Shit, son, I fucking *pwnd* you," Rico jeered.

"The controller wasn't working. It was, like, stuck or something."

"Sure, sure." A machine gun blast, then: "Damn, man, I keep thinking of that little Puerto Rican girl in the pink bikini."

"The one with the bangs?"

"No, the one with the pierced belly button. Cute, cute, cute."

Willie laughed so hard he started to cough. "Dude, she called you a douche bag. I don't think she's that into you, man. Plus she's here with, like, twenty girlfriends. No way can we get her alone."

"No, man, look—here's what we're gonna do. We're gonna go to the garage and get the Ferrari. Then we're gonna drive it around to the patio with the bass thumping. They are gonna swarm us, man. Bitches love Ferraris." He held up his controller and jammed over and over again on one of the buttons. "Then we'll load up the honeys and take 'em to Taco Bell."

"Taco Bell? Man, there's, like, smoked salmon and asparagus in truffle oil and, like, crudités downstairs. Why the hell do you want to go to Taco Bell?"

Rico shrugged. "I like their chalupas."

Willie's voice went dreamy. "Oh, yeah. Those are *awesome*."

Rico stood halfway up, then fell back into the sofa, laughing hysterically.

Oh, shit. The stoners are on the move. Willie was helping Rico to his feet. *Not very quickly, or efficiently . . . but on the move nonetheless. Time to exit.*

She backed up a few steps, then turned on her heel and went back the way she'd come. If she hurried, she'd have time to duck into one of the other rooms, hide behind the door until they passed. She rounded the corner and pushed her way into the library . . .

. . . and right into Eduardo.

CHAPTER NINETEEN

A short, shrill scream burst out of her throat before she could stop it. Eduardo grabbed her by the bicep, his fingers digging into her bare flesh. He dragged her farther into the library behind him.

"How the fuck did you get back here?" Spittle flew from his mouth. She instinctively shrank away from him, but he had an iron grip on her arm.

The sound of footsteps pounded along the corridor outside. Rico burst into the room, Willie on his heels.

"What's going on?" Rico stopped in his tracks and stared. Behind him, Willie went pale, his eyes round.

Eduardo shook her roughly back and forth. Her teeth clattered against one another with the impact. She gave another little cry of pain, her breath short and shaky.

"*This* little bitch is wandering around where she shouldn't be." His words came in a wild cascade, tumbling in rapid-fire bursts out of his mouth. He sniffed loudly. "What the fuck, Rico? She one of yours? You can't just let people wander around this place, *ése.*"

He sniffed again, as if he were allergic to something in the room.

Dilated pupils, runny nose, diarrhea of the mouth: some-

one's been sampling the company product. Her eyes fell on an ugly gilded clock on the mantel, naked cherubs gesturing toward the face. It was just after ten thirty—almost fifteen minutes since she'd called Lamb.

Rico held up both hands. "It wasn't me. I've never seen this chick." He gave her an appraising look, his lids heavy. "I'd remember."

"Eduardo, man, I think you're hurting her," Willie said, his voice uneasy. "Why don't you let her go?"

"Shut the fuck up, Willie." Eduardo jerked Veronica close to his body, his face only inches from hers. The smooth-talking flirt of the night before was gone. This Eduardo was taut and aggressive. Tendons strained in his neck and arms, and his hair stuck up where he'd been running his fingers through it. Between that and his bulging eyes, he looked quite mad.

Tears sprang to her eyes, but she didn't try to hide them. She wanted to look as defenseless, as nonthreatening, as possible. "Don't you remember me? We talked the other night, down by the pool. We were going to take a walk on the beach, but I was here with my boyfriend. I came back tonight to find you. I didn't mean to do anything wrong."

"You think I'm some kind of idiot?" he spat. "I want to know who you're working for!"

She glanced over at Willie and Rico. She didn't know what she was hoping to see in their faces—sympathy, maybe, or even exasperation. Instead, Willie was looking studiously away, his twitching rabbit eyes darting around the edges of the room, as if he were politely trying not to notice the way Eduardo was twisting her arm. Rico, on the other hand, grinned foolishly. He looked like he thought he was in for a treat.

"I'm really sorry," she whispered. Her vision blurred for a moment, and a tear cut down the side of her cheek. She held very still, trying to keep her focus steady. "I didn't mean to do anything wrong. Please, just let me go, and I'll go back down to the party. I won't bother you. I'll leave, if you want, and never come back."

"Hey, man, that seems fair." Willie shifted his weight. "She didn't hurt anything. Let's just take her back out front and leave her alone."

"Get lost, Willie." It was Rico who spoke this time, his voice soft and slow. "We need some privacy."

Willie licked his lips. She caught a whiff of sweat and patchouli as he rubbed the back of his neck with one hand. "Sure, Rico. Sure, I'll just . . . I'll head back to the party, okay?" He edged toward the door, slowly at first, as if he couldn't quite get his speed up. Then he disappeared down the hall. Veronica could hear a distant door open and close. And just like that, she was alone with the Gutiérrez cousins.

Rico turned to shut the library's double doors with a soft *click*. Eduardo stood stone still, his eyes boring into hers, his grip tight.

"I'm not sure what I did wrong," Veronica said feebly. "The door was open. I just came in and looked around."

"The door wasn't open, *mami*." All of a sudden he let go of her. She staggered a few feet back, rubbing her arm, as a wolfish smile spread over his face. It was a lot like the smile he'd given her just the night before, on the terrace. Both times she felt hunted, but this time, she felt teeth.

"The door wasn't open, and we both know it. So why don't we cut the *shit*?" He shouted the last word and swept an armful of books off the shelf as he passed, sending them crashing to the floor. Rico walked around the other side, flanking her with an expression of stupid amusement.

She took a step backward and felt one of the bookshelves pressing against her spine. Rico laughed, stopping a short distance away from her. She felt around behind her for something, anything, that she could use as a weapon, but there were only books.

"Who . . . sent . . . you?" Eduardo's voice had escalated to a furious scream. He lunged toward her, his lips pulled back in a snarl. She flinched away from him, stumbling over a fallen book.

"I don't know what you're talking about!" she cried. She looked from one to the other, truly confused. Did they know she was a PI? Did they think she was a cop?

"She's not gonna make it easy, Eddie," Rico said thickly. He grinned at her. "But she's gonna make it fun."

When she looked at Eduardo, he was reaching behind his back, fumbling at something she couldn't see. A moment later her heart stuttered painfully in her chest.

He had a knife.

"Who are you with? The Sonoras? The Zetas?" Eduardo turned the blade back and forth, the firelight running along the steel in bright and shifting patterns. It was a Bowie knife, six inches long, and he held it up in a ready stance. *"Los Caballeros Templarios?"*

She gaped at him, her brain on fire. He thought she was an assassin? Someone from a rival cartel? That was *insane*. Certifiably, beyond a doubt insane. But he was deadly serious. A tight, panicked feeling was starting to close in on Veronica's chest, pressing down on her lungs, on her heart.

"I'm not with anyone," she whispered. She mentally took the measurements of the room around her. Rico and Eduardo flanked her, each a few feet away. Behind her were the bookshelves; in front of her, a low chaise longue she might be able to launch herself across. *But how fast is he with that knife?* He held it like he'd used it before. She wasn't sure she'd be able to make it to the door.

"That's what they all say," Rico said. He grinned, and she thought she saw a mischievous gleam in his eye. *He doesn't think I'm in a cartel,* she realized. *He's just egging Eduardo on—because he thinks it's* funny. The thought didn't make her feel any better.

"We know your people've been in town for a while now." Eduardo's pupils were so wide she could see the room reflected in their depths. He wiped his nose quickly with the back of his left hand. "Watching, waiting for an opportunity. Looking for your chance to send a message to El Oso."

Veronica wondered distantly if this was what had happened to Hayley. To Aurora. If, instead of discovering something, they'd simply been on the receiving end of Eduardo's paranoia and Rico's thirst for blood. She took a step sideways and bumped into a heavy pedestal with a musty dictionary perched on top. "I don't know what you're talking about."

"Stop. *Lying.*" Eduardo's voice rose, a ragged cry of rage. She saw his legs tense in the split second before he sprang at her, and she took her one desperate chance, throwing her body at the chaise longue in the hopes she could scramble over it. But a fist closed in her hair. She was jerked backward against someone's hard, heaving chest. The knife flashed against her throat.

"'Tell me who sent you." Eduardo's breath was hot against her cheek.

"No one!" Her scalp burned. She writhed in his grip, struggling to twist out of his grasp, but he had her pinned.

She felt the edge of the blade pressing into her flesh. A thin ribbon of blood trickled down her throat. "Tell me!"

She didn't answer. She closed her eyes and waited for the pain.

Then an explosion of noise blasted through the room.

The French doors burst. A group of girls poured through, laughing and jostling. At the head of the crowd was Willie Murphy, looking like he was leading a marching band as he gestured for the crowd to follow him. Absurdly, bringing up the rear was Dick Casablancas, plastic cup in hand. The sound of music drifted down the hallway and filled the room.

"This way, ladies—there's more Cristal in here!" Willie opened a bottle of champagne with a loud pop. Behind him the group cheered. He gestured at a buxom black-haired girl in a bright pink bikini. "Rico, man, look who I found. Selena here is totes down with our Taco Bell plan, brah!"

Eduardo's grip on her loosened, the knife flashing away out of sight of the crowd. The moment she was free, Veronica staggered toward Dick. "Dick, baby, where have you been? I've been looking all over for you."

He tried to take an instinctive step backward as she advanced, but she was already flinging her arms around his neck and pulling him toward her. She showered him with kisses, and as she leaned up to plant one firmly on his lips, she caught a glimpse of his sea-blue eyes, frozen wide in a kind of mesmerized horror.

But Eduardo wasn't even looking at her and Dick. He had eyes for no one but Willie.

For just a moment, she caught sight of Willie's face. His complexion was like curdled milk, his eyes wide and darting. His hands trembled so bad he could barely pour the champagne.

He looked almost as scared as Veronica felt.

A few of the bodyguards burst in, looking abashed, trying—and failing—to herd everyone back down the hall to the main floor. Girls climbed up on the antique chairs, gyrating their hips to the music pouring in from the other room. An inflatable beach ball had manifested from somewhere and floated through the room from fist to fist. Rico was already chatting up a little cluster of girls, easily distracted from bloodshed to booty.

Then another kind of noise filled the hallway.

"Attention. Attention. Evacuate the premises immediately. This is an order. I repeat: this is an order."

Bullhorns. Mechanical, blaring voices.

Cops.

All hell broke loose. At once the spring breakers flew into motion, some running straight for the door, some rooted to the spot in confusion and fear. Dick released Veronica, looking baffled. She saw Eduardo stepping back with his hands up and a resigned expression on his face. Rico scowled, annoyed, as the little group of girls scattered.

Willie Murphy, though, reacted with the knee-jerk panic of a man who'd been hunted half his life. He ran toward the door in blind terror. He sidestepped a brutish-looking deputy in khaki only to be headed off by another, this one with a baton swinging in his fist. Then he scrambled backward, eyes rolling like a cornered animal. Veronica saw the familiar white flash of a Taser, and Willie hit the ground hard.

Suddenly Lamb was there, bullhorn in hand. His voice screeched painfully through the room, echoing off the glossy furniture. Several of the remaining spring breakers covered their ears, cringing.

"Clear this room. Clear it out, people, this is your last warning or we'll bring in the tear gas. Out to the front lawn where our friendly officers will meet and process you. Go on."

A few feet away, one of the officers was getting Murphy's wrists in cuffs.

"Willie Murphy, you are under arrest. You have the right to remain silent. Anything you say can and will be used against you in a court of law. You have the right to an attorney. If you cannot afford an attorney, one will be provided for you. Do you understand the rights I have just read to you?"

Lamb took the bullhorn away from his lips, leaning in to talk to Eduardo, who nodded slowly at whatever he said. A surge of anger propelled Veronica forward, her eyes blazing. Lamb's eyes narrowed when he saw her.

"Mars. Going in guns blazing as usual, I see. You should have let us handle this."

She jabbed an index finger toward Eduardo. "This asshole had a knife to my throat, Lamb. I want to press charges."

Lamb glanced at Eduardo, then put a firm hand on her back to propel her out the door. "Come on, Mars, this has been a crazy night for you. Let's not say anything we'll regret later."

She shook him off. "Are you kidding me? He assaulted me. He drew blood. Do your fucking job for once and arrest him!"

Eduardo quickly stepped forward, giving Lamb an abashed look. "Sheriff, I did do as this girl said. Mars, you said her name was? I overreacted. I found her in my private rooms and thought she was an intruder. I did not know she was a friend of yours."

Veronica's mouth fell open. But Lamb just smirked.

"I told you not to go sneaking around peoples' houses, buttercup. Hell, I could actually take you in for trespassing right now, you know that?"

"There's no need for that," said Eduardo benevolently. "It was an honest mistake." He gave a little bow toward Veronica, a mocking smile playing at the edges of his lips.

She stared at the two of them, standing close together now, talking in low voices about Willie Murphy. Willie Murphy, the low-hanging fruit that would be enough to get the press off Lamb's back without requiring any real police work—and without requiring him to piss off the cartel.

Then she swallowed it. The rage, the fear—it went down hard. It made a knot in the pit of her stomach. She didn't speak but let an officer lead her out the door and down the stairs, toward the clean, cool air outside.

CHAPTER TWENTY

"Look, I'm telling you, I'm fine. I don't need a sedative."

It was almost three in the morning, and Veronica sat at the edge of the hospital bed, a plaid blanket tucked around her shoulders. She wore a set of light blue scrubs, three sizes too big—she'd still been in her bikini when she'd arrived at the ER waiting room an hour and a half ago, shivering and exposed. Now she held up her hands to ward off the tiny Dixie cup the nurse was trying to hand her and accidentally knocked it to the floor. Two blue pills scattered across the scuffed linoleum.

The nurse, a short, plump man with a buzz cut and glasses perched on the edge of his nose, gave her a stern what-did-I-tell-you look before stooping to scoop them back up. "You don't, huh? Except for the fact that you're shaking like a leaf."

Back at the mansion, the EMTs had taken one look at her neck and insisted on taking her straight to Neptune General. Once the doctor had swabbed the blood away, the cut turned out to be shallow, only about three centimeters long, but they'd had her lie still for a while so they could monitor any possible shock.

"Sorry," she muttered. "My friend's on his way to pick me up. I'll be okay then."

On the other side of the thin cotton curtain around her bed, she heard the sound of someone violently puking into a bin. The ER was full of gray-faced undergraduates, most of them with alcohol poisoning. The nurse sighed heavily, gave her one last argumentative look, and turned to go and check on her neighbor. Veronica pulled the blanket tighter around her shoulders, relieved to be alone.

The nurse was right—it wasn't just the chill air that made her shiver. All the adrenaline of the last few hours had curdled in her blood, leaving her weak limbed and nauseated. Her arm ached where Eduardo had grabbed her, and a half dozen dull, throbbing pains were blooming across her body from the struggle. And then there was the thin line across her throat, still burning from the touch of that blade. Superficial as the wound was, she felt it most of all.

But she didn't want to take any pills that would make her slow or stupid—not yet. Not while she might still have to think on her feet.

The curtain fluttered open. A second nurse put her head through. "Miss Mars? Your friend's arrived. He's in the waiting room whenever you're ready to go."

She jumped off the bed. "Okay. Thank you."

Wallace stood in the lime-green waiting room wearing a pair of baggy sweats and a T-shirt. Her call had obviously woken him up; he was sleep rumpled, but his warm brown eyes were alert. He was pretending to read a poster about proper hand washing when she came in the room, but he looked up with a gentle, concerned expression, taking in her scrubs, her tangled hair, and the dark red scratch on her neck.

She paused in the doorway. Then, all at once, her lip started to shudder, and she burst into tears.

It was a sudden storm, coming on without warning and gone almost as soon as it'd started. Wallace pulled her against his side in a rough hug and didn't speak. They stood there for a few minutes, him patting her shaking shoulder. Finally, she wiped her eyes frantically, embarrassed, unable to speak. Then she laughed shakily.

"Let's get out of here, okay?"

"Yeah, okay." He squeezed her shoulder and then let go.

The streets were still busy, even at 3:00 a.m. Most of the bars kept extended hours during spring break, and they passed a few, fluttering with light. An ambulance streaked in the opposite direction, back toward the hospital. She leaned her head back against the seat and looked over at Wallace.

"Thanks for coming to get me," she said. "Dad's not cleared to drive yet."

"It's no problem," Wallace said. "You gonna tell me what happened?"

She watched his knuckles tighten around the steering wheel as she told him about the night—how she'd gone back to the party to find Willie Murphy, how she'd gotten caught sneaking around the upstairs rooms. How the cousins had closed in on her—only to be interrupted by Murphy himself, leading an impromptu parade through the library.

"You know, you didn't have to go back in there alone." She could hear a hint of restrained anger in his voice. "I would've gone with you."

She gave a sad smile. "No, you would have tried to talk me out of it. Probably with good reason." Her hand flew up to her throat. "But I had to find Murphy, Wallace. I had to take the chance."

"You always do, don't you?" He glanced at her, then looked quickly back to the road. "Look, I'm not mad, Veronica. I'm just worried that someday the unstoppable force is gonna meet the immovable object."

"Wait, which one am I?" she joked. "No, don't answer that."

He snorted. "So you found this Murphy guy. Do you think he did it? Took the girls?"

She stared out at the world rolling away outside her window. "I don't know anymore. I went in thinking Willie Murphy was the one behind the disappearances. But you should have seen the guy's face when Eduardo grabbed me—he was terrified. And he waltzed back in with Dick and those girls and probably saved my life."

"Yeah, but he had that necklace, right?" Wallace glanced at her, his fingers drumming along the steering wheel. "He had to be involved somehow."

He was right. But she couldn't shake the feeling that something didn't fit. Willie Murphy didn't look like a guy who could *handle* violence, much less one who *liked* it. And he'd come back—scared as he was, he'd come back, because it was the only way he knew to keep Eduardo from killing her.

"Maybe Murphy's just their cleanup crew," she said, thinking out loud. "Maybe Eduardo or Rico—or both of them—killed Hayley and Aurora, either because the girls found out something they shouldn't have or because the guys just like killing. Or maybe Eduardo assumes anyone who's caught sneaking around the house is an assassin. He's pretty jumpy. Then they call in Murphy to clean up, dispose of the bodies. And Murphy saw the necklace and just couldn't help himself." She rubbed her forehead. "Well, it doesn't matter. Lamb's going to hang him out to dry. Willie Murphy is the definition of low-hanging fruit. He's got a record, and he looks sketchy as hell."

Wallace was quiet for a moment. Then he spoke. "So you think the girls are dead?"

She didn't answer. The raw cut along her throat throbbed gently. There wasn't any way of knowing for sure what had happened to those girls—but after what she'd just been through, the little flicker of hope that she'd been holding on to throughout her investigation was guttering.

They turned left into Veronica's neighborhood. Here the houses were dark and silent, their occupants still asleep. Somewhere a dog barked, deep voiced and lonely.

They pulled up in front of the bungalow. She suddenly realized she'd have to tell Keith what had happened in a few short hours. That would be a nightmare. *Thank goodness for the U.S. Navy. I can at least put off telling Logan. The last thing I need is for my boyfriend to pick a fight with an international crime syndicate.*

"You want me to come in with you?" Wallace turned his head to look at her, his brow furrowed. She shook her head.

"No. I don't want to wake up Dad." She reached across to pat his arm with a forced joviality. "I'm okay. I'll call you tomorrow. At a reasonable hour this time."

"Veronica . . ." He hesitated, then shook his head. "You sure you're okay?"

She gave a weak smile. "I'm always okay." Then, seeing he wasn't buying it, she hugged him around the neck.

"Thanks again, Wallace. For everything."

She jumped out of the car and headed up the stairs to

her house. He waited until she'd gotten in the door before driving back out to the street.

And for about the millionth time in her life she felt an overwhelming gratitude for her best friend. Because she knew he wouldn't mention this afterward; she knew he wouldn't take it as a sign that she was losing her nerve or was in too deep. There weren't many people in this world who would let you be vulnerable and still believe you were strong.

CHAPTER TWENTY-ONE

The sun was thin and pale on the courthouse steps the next morning as the crowd of reporters gathered before it, cameras at the ready. The dramatic capture of Willie Murphy by the Balboa County Sheriff's Department had made the early morning news, and Lamb had called a 9:00 a.m. press conference to make it all official. A low buzz rippled over the crowd as well-coiffed newscasters murmured to their viewers that in just minutes, they'd have exclusive live coverage involving the missing Neptune spring breakers.

Veronica was facing the podium, Keith on one side of her and Mac on the other. She would have been happy to watch the coverage from home, but Petra Landros had called her a little over an hour earlier asking her to be there. She hadn't been able to sleep; her nerves had been too ragged. But she'd showered and pinned her hair in a sleek, professional bun. Somewhat passive-aggressively, she wore a scoop-neck top under her blazer, making the long red line across her neck as obvious as she could. *Go on and let someone ask me about it,* she thought. *I'll let them know who did this in no uncertain terms.*

She looked out of the corner of her eye at Keith. He stood with both hands propped on the head of his cane, his expression stony. That morning he'd been silent, his face drawn as he listened to her describe the events of the night before. Then he'd hugged her close, seemingly unable to speak. She'd seen his eyes dart to the revolver in the wooden box, but Keith refrained from lecturing her. By the time she'd come out of her room, groomed and ready to go to the courthouse, he'd been in a suit and tie, waiting by the door. And he must have called Mac, because she met them there, bleary-eyed but anxious, with three coffees in to-go cups.

Veronica was grateful. Standing in front of all these people alone, waiting to hear Lamb act as though the case were solved while ignoring the most important piece—the violent cartel cousins—might have put her over the edge.

She glanced around the crowd. The Dewalts stood a few yards away, Mike's arms wrapped around Ella's shoulders from behind. Crane looked strained, edgy, his eyes wide and panicked. Tears rolled down Margie's cheeks. Veronica glanced around to look for her mother and found her, near the back of the crowd, with Hunter gathered in her arms, her face buried in his neck. Next to her, Tanner stood and stared blankly around like a man who didn't know where he was. She wondered if Petra had asked them to come too, or if they were as desperate for information as the reporters.

"Ms. Mars?"

She turned around, startled, to see Petra Landros right in front of her. Her thick dark hair was pinned back in a somber twist, and her Armani suit was an understated charcoal gray tailored to hug her curves.

"You must be proud," Petra said, shaking Veronica's hand. "You caught the bad guy." She turned to face Keith. "And you must be the notorious Mr. Mars. I'm so pleased to meet you."

Keith's eyebrows shot up. "Notorious?"

"Your tenure as sheriff wasn't the most probusiness we've ever had, you know. But your name came up again and again as the Chamber talked about whom we should hire to find Hayley. Everyone says you're the best." The hint of a smile tugged her lips upward. "In any case, your daughter's certainly upheld your firm's reputation." She turned back to Veronica. "Now, shall I wire you payment, or would you like to come to my office for a check right now?"

Veronica frowned. "Usually I don't get paid until the case is closed, Ms. Landros. We still haven't found those girls."

Petra's smile faded quickly. She adopted a concerned, sincere expression.

"Of course," she said. "If we can recover the girls, we'd love to do that for the families."

Veronica's jaw tightened involuntarily. It wasn't hard to read the writing on the wall. As far as the Chamber of Commerce was concerned, the case was resolved. Willie Murphy was a perfect suspect, whether he'd done anything to the missing girls or not.

The semblance of law and order is just as good as the real thing, right? As long as it keeps the tourist dollars flowing, who cares if we've got the right guy?

The crowd suddenly went still as Lamb made his way to the podium. Cameras shuffled around, microphones bristling forward. Veronica straightened up a little. Lamb's khaki uniform was perfectly pressed, each button gleaming in the sun. He gave a dramatic pause as he stared arrogantly around the gathered crowd, then looked down at his notes.

"Early this morning, at just after twelve a.m., we arrested a suspect in the disappearances of Hayley Dewalt and

Aurora Scott. William Murphy, age twenty-four, was seen with both girls prior to their disappearances. I can't discuss the evidence in an ongoing case, but . . ."

The reporters broke into a clamor. Next to her, her father stood with his knuckles white on the handle of his cane. Mac gave a contemptuous little grimace, shifting her weight. At the podium Lamb lifted his hands with a benevolent, patronizing smile. "One at a time, please. One at a time."

"What are you charging him with?" shouted a bespectacled man with wisps of hair across his scalp. "Do you know what happened to Hayley and Aurora?"

"Has Murphy confessed?" asked a dark-haired woman in a violet-flowered suit. "Or do you have some physical evidence linking him to the crime?"

"Where are the girls?" Veronica couldn't tell where the voice came from, but the question was echoed a few more times around the courtyard.

"Where are Hayley and Aurora?"

"Are you going to be able to bring them home?"

Lamb cleared his throat. "At this time, we are moving ahead with a murder investigation."

A spike of sound went up from the crowd. A few gasps, a ragged sob. Veronica exchanged a glance with Keith. Had Murphy copped to something, or was Lamb going for maximum effect?

"Again, I'm not at liberty to discuss the specifics of the case at this time, because we are still talking with the DA about how to move ahead. But the important thing is that we've got this guy off the street, and Neptune is safe again."

"Sheriff Lamb, some people are saying that Murphy is

involved with a larger criminal organization. Can you speak to these rumors?"

So they weren't completely stupid. Veronica wasn't surprised that the question had come from Martina Vasquez, a reporter for San Diego's local news station. Lamb's eyes darted toward her, his mouth gaping for just a moment before he collected himself.

"Well, Martina, I can't respond to rampant speculation, and frankly, I think it's irresponsible for the media to report hearsay as fact." He leaned one arm on the lectern, smiling at Martina as if she'd just made some cute and childish mistake.

Mac made a strangled noise in the back of her throat.

"Hard to believe he's single, isn't it?" Veronica whispered. But she couldn't hide her grin. If anyone was going to dig a little deeper, it would be Martina Vasquez, who seemed to like the Sheriff's Department about as much as Veronica did. Maybe she could even send Martina an anonymous tip or two about the Gutiérrez boys. A little media attention might help Lamb take an interest in the cartel's laundering operation.

"Do you think Murphy will lead you to the girls' bodies?" someone asked from the crowd.

Lamb fidgeted with the note cards he'd prepared. "So far he's not offering any information. But I have faith we'll get it out of him sooner or later. Once he realizes he's got no choice, it'll just be a matter of time."

Next to her, Veronica heard Keith exhale a small, exasperated sigh. His jaw was tight, but he watched the proceedings without any other reaction. She knew that poker face from experience. The deeper the anger, the harder the puzzle, the higher the stakes, the calmer Keith Mars looked. Which meant that right now, he was pissed.

A few yards away, Margie Dewalt wept silently into her handkerchief. Veronica met Ella's eyes for one long, awful moment, forcing herself not to look away. Her breath felt tight in her chest. She saw Mr. Dewalt, pulling his phone out of his pocket, sticking his finger in his left ear to block out the sound of the crowd as he answered. His expression was confused. Then the crowd shifted, obscuring him from sight for a moment.

"All right, if there are no further questions—"

"Oh my god! She's alive!"

People turned and craned their necks to see where the sudden cry had come from. A moment later Veronica caught sight of Mike Dewalt, his face a mask of anxious astonishment. He had a cell phone clamped to one ear.

A murmur went up from the crowd, only to die down as Mike spoke. "Hayley's still alive." His voice was a breathy croak. His eyes looked wild. "And so's the other girl. They're still alive."

He held up the cell phone, as if it was some kind of proof. His eyes were fearful and excited all at once.

"Their kidnappers just called. And they want a ransom."

CHAPTER TWENTY-TWO

Interrogation room B hadn't changed at all in the almost ten years Veronica had been away. Dark wood wainscoting, dingy yellow paint, a chalkboard scrawled with what at first looked to be clues to some convoluted mystery but that turned out to be fantasy football scores. It was just like stepping into a time warp.

Except instead of a vain, lazy, incompetent Sheriff Lamb, now we've got a vain, lazy, corrupt Sheriff Lamb. She looked across the table at Lamb's glowering face. He'd just been upstaged, and he wasn't happy.

The room was at capacity. Veronica and Keith sat across from Dan Lamb and Petra Landros. Mike, Margie, and Ella Dewalt sat close together on the side to Veronica's left, Crane standing behind them. To Keith's right sat the Scotts. Lianne was inches from Keith, which sent an anxious, electric charge up the back of Veronica's neck every time she glanced their way.

Keith and Lianne hadn't seen each other in more than ten years now; their divorce had been quick and uncontested, a signature on a piece of paper. Veronica had worried their presence in the same room would be like matter and antimatter, exploding on contact in a rush of blinding light.

But all that had happened had been a smile, a handshake. A civil exchange.

"Hello, Keith."

"Lianne. It's good to see you. I'm sorry for the circumstances, though."

And then they'd sat down. That was all.

Veronica looked around the table at the other faces. Mike Dewalt's eyes were bright with relief. Margie couldn't stop crying, her face hidden behind her enormous handkerchief. Ella looked pale, her lips and eyes like dark marks on paper. Behind them, Crane clutched the back of a chair, his fingers white. On the other side of the table, Tanner and Lianne held hands. Hunter sat on her lap, resting his head against her shoulder and looking at no one.

They'd all just heard that their daughters had been murdered, only to get what felt like a reprieve minutes later. A sense of cautious relief hung on the air.

"The e-mail address it came from is just a bunch of scrambled numbers," Mike said, setting his phone on the table. "But it had a . . . a sound file in it. What's it called, sweetie?"

"MP three," Ella said, in a soft, distant voice.

"MP three," he repeated. "Here, listen."

He hit Play. A man's voice came through the speaker, garbled through some kind of voice modulator so it sounded like a child's toy robot.

"*Dewalts: Your daughter is alive. If you want to see her again, follow our instructions to the letter. We want six hundred thousand dollars in unmarked, nonsequential bills. Pack it in a small suitcase. Do not try to put any trackers or dye into the money; this will result in your daughter's immediate* death. Do not involve the cops; this will result in your daughter's immediate death. We will be in contact on the evening of the twenty-sixth to instruct you on where to leave the money. Do not try to set up some kind of sting, as we are watching every move you make.

"For the time being she is safe and comfortable, but very scared. To prove she's alive we asked her to tell us something only she would know. She said you once let slip that she'd been conceived to Meat Loaf's 'I'd Do Anything for Love.' She said only you, Mrs. Dewalt, Mr. Dewalt, and she know that fact.

"Do not try to outsmart us. If you follow the instructions to a T, you will have your daughter back again by the weekend. We do not want to be violent, but if we have to, we will."

Margie hid her face entirely now, her sobs loud and ringing in the quiet room. Ella wrapped a slender arm around her mother's neck, her face pinched and scared. For a moment, no one spoke.

"Someone's been tracking the money on the website," Veronica said. Her voice felt too loud in the quiet room. "They're asking for the exact amount of money raised. That's not an accident."

"Ours is almost the same," Tanner finally said. He wore a T-shirt with a picture of his daughter printed across the front. It said FIND AURORA in large dark pink letters across her forehead. The creases in his face seemed deeper, more graven than before. He thumbed a button on his phone to play the message.

He was right; it was the same, word for word, until it got to the paragraph on proof of life.

"Aurora said she and Lianne made gingerbread pancakes together in the middle of the night during Tanner's last relapse.

You were waiting for him to come home, and you made the pancakes to kill time and fed them to the dog."

"That was years ago," Lianne whispered. "She was twelve or thirteen. I don't think we've ever talked about it since." She took a shuddering breath and looked around the room, her eyes round, hopeful. "But this is good news, right? It means the girls are still alive. It means we can get them back."

Lamb cleared his throat. He seemed to be fighting to keep his face sympathetic, but it wasn't a natural expression for him—the effect came across almost passive-aggressive, like he actually *was* going to kill someone with kindness.

"I don't want to dash your hopes, folks, but there are almost always hoax ransom demands that come in after a disappearance. The Lindbergh baby, JonBenét . . . it's possible that this is some kind of prank or con."

Margie let out a gasping sob. "There's no way Hayley would have told anyone about that song. She was so embarrassed. It came on the radio one night when we were making dinner, and I . . . I thought it was funny. I couldn't help myself. I had to tell her. But she ran to her room and hid for the rest of the night."

"She might have told a friend, a boyfriend . . . ," Lamb said.

"No. You don't know Hayley like I do. She was furious that I told her. I can't imagine her telling anyone else."

Lamb sighed. "Look, I just want to caution you all to not get your hopes up. We'll look into every possible lead here, but the fact is, we have a suspect in custody who we can place at the scene of both crimes. And we have physical evidence tying him to one of the disappearances. The signs are not looking good, and it would be a mistake to comply with these demands."

That was when Lianne spoke, and Veronica saw it—saw a glimpse of her mother, the woman who'd been married to a cop, who'd been willing to fight for things she loved when the vodka wasn't pickling her brain.

"A mistake?" Lianne leaned forward. "Listen to me, Sheriff. As long as there's a chance of finding Aurora alive, we'll take it. We'll do anything we have to do to get her back."

Landros, her face much more convincing than Lamb's in its mask of sympathy, held up her hands. Her pillowy lips were turned down, her dark eyes gentle. "Please, Mrs. Scott. We're here to help. Rest assured that we will do everything in our power to bring the girls home, alive and well."

With startling intensity, Lianne whipped her head around to face Keith and Veronica. "What do you think, Keith?"

Keith shook his head. "I haven't been working this case. I can't really speak to the details. It's Veronica we should be asking."

All eyes settled on Veronica. Her heart picked up speed, and her hand, almost unconsciously, drifted up to touch the cut at her neck.

"Well," she said carefully. "I don't know anything for sure. But I'm not convinced Willie Murphy's our guy."

Lamb looked at her incredulously. "You're the one who brought me the evidence, Mars. Now you're saying—"

"I'm *saying* that we don't know the whole story yet," she said, speaking over him. "Murphy risked his life to help me back at the Gutiérrez house. I think he knows something about what happened to the girls—but I'm not convinced he's a kidnapper. Or a murderer. And we're all ignoring the fact that he was in custody when the ransom notes came in. Either he has an accomplice—or he didn't do it."

They stared at each other across the Formica, the space between them electric with mutual loathing. She kept her gaze level, her chin slightly raised.

On the adjacent side of the table, Margie Dewalt looked up from her handkerchief. "Can we use the money from the reward funds to pay the ransom? Is that . . . is that something we're allowed to do, Ms. Landros? I know it was supposed to pay for the reward, but so far it hasn't helped us find her. Maybe it can help us bring her home."

Crane suddenly spoke, his voice loud and sneering. "Look, this guy they arrested had her *necklace*. He obviously killed her." He jerked his head toward Veronica. "Like she said, Willie was already in jail when the e-mails were sent. Whoever sent these notes, they're just trying to get your money."

Mike Dewalt shot to his feet. His face was terrifying, his thick bushy brows low over his eyes. Wordlessly, he grabbed his son's shirtfront, pulling Crane roughly toward him. Margie shrieked, shoving her chair away from them both. Veronica caught sight of Ella's face, a sudden, protective blank.

Before anyone else could move, Keith stood from his chair. He held both hands up nonthreateningly, but he took a few careful steps toward the two men. "Mr. Dewalt. Please—you're in a courthouse. I don't want to see you in the lockup. Not when we should be focused on how to bring Hayley home."

His voice was quiet but firm, a tone that was more compassionate than chastising. The room was otherwise silent. Veronica realized she was holding her breath, her muscles tense. Mike froze, staring down into his son's face for another beat. Then he let go. Crane leaned against the wall, shaking—whether from anger or fear, Veronica didn't know.

Petra waited until Mike had sat back down before speaking again. "As to your question, Mrs. Dewalt, I will talk to the lawyers this afternoon to make certain, but I see no reason not to use the donations any way we must."

It was Tanner who broke the silence.

"What about a ransom specialist?"

The gravity in the room shifted, all eyes moving down the table to his exhausted face. He looked around at them all.

"A what?" Petra stared at him blankly. He looked apologetic, like bringing it up was somehow awkward.

"You know—the people who handle the ransom so it all goes off according to plan? They had a thing about it on *Dateline* a couple years back. Lots of security firms are doing that kind of thing these days." He licked his dry lips, looking around the table. Margie glanced at her husband, obviously interested in the idea. Lamb scowled but remained silent.

"Well, of course, if you feel it's the best way to handle the situation—" Petra began. Lianne stood up abruptly, holding Hunter against her chest.

"I think we do." She gave Lamb a withering look. "I'd feel a little safer with a professional on my side."

Veronica knew the barb was directed at Lamb, but she still flinched internally. As if she weren't a professional; as if she hadn't done her best to bring the girls home. But Lianne was already halfway out the door, Hunter in her arms. Tanner gave the table an awkward smile and hurried after her.

With that, the meeting seemed to be adjourned. Crane

stormed out ahead of his family, shoving violently through the door. Everyone else rose slowly, gathering their belongings with tentative movements. Veronica took one last look at Lamb then left, Keith close behind her.

"You okay?" Keith asked Veronica when they were on the steps outside. She smiled faintly.

"Yeah. I'm okay."

But her heart felt heavy as they walked back to the car together. For once, she had a feeling that Lamb might be right—not about Willie Murphy, but about those e-mails being a hoax. And somewhere in the pit of her stomach she had the uneasy feeling that the girls weren't going to make it home. If the families paid out, someone was going to get away with fraud at best—and at worst, murder.

CHAPTER TWENTY-THREE

Veronica's hands wouldn't stop shaking. She held the revolver straight out from her body and breathed slowly, deeply, the hot-metal smell stinging her nostrils. She tried to relax her shoulders. Then she pulled the trigger.

It was early afternoon on Saturday. She'd come to the range by herself, slipping out the door once she'd heard her dad start his lawnmower in the backyard. She didn't want him to see her sneak into the kitchen like a thief and take the gun from where they'd both left it on the kitchen island.

She knew she was being stupid. Keith was a good shot—he should be teaching her. But for some reason she wanted to do it alone. Perhaps it was that she wasn't ready to eat crow after their argument, even though he wouldn't try to rub it in. More likely, it was that she didn't want him to see how scared she was, holding a thing that was intended to hurt someone. To kill someone. She didn't want him to know that the idea of using it made her feel sick to her stomach. Because she knew he'd see it as a weakness, a sign that she really wasn't ready for this kind of work. So instead she'd spent the morning googling how to load and shoot a revolver. She found a video blog giving step-by-step instructions, starring a plump, cheerful ex-cop from Florida who managed to put a hole through the target's head every single time.

Veronica took aim again downrange, trying to focus on the target, and fired.

The only other people at the range were a heavyset man with two teenage sons, all of them in camo. The man had a slabby jaw and short, bristling hair. His sons wore matching baseball caps in neon orange. They had a dozen guns between them and were taking turns in a variety of Rambo poses, jeering at one another for every missed shot. Veronica couldn't hear them through the enormous plastic earmuffs, but she got the gist. A few times their eyes twitched slyly toward her, and she caught an *ain't-she-cute* smile on the dad's face once when he thought she wasn't looking.

She fired again, thinking about the party and the knife Eduardo had pressed against her throat. She tried to get angry enough to enjoy this—to hate Eduardo enough to imagine his face on the target. And she did hate Eduardo. But the idea of killing him held no joy for her. She wanted to hurt him, it was true. She wanted revenge. But not like this.

The gun was a snub-nosed .38 Special, pocket-size. It didn't look like a lot of gun. But the recoil slammed through her body with every shot. She reloaded, stood wide legged, squared to the target, and shot all five rounds, slow and deliberate. Then she pushed the button that pulled the target back to her. It ran slowly back up the range, fluttering as it went.

She'd hit it twice, once on the bare edge of the page, and another time in what would be the victim's shoulder. *Victim—is that how you're supposed to think of it? Or is it a perp?* She gritted her teeth and hit the button to send the target back out. There was no sense in putting up a new one—she'd barely dented her first.

She was turning to reload her gun when a hand touched her shoulder. She gave a start and whirled around.

Weevil Navarro stood a few feet behind her, in a glossy black motorcycle jacket and jeans. His trim goatee framed lips that were pursed in a look that was part pensive, part tough guy. Outsize diamond studs punctuated both earlobes, and she could just make out the edges of the tattoos that climbed up his neck and down his arms.

She carefully set the revolver down in its case, then took one muff off her ear. "I don't think you're supposed to sneak up on someone holding a gun."

"You wanna keep your knees soft. Bent a little, to absorb the shock." He lifted his head up, then down, a short appraising nod.

Veronica gave him a skeptical smirk. "Huh. I'm not actually sure if it's a good or bad idea to take advice from someone with a stolen weapons rap."

"Hey, you know as well as I do that Glock was planted." He straightened up and moved into a shooting stance to show her, bouncing a little on the balls of his feet. "You can lean forward a little from the waist too. It'll help with balance."

She watched him for a moment but didn't move to pick up the gun.

She and Weevil went way back, and while she was pretty sure she could call him a friend, the relationship had sometimes been . . . complicated. In high school he'd headed the PCH Bike Club, and there'd been a whole mutual back-scratching agreement between them. Veronica knew she could call him in for muscle if she needed it, and sometimes he was good for information on Neptune's underworld. Veronica, for her part, had helped him out of a few tight spots, including juvie. But she'd seen just how far he would go to stay on top—and just how much destruction he could cause.

When she'd returned to Neptune a few short months ago, he'd been on the straight and narrow. She'd seen with her own eyes how he looked at his wife, and it had made her feel—what? Happy for him? Jealous, that even Eli "Weevil" Navarro could settle down and find some kind of peace, when she thought she'd go out of her skin if she had one more long, quiet, calm afternoon?

But when Celeste Kane shot him, claiming self-defense, a stolen gun had ended up in his unconscious hands. Since then something had changed. He was back on the bike, roaring through the streets of Neptune with his old gang, believing that if the system was rigged, this was the only way to give himself a fighting chance.

And suddenly the thought made her deeply, achingly sad. Because they were both back in it. Because it looked like neither one of them would ever be able to walk away from the past, no matter how hard they tried.

"So what are you doing here, anyway?" Veronica asked.

"I saw that fancy car you've been driving in the parking lot, and thought to myself, *I gotta see this*. Veronica Mars with a gun. Like you weren't scary enough already."

She looked down at the revolver, nestled against the bright foam packing. "Dad wants me to learn."

"Smart man." Weevil picked up the gun and weighed it in his hands. "This is a shit town. You gotta look out for yourself." He aimed out downrange, cowboy style, gun in one hand. "I heard you got into it up at the Gutiérrez party."

"Who told you that?"

"Oh, you know. I follow you on Twitter, @too_nosy_for_her_own_damn_good."

Veronica faked a smirk, then became serious. "So you know the Gutiérrez cousins?"

He turned to look at her, pointing the gun carefully downward. "I know *of* them. Trust me, V. There are some things in this town even I stay clear of. I'd say you should take my example, but you've never been smart enough to listen to good advice."

She shook her head. "Weevil, there are two missing girls. I have to try to find them."

"Yeah? I heard they got the guy who killed them."

She grimaced. "Willie Murphy? I have my doubts. Yesterday the families got ransom messages from someone who claims the girls are still alive. If you know anything about these guys that can help me find those girls . . ."

Weevil sighed and set the gun down. He rubbed the corner of his jaw with his thumb. "Look, like I said, I steer clear of that whole scene. I don't know much. But I can tell you this—the Milenios don't do any kind of business in this town."

She frowned. "But Eduardo and Rico—"

"—are two squeaky-clean schoolboys with no records. And you bet your ass they want to keep it that way. They got a good thing going here—they're out of the line of fire, they're getting educated, and they have a chance to wash all that dirty money clean by dumping it straight into a legitimate business."

"But the Milenios are known for taking hostages, holding people ransom. There are hundreds ' of documented cases where they take some university student right off the streets," Veronica argued.

"In *Mexico*," he said. He shook his head. "Use your brain, V. What kingpin in his right mind is gonna order the kidnapping of two white American girls? He'd risk bringing the FBI or the DEA right down on his head, when he's got such a nice arrangement here."

"One point two million in ransom is a lot of money."

"That's chump change to these guys." He shoved his hands in his pockets. "I don't know. It's possible *los primos* Gutiérrez have gone rogue. Maybe they're trying to get a bigger piece."

"Maybe they just like hurting people, and no one has ever told them no." Veronica's voice was low and tense.

Weevil shrugged. "Maybe. But all I'm saying is, these guys don't shit where they eat. There's no way El Oso sanctioned any of this. Not a kidnapping, not a murder. And if he found out those kids went off book, I'm guessing there'd be hell to pay." Then he shrugged again. "But like I said. I don't ask too many questions about those guys. So maybe I don't know what I'm talking about."

Veronica nodded slowly. She picked up the gun and ejected the cylinder. Her fingers weren't shaking anymore. She loaded five more rounds.

"Did they hurt you?" Weevil's voice was quiet behind her. A few bays away the teen boys and their father were packing up their guns. One of the kids was watching her and Weevil with watery, pale eyes. She curled her lip at him, and he turned away, blushing.

"I'm okay." Then she shut the cylinder with a click. "You should put some earmuffs on."

Then she shot five more times in quick succession. The sound echoed distantly around her skull, the powder sharp and oddly sweet in her nose.

When she hit the button to call the target back, she'd gotten two more shots into the perp's silhouette. One was low, in the gut. And the other went right through his head.

CHAPTER TWENTY-FOUR

The Sheriff's Department was thrumming with energy when she arrived on Sunday morning. In the parking lot out front, reporters stood vigil, waiting for new information. Veronica caught sight of Martina Vasquez, taking a few quick drags on her cigarette before picking up her microphone and smiling into the camera.

She wanted to talk to Willie Murphy. She knew it'd be a long shot. Now that Lamb had him in custody, a perfect patsy, he wouldn't want anyone digging too much deeper. But she had to try, because otherwise, she was out of sources on the Gutiérrez cousins.

"Care to tell our viewers what you think of the sheriff's handling of the Dewalt-Scott kidnapping case, miss?" A man with Ken-doll hair thrust a microphone under her chin. She scuttled backward, away from him.

"No, thank you," she said. She turned where the door to the building should be and walked right into someone.

It was Crane Dewalt, pale and slouching. Behind him stood the rest of his family, and a fifth person, a short, stocky man.

"Hi, Mr. and Mrs. Dewalt. Crane. Ella. How are you guys holding up?"

Hayley's mother stepped forward and took Veronica's hand. "As well as can be expected, I suppose."

"Have there been any new messages about Hayley?"

"Don't answer that," said the man. Veronica turned to frown at him. "No offense," he added. "We just want to keep the information very controlled right now."

He was dressed in a rumpled button-down shirt and ill-fitting chinos—no tie, no jacket—and had a jowly, sagging face. The hair on the top of his head was thin and receding, but behind that it was curly and overgrown. A pair of thick-lensed glasses magnified his eyes and gave him an expression of mild surprise. More than anything, he looked like a particularly disgruntled civics teacher.

Mrs. Dewalt gestured toward him. "Veronica Mars, this is Miles Oxman."

"I'm a private security consultant," he said. A card manifested from somewhere in his jacket, the corners creased. GULL AND ASSOCIATES was printed at the top, above his name. She slid it into her purse.

"Mr. Oxman is helping us with the details of the ransom," Mrs. Dewalt said, wringing her hands in front of her. "We don't want to make any mistakes."

Veronica shrugged the straps of her purse more securely into place. "So were you here questioning Murphy?"

Oxman's wide mouth stretched a little wider, his jowls tucking back into a smile. "At this point, Ms. Mars, I'm not interested in who took Hayley. I'm here to make sure the ransom exchange goes smoothly and that we get Hayley back in one piece."

"We can't sit around hoping that someone will catch the

criminals who took her. All we can do is follow their orders and get our daughter back." Mrs. Dewalt's gentle blue eyes were moist and tired. "Not that we don't appreciate all your help. You did your best for us."

"Unlike some," spat her husband, speaking for the first time. "No offense, ma'am, but is everyone in this town a moron? How'd that idiot ever get elected sheriff?"

"Mike," whispered Mrs. Dewalt, but without real conviction.

"It's okay, Mrs. Dewalt. It's not the first time someone has said exactly what I'm thinking." Veronica looked at Oxman. "What about the Scotts, are you working with them too?"

Mrs. Dewalt's lips went thin. "We talked to them about it. We thought it'd be easier, safer even, to have one expert managing both cases. But they weren't interested. They said they had their own guy."

"They say who they're working with?" Oxman asked, rocking slightly on the balls of his feet.

"Um, the Meridian Group, I think? Someone named Lee Jackson?"

"Oh, yeah, they're good. Lee's got a great reputation." Oxman seemed unconcerned with the competition. "Very good."

A cry suddenly went up a few feet away. Mrs. Dewalt jumped, clutching at her throat. The rest of them whirled around to see what was happening.

Ella stood hugging herself, backed against a lamppost by the same plastic-haired reporter who had tried to chase Veronica. He waved the microphone almost threateningly at her. "Do you have anything to say to your sister? What about to her captors? How's it all been for you, Ella? Are you scared?"

It happened so fast no one could stop it. Crane slapped the microphone away. Then he pulled back his fist and landed an uppercut right into Ken-doll's jaw, sending the reporter staggering backward into his cameraman. Somewhere across the parking lot someone screamed. There was the sound of people running, and then four officers in Sheriff's Department khakis came pushing out the doors. A moment later, Lamb came striding behind them. He must have sensed an opportunity to posture in front of the media—he wore mirrored aviator shades that he no doubt grabbed the moment he heard raised voices.

"Stay away from my fucking sister," Crane screamed, fists clenched at his sides. Behind him, Ella was crying silently, big blobby tears rolling down her cheeks. Mrs. Dewalt ran to her, pulling her close and staring wildly around. The reporter was on the ground, a dazed and distant expression on his face. A deputy touched Crane's arm, and he jerked away.

Other reporters sprinted across the parking lot as they scented blood, and already, cameras were flashing. One deputy helped the fallen reporter to his feet while Lamb himself stepped in front of Crane. "I'm going to have to ask you to step inside, Mr. Dewalt."

"Oh, you got off your asses for this, huh?" Crane sneered. The veins on his forearms strained against his skin, Hulk style. He stood, shoulders back, ready to take another swing if he had to. "I finally figured out what it takes, then."

A deputy kneeled down to inspect the reporter's injuries. Another gently led Ella and her mother back toward the glass double doors. Crane's chest heaved visibly. For a horrible, wonderful moment, Veronica thought he might swing a punch at Lamb. Then he seemed to collapse, the rage dissipating all at once. He held up his hands, both a surrender and a mark of disgust. Lamb watched one of the remaining officers lead him to the doors. Mr. Dewalt followed, flushed beet red.

"It's all under control, everyone." Lamb turned toward the cluster of reporters, whipping his shades off with a flourish. "Just a scuffle. You all right, Langston? Come on, get him inside. We'll go ahead and take a statement."

Lamb basked in the camera flashes for a few minutes until the reporters lost interest. As they started to draw away he turned to the doors. That was when he caught sight of Veronica. His eyes narrowed.

"What are you doing here?"

A hundred smartassed answers sprang to her lips. But for once she swallowed them. She forced a smile that could charitably be called "polite."

"I was hoping to ask Willie Murphy a few questions—"

But Lamb was already shaking his head no. "Forget it, Mars. Even if I wanted to let you in—which, by the way, I don't— Murphy isn't taking any visitors." He smirked. "And I doubt he'd talk to you, anyway. You don't accuse a man of kidnapping and murder one day, then ask him out for coffee the next."

"I didn't . . . Okay, there are so many things wrong with that statement I'm not even going to bother." She gave him an exasperated look. *Should have gone with the smartassed answer after all. At least then I'd have the satisfaction of a job well done.*

"Now if you'll excuse me, I have to go talk to young Mr.

Dewalt about his attitude." He gave her another smug little grin, turned to nod at Oxman, and went back inside.

"They'll have to book the kid. They can't let him get away with that," Oxman said conversationally. He yawned, revealing a mouthful of coffee-yellowed teeth. "Are you still working the case?"

"Yeah, I am. At least until I find out what happened to Aurora and Hayley."

He adjusted his collar. She caught sight of the sweat stains beneath his arms. "The best thing you can do for the safety of these girls is to step back and let us do our thing." He lowered his voice. "These cartels don't play games. I know—I've been dealing with them for more than a decade."

"So you think the Milenios have her?"

"I didn't say that." His eyes darted around the parking lot. Veronica blinked. The very word "Milenios" seemed to make him jump. "I don't know who took Hayley Dewalt, and frankly, I don't want to know. But I'll tell you this. Three hours ago Murphy dismissed his public defender. Now he's got Schultz and Associates representing him."

"Schultz? They're huge. And expensive." She frowned. "How is Willie Murphy affording that kind of firepower?"

"Exactly." He stabbed at the air with one index finger.

Maybe Weevil had it wrong after all. Schultz and Associates were high profile, and they weren't always easy to get even if you had the money. You had to be connected, important, and as far as she knew Willie Murphy didn't even have a permanent home to call his own. Someone wanted him protected—someone with leverage. But did Eduardo and Rico want him protected to cover up murder and kidnapping—or something else?

"Look, I can't tell you what to do, kid, but proceed with caution." Oxman rubbed his nose between his index finger and thumb, then sighed. "One of my colleagues got snatched down in Oaxaca last year. Disappeared without a trace while he was working a case. So they're not above taking the so-called experts in order to keep us out of their business." He shrugged. "And you might do us all a favor and wait until we have the girls back home before you go stirring up too much shit."

As he took a few steps toward the parking lot, an idea dawned on her.

"Hey, did you catch the name of the public defender who got fired?"

Oxman shrugged. "Can't remember. But I understand it was some low-rent local guy." He thought about it for a moment. "McSomething."

A slow smile stretched over Veronica's face. *Bingo.*

CHAPTER TWENTY-FIVE

The wind picked up as Veronica arrived at the Scotts' condo later that day. Thin clouds skidded across the sky, and the trees murmured softly as their branches caught each gust. She grabbed a pink box from the passenger seat of the BMW and walked slowly toward the front door.

At first Veronica hadn't realized the date—not until she was leaving her third message on Cliff McCormack's voice mail. "I need to talk to you. It's urgent. It's Sunday, March twenty-third, just after three. Call me back." And as she hung up the phone, the date had burned on her lips. March twenty-third, her mother's birthday.

She really didn't want to admit that she still remembered it. But there it was, written in indelible ink in some part of her mind. It went with a handful of memories she didn't love to relive—Lianne, tossing back cheap martinis at the midrange steakhouse where they'd celebrated her birthday, getting so drunk she fell on the dessert cart. Another year, when they'd thrown a party for her at the house and she hadn't even shown up. When she'd staggered in the door at three that morning she and Keith had had one of the few truly nasty fights. And other memories that were, in a way, even worse—the year they'd taken an afternoon dinner cruise, and the three of them had stood silent and peaceful on the deck watching whales play in the wake of the ship. The year Keith brought home Backup, a tiny, wiggly puppy with an enormous bow around his neck, and Lianne had carried him in her arms like a baby all afternoon.

Veronica adjusted the box in her hands. Was it tacky to get a cake during a hostage crisis? What was the protocol? She pictured chocolate frosting with white lettering: HAPPY BIRTHDAY. HOPE YOUR DAUGHTER ISN'T DEAD. But this year was her fiftieth, a year with a zero. Veronica had to do something. So on her way to the condo she'd swung by a bakery and picked up a small German chocolate cake. It was her mom's favorite—or at least it had been, a decade ago.

Lianne jerked the door open moments after the doorbell rang, as if she'd been waiting for it. She gave a little jolt when she saw Veronica. Then she opened the door a little wider. "Veronica. Hi. Sorry, I was expecting . . . Come on in. We're on the terrace."

She followed her mother through the house. It looked much the same, if a bit more lived-in. A hodgepodge of instruments was strewn across the living room floor—a plastic toy accordion, a miniature xylophone, a full-size tambourine with half the zils missing. Half-empty glasses cluttered the coffee table, next to a small stack of newspaper crossword puzzles pocked with eraser marks. A greasy smell hung on the air, the remnants of a week of hastily eaten fast food.

Lianne opened the glass doors and led her out to a balcony jutting out over the bluff. It was decorated with cool slate tile, a wrought-iron railing, and a retractable sunshade. Large earthen pots of bougainvillea and philodendron sat in every corner and cranny, giving the deck a lush, jungly look.

At the far end of the balcony, Tanner sat submerged in a sleekly curving Jacuzzi tub, head resting back against an inflatable pillow. He waved as they came in. "Veronica! We weren't expecting you."

"Hi, Mr. Scott," she said. Then, as an afterthought: "Tanner."

Hunter sat at a round glass table with an ancient Casio synthesizer, the rhythm set to bossa nova, plucking at the keys one finger at a time. His hair stuck up in the back, and there was a smear of something—barbecue sauce, maybe—at the corner of his mouth. Veronica smiled at him as she set the box down on the table. "Hi, Hunter. How's it going?"

He shrugged, his eyes wary.

"I thought you were the kidnapping specialist," Lianne said, sliding the glass doors shut. "He's supposed to arrive any minute."

"So you guys are going to pay the ransom?"

"Of course we are." Lianne took a few steps around the deck, aimless and tense. She wore the same FIND AURORA T-shirt Tanner had been wearing on Friday. Aurora's face looked strangely stretched out, almost like it was warped with pain.

Veronica watched her mother's movements—simultaneously jerky and controlled, as if she was thinking about every step, every reach. Like she was just waiting for someone to jump out of the bushes and scream, "Boo!" It was familiar. Painfully familiar. That was how Lianne had always acted in the days before a relapse.

"What's *this* for?"

They all turned to look at Hunter, who'd taken the lid off

the box and was staring down at the cake. Veronica gave an uncomfortable little laugh.

"Oh. That. Well . . ." She gave Lianne a nervous smile. "I know it's not exactly a happy birthday, but I thought we should at least have some cake."

Lianne's eyes fell on the box, then darted up to meet Veronica's. For a moment they stared at each other. Lianne's mouth fell open, her cheeks pink as well. "Birthday?" Tanner glanced from Lianne to Veronica and back again. "It's . . . oh Christ, I forgot again, didn't I?"

He heaved himself out of the Jacuzzi, water slopping against the sides of the tub. His swim trunks were bright green with a palm-tree print all over them. A few old scars ran across his torso, white against his suntanned skin.

"It's fine, Tanner. There's been so much going on. I almost forgot it myself."

"We should have planned something." He toweled off, then put a damp arm around Lianne's shoulders and kissed the side of her head. "Hunter, we forgot your mama's birthday. We're gonna have to make it up to her."

"How come *she* remembered it?" Hunter asked, staring at Veronica.

The bossa nova drumbeat grooved its way into the silence that stretched out between them all. Was this the moment to tell a six-year-old that, by the way, his mom had another kid? To try to explain why Veronica wasn't a part of their life? Hunter's brow was rumpled up in a painfully familiar way—the family forehead, skeptical and anxious. The forehead of a kid who saw everything, heard everything, even if he didn't understand what he was seeing or hearing yet.

Veronica's and Lianne's eyes met over the top of the little boy's head. Then Lianne slowly sat down at the table next to Hunter, putting a hand on each arm so that he'd look at her.

"Hunter, we haven't been totally honest with you," she said, her voice trembling. "You know how Rory's your half sister, from your dad's previous marriage? Well, Veronica's your half sister on the other side. She's my daughter. She's your sister."

Hunter's little brow furrowed deeper. For a moment Veronica wondered if he was about to cry. She realized she was holding her breath, her heart racing, and she almost laughed. How was it, after the week she'd had, that a six-year-old's reaction to the news that she was his sister could make her so nervous?

Then Hunter looked back at the cake. "So are we going to eat it?"

Lianne's lips trembled. She leaned forward to hug Hunter, a single tear rolling down her cheek. "Yes, baby, we're going to eat it. I'll get a knife. Can you say thank you to Veronica?"

"Thanks for the cake," he said. Then he hit a few experimental keys on the keyboard and sang it. "Thanks . . . for the caaaaake."

Lianne went into the house to get plates and silverware, Hunter following at her heels and singing to himself. Tanner and Veronica were alone. The awkwardness was almost deafening.

"Thanks so much for making sure your mom had a nice birthday, Veronica." He shook his head. "I'd like to say I forgot because of . . . all this. Aurora being missing and all. But the truth is, I'm pretty bad at birthdays. It's a flaw of mine.

But it's not for lack of caring. I just killed too many damn brain cells." He gave a hoarse laugh and sat down across the table from her. His blue eyes were the only part of him that didn't look somehow faded.

Veronica wasn't sure what to say. She'd never had that problem. Neither she nor her dad had ever forgotten a birthday. They took any excuse to appreciate each other. They'd taken any excuse to try to make Lianne feel loved. And it hadn't been enough. It had never been enough.

But somehow, here Lianne was, with someone new. And she knew it wasn't fair—she barely knew Tanner—but she couldn't figure out how Tanner had kept her mother when Keith hadn't been able to.

Tanner seemed to read something in her face, and he gave a crooked grin. With quick, careful fingers he picked up a pack of cigarettes from the table. When he lit up, he was careful to blow the smoke away from her.

"I'd quit before all this," he said, holding up his cigarette with a sheepish look on his face. "But, you know. Stress." For a moment he stared out over the skyline. Then he turned to look at Veronica again. "Your mom's worked real hard to keep clean. And I know . . . I know the two of you probably have a lot of unfinished business between you. If anyone knows that, I do. Me and Rory's mom . . ." He trailed off, then took another quick drag. "You're a grown-up woman so I'm not going to tell you how you've got to feel. And it's not my place to interfere between a mother and her daughter. All I can say to you is that sometimes, it's easier to be with your own kind. And your mom was never of a kind with your daddy. I'm not saying anything bad about him. Maybe the opposite, even. It's hard to look the people you love in the face when they've seen you fuck up everything you touch. Sometimes, it's easier to rebuild your life if you're with someone who's been as low as you've been."

Veronica was spared having to answer when Hunter came running back outside. "He's here!"

Lianne came out onto the patio, her hands empty, followed by a tall African-American man in a perfectly cut suit. Tanner stood up, and Veronica did too, a half second later. "Mr. Jackson?"

The man held out a long, fine-boned hand and shook with Tanner. "Pleased to meet you, Mr. Scott. I'm so sorry for all you're going through."

He was in his midforties, clean-shaven, with a deep and reassuring voice. His broad shoulders stayed perfectly level, and he moved with studied economy. Next to Lianne's anxious fidgeting and Tanner's quick, aggressive motions he seemed unbelievably graceful.

"And this is my daughter, Veronica Mars," Lianne said. Jackson shook her hand too. His grip was firm and cool.

"She's a private detective," Tanner added. "She's been helping us with the case."

Jackson looked at her more intently now. "Interesting." Then he released her hand.

"Can I . . . can I get you anything? Water, iced tea? I can put on some coffee if you like," Lianne offered.

"No thank you, Mrs. Scott." He set down his briefcase and straightened his lapels. "Before we start, let me give you some reassurance. I know you're both scared. You've been through hell. But I want you to know you're in good hands. I've handled more than a hundred of these cases, in countries all over the world. These guys just want to get their money—as long as you trust me, and give me free rein to deal with them, I believe that we have a very good chance of getting her back." He glanced at Veronica. "But that means we've got to play by the rules. And I don't want to endanger Aurora's life with any unnecessary poking around. I'm sure you can appreciate that."

"So the plan is to give the kidnappers what they want? And then what?" Veronica frowned. "Don't you want to know who it is so they can be held accountable? So we can stop them?"

"The plan, Miss Mars," Jackson said calmly, "is to bring Aurora Scott home. That is what I do. That is all that matters. And I would ask you to think very carefully about interfering with that plan. This is a delicate operation. One mistake could cost us everything."

His eyes locked on hers. Veronica didn't flinch. She stared back at him, shoulders squared.

"Veronica." Her mother's voice was brittle, shaking. "Please."

She looked up. Lianne's eyes were wide and scared.

For a moment she felt rooted to the spot. Everyone watched her, waiting, tense. Out below the patio, a gust of wind rattled the leaves in the trees. She picked up her purse.

"Look, don't worry. I'm not going to interfere with your negotiations."

She headed toward the door.

"Good luck," she said over her shoulder. "And happy birthday."

CHAPTER TWENTY-SIX

It was nearly 11:00 p.m. when she walked into her bedroom to see if Logan was online. He hadn't replied to her e-mail earlier in the week, but that didn't mean anything. His schedule was as uncertain as hers, and she didn't want to miss him if he did manage to score some computer time. So after watching the evening news with Keith—images of the dramatically interrupted press conference were being mined with a vengeance—she'd kissed his forehead and gone back to her room to get ready.

She stood in the mirror, running her fingers through her hair. For one ridiculous moment she considered changing into something sexier—at least from the waist up, as that was all he'd see on his camera—but decided not to bother. Logan had fallen in love with her in striped T-shirts and jeans. There was no need to mess with a winning formula.

She looked around her bedroom, a sudden strange weight pressing down on her chest. The hazard of living in a place where you had so much history—so much pain and so much rage and so much love—was that every item could turn on you in a flash. Sure, the photo of her at Disneyland that perched on the bookcase? Cute as a button. But then she had to remember that Lianne had taken it. And even if she took the picture down, how many other belongings were just waiting to remind her of everything she'd ever lost? There was the teddy bear she'd kept since Duncan Kane won it for her at the Winter Carnival sophomore year. There was Lilly Kane's necklace, twinkling from a jewelry tree on her dresser. There was Logan's T-shirt, left behind after the days they'd spent together, which she kept draped over the back of a chair.

Veronica suddenly missed him worse than she had in weeks. She steeled herself. *Dealing with Mom has got you maudlin. Remember the rules, Mars—no pining, no whining. Keep it light.*

She was adjusting the angle of the lampshade on her desk when she heard the singsong chime that meant a call was coming in.

And then he was there, at the top of her screen. He wore his sage-green flight suit, unbuttoned partly to show the black T-shirt underneath. This time his eyes seemed to meet hers; the camera must have been adjusted properly. And even though she knew it was an illusion and that their eye contact was being filtered through lenses and wires, it sent a little shiver down her spine.

He smiled. "There you are," he said.

"Here I am," she answered.

For a moment they just grinned at each other, each taking in the other's presence.

"How long do you have?"

It took him a beat too long to answer. They must have a lag.

"Not long enough. Fifteen, twenty minutes? There's a

wait list for the computers." He smiled ruefully. "Hey, so, sorry I had to miss our last date. I, uh, lost my Internet privileges. Something about insubordination."

"That doesn't sound like you," she said, eyes wide.

"It was a frame job, I tell you."

"So, business as usual."

He laughed softly, and the image froze for a moment, streaky digital lines across his face. She held her breath, waiting. After a moment it came unstuck again.

"Can you see me now?" She tried not to cringe at her words. It seemed like half of their scant and precious time together was spent asking that. *Can you see me? Can you hear me? Still there? This fucking computer.* Mac had helped her optimize her video chat capabilities, but Logan was approximately eight thousand miles away, floating, as he put it, in a giant metal box, surrounded by God knew what kind of equipment interfering with their connection.

. He smirked. "Billions of dollars of defense technology at work."

They were quiet for another moment, awkward. Then his face softened. "You look great."

"Thanks," she whispered. "How're you doing?"

"I'm okay. The flight surgeon cleared me yesterday. I'll be on deck for a mission this afternoon, so it may be a few days before I can e-mail you again." He licked his lips. "So how's Lianne?"

"Well, she's clean now. She's got a new family, a new life."

"Yeah? How're *you* doing?"

She hesitated.

"I'm . . . fine," she said softly. "I mean, it hasn't been easy, seeing her again like this. But I made my choice a long time ago. And so did she." She gave a short, heavy laugh. "It seems like she was really happy, before all this happened. Apparently no one in her new life drives her to drink."

Logan's brow furrowed. "Veronica. You know she didn't leave because of you, right?"

She didn't answer. She felt impossibly adolescent again. *Does Mommy love me?* was the kind of thing you scrawled in a diary, not the kind of thing you discussed at twenty-eight years old with your boyfriend.

Logan said something else then, but the screen froze again, his voice so broken up she couldn't make out the words.

"Logan?"

"You . . . better . . . your dad," he finished. She smacked the side of the desk, more out of frustration than in the hopes it'd provide better reception. But she didn't have the heart to ask him to repeat himself, to spend another fifteen minutes laboring over the same twenty words, as they'd done several times before. She just nodded.

"Are you there?" he asked. He leaned forward and frowned at the camera.

"Yeah, I can hear you. Logan?"

"Veronica? Are you there?"

Her heart sank. She craned her neck at the monitor, hoping the connection would correct itself, that his voice would come clear through the digital noise. His image shifted jerkily once, twice. She caught the sound of his voice deconstructed into halting and meaningless syllables. And then the window went dark.

She stayed in her chair for a long time. A dark hollow seemed to carve itself out under her chest, frustration and despair curling her fists at her sides. She knew not to worry about the sudden disconnect—he'd often warned her it was just the connection, not some kind of emergency or attack. But now she felt more cut off from him than she had before their awkward, aborted chat.

After a few minutes, she powered down her computer. Logan had said out loud what everyone else had danced around: the fact that, no matter how "professional" and detached Veronica tried to be, Lianne was still the woman who'd left. Still the woman who'd cut and run when things got too hard. And watching her soldier through the search for a missing stepdaughter hurt some deep, childish part of Veronica more than she wanted to admit.

In the hall outside her room, she heard her father's uneven steps as he made his way to bed. Veronica stood up from her desk, staring at the faint outline of her face reflected in the darkened window. Logan had seen through her; that was one of the reasons she loved him. He could tell her things she couldn't bear to tell herself sometimes. But what good did it do to dwell on all the ways Lianne had let her down? The bridges between them had burned to ash a long time ago. She couldn't go back in time. She couldn't fix what had gone wrong. She couldn't make Lianne love her.

She touched the surface of Aurora's diary where it sat on her desk. Not for the first time, she felt a connection to the girl, an ache of recognition.

Both of us are lost, she thought. *But maybe, just maybe, I'll be able to bring one of us home.*

CHAPTER TWENTY-SEVEN

The Balboa County Public Defender's Office was a utilitarian concrete slab of a building, conveniently located a few blocks away from the Sheriff's Department in downtown Neptune. Veronica arrived at 1:00 p.m. the next afternoon with lasagna from Mama Leone's and a smile and took the elevator up to the sixth floor, where Cliff McCormack's office was situated.

Cliff and her dad had been friends for almost twenty years now, and Mars Investigations had cleared more than a few of his clients of wrongdoing. Of course, evidence gathered by Mars Investigations had also put a handful of his clients away—but that was life in the seedy underbelly of the criminal justice system. Sometimes you had to defend the indefensible.

As far as she knew, there wasn't another McSomething working for the Public Defender's Office. Which meant that Cliff, the low-rent local lawyer near and dear to her heart, was her best shot at getting access to Willie Murphy's statement. But as cynical as Cliff pretended to be, he sometimes got a tiny bit hung up on ethics—especially on sticky little issues like attorney-client privilege. Veronica hoped the piping hot lasagna currently turning the white bag translucent would coax him toward a moral gray area.

His door was open, but she knocked lightly on the frame. Cliff looked up from his desk, where he sat thumbing through the contents of a manila folder. When he saw her, his eyebrows furrowed.

"I brought lunch" she sang, dangling the bag tantalizingly in front of her. "Fresh from Mama Leone's"

"How cheap do you think I am?" His nostrils flared. "Don't answer that."

She took a few steps into his office, closing the door softly behind her. It was a windowless closet of a room with walls painted in a soul-killing greenish gray. A heavy bookshelf took up the greater part of a wall, covered in dusty law books and three-ring binders. The desk was a disaster site, strewn with manila folders and stray scraps of paper, interspersed with sandwich wrappers and a half-eaten box of Cheez-Its. She sat down in a stiff-backed chair across from him.

"You've been dodging my calls, Cliffy."

Cliff scowled. He was a tall, rangy man, his dark hair slicked with pomade. His lips were always on the verge of a sour smile, his brows expressive and skeptical. He watched warily as she uncovered a to-go portion of lasagna, stuck a plastic fork in the still bubbling cheese, and handed it across the desk to him.

"Contrary to what you and your father may think, I do have a life." Cliff closed his eyes for a moment to inhale the savory aroma, then frowned. "It just so happened that I had plans yesterday."

"Was it double-coupon day at Les Girls already? My, time flies."

"If you must know, I was at a winery, with a friend. A *lady* friend. And it turns out lady friends are much less *friendly* when you interrupt a date to answer a call from a perky young blonde. Especially a perky young blonde who has a habit of asking for favors." He gave her a pointed look, picked up the loaded fork, and took a large bite.

"What are favors between old friends?" She cocked her head to the side.

"What do you want, Veronica?" His mouth was full as he spoke, sauce spattering along the length of his ten-dollar tie.

"I heard you lost a client on Saturday." She nibbled a piece of her own lasagna. "Any idea why?"

"At a guess? Probably because someone wanted him to win his case."

"Someone . . . like the Gutiérrez cousins?"

"Someone like that, yes." He set down his fork. "Honestly I'm glad. Cases where stupid people do stupid things are really more my forte. Like this guy." He picked up a folder from the mess on his desk. "He updated his Facebook account from inside a house he was robbing. Classic Cliff McCormack material. I'll leave the murderers to someone who knows what he's doing."

"So you think he did it?" Veronica leaned forward. "You think Willie Murphy killed those girls?"

Cliff counted off on his fingers. "Well, let's see. He was at the parties where both victims were last seen; he tried to pawn the property of the first victim; and strands of the first victim's hair were found on the passenger seat of his car. Add that to the fact that the guy has priors and that he had a pharmacopoeia of narcotics in his bloodstream the night of his arrest, and all signs point to—"

Veronica sat up straight. "He had Hayley Dewalt's hair in his car?"

"They're still waiting for the lab tests to confirm it, but it looks like a perfect match with hair found in her brush." He shrugged. "Sometimes, if it looks like a murderous duck and quacks like a murderous duck . . . well, you know."

She laced her fingers together and rested her chin on her hands, frowning. Cliff's eyes narrowed. "It scares me to see you thinking that hard."

"Something about this just isn't adding up, Cliff."

Cliff shook his head. "Look, kid, I'm no fancy Columbia-educated profiler, but I've worked with the 'ethically challenged' for a long time. They call it 'deviant behavior' for a reason—it's hard to predict and doesn't make a lot of sense. Believe me. If you'd heard the guy's story your bullshit detector would be—"

"So you got his story?"

He closed his eyes for a moment and sighed. "Yes. I got his story. And no, I can't tell you anything about it."

"Sure, of course, I know that. Attorney-client privilege." She scooted her chair forward confidentially. "I *did* go to law school, after all." She paused. "I'm just wondering if he said anything about what he did *with* the girls. Because you know as well as I do that if Lamb can get a conviction, he'll consider that the end of it. He doesn't care if we find the bodies."

She sat on the edge of her chair, watching him. Some sort of battle seemed to be raging in his face. His jaw tensed. His eyes locked on hers and then looked away thoughtfully. After a few seconds, his face relaxed, and he sighed and stood up.

"Well, this has been a fun conversation, but I have a meeting in just a few minutes." She started to stand up, an argument leaping to her throat, but he held up a hand. "Hey,

I know your administrative skills are probably rusty after all this time, but if you wanted to really do me a solid you could clean up my desk. Since we're talking favors and all." He looked at her from under heavy, exasperated brows. "I'll just close the door so no one comes in to bother you. Lock it on the way out."

He buttoned his suit jacket, brushed a thick coil of hair off his forehead, and, giving her one last pointed look, left the room.

Veronica stared down at the expanse of his desk. Stacks of paperwork cascaded across it. Three different coffee mugs sat with a rime of scum across the bottom of each. One of the mugs said KEITH MARS FOR SHERIFF. Another said NEPTUNE IS FOR LOVERS. A small smile played at the corners of her lips. She cracked her knuckles.

Twenty minutes later, the wastebasket was full, the mugs were in a drying rack in the break room down the hall, the paperwork had been sorted, collated, and alphabetized—and she had Willie Murphy's file spread across her lap. She flipped through it page by page, past his rap sheet and his mug shot, until she found it—a transcription of the statement he made to Cliff.

She glanced at the door one more time. Then she started to read.

CM: So here's thing, Mr. Murphy—the
sheriff is building a case against you
as we speak. They know you were at the
parties where both girls disappeared. They
have the necklace you cleverly pawned two
days after Hayley Dewalt's disappearance.

And they've found three long brown hairs
in the passenger seat of your car. We're
still waiting on the forensic report, but
they look identical to hair pulled from
Hayley's brush back home. It's not looking
good.

WM: Look, man, I don't know what you're
talking about. I never killed anyone. I'm
not into that kind of shit. It's not . . .
I don't even like the sight of blood, okay?
I mean, okay, yes, she was in my car that
night. But I didn't, like, hurt her. I mean,
I was trying to do her a fucking favor.

CM: A favor?

WM: Yeah, man. I mean, fine, we talked
a little at the party. She was getting
friendly with a friend of mine—like, real
friendly, if you know what I mean—and then
all of a sudden she freaked out.

CM: What do you mean she freaked out?

WM: I don't know, man, one minute she was
curled on the couch nibbling Rico's earlobe,
and the next minute she was running around
the party asking if anyone could give her
a ride north. Rico was pissed. He'd been
working on her all night long and suddenly
she's running for the hills.

CM: This would be Federico Gutiérrez
Ortega?

WM: Yeah.

CM: What did he do?

WM: He called her a cocktease. She
didn't care, though. She wanted to go to
Bakersfield. Like, right then and there.
She was desperate. I felt bad for her. I
told her if she had gas money I'd take
her.

CM: So you expect me—and more
importantly, the jurors—to believe that a
girl you didn't even know decided to head
to the middle of nowhere in the middle of
the night, and you gallantly offered to
drive her? That's like, what, four hours?

WM: Three. And yeah. That's what
happened.

CM: And you did this out of the goodness
of your heart, did you?

WM: Look, man, I thought she was
flirting with me. I figured, she's a damsel
in distress, I'm a knight with an '86 El
Camino—maybe a little chivalry would get me
an in, you know what I'm saying?

CM: Okay. So what did you do once you got
to Bakersfield?

WM: She had me pull into a truck stop
just outside town—said she wanted a Coke.
Then when I got out to fill up the tank, she
bolted. Ran right across I-5. I don't know
where she was going. I called after her,
but, like, I'm not chasing after some crazy
bitch at four in the morning in the middle

of nowhere. I went and had some breakfast
in the diner, just to give her some time to
come back. But she didn't. So I went home
and went to bed. She never even paid me for
the gas.

CM: So how do you explain how you got
your hands on her necklace?

WM: When I got back to my car from the
diner it was in the passenger seat. It must
have come loose or something on the way
up. I don't know—I'd just used a whole tank
of gas getting her there. Six hours round
trip! I wanted to cover my losses, so I
sold the stupid thing. I didn't know she
was missing. If I'd known I would have just
thrown it in the bushes.

CM: Right. And what about Aurora Scott?
Did she express an urgent need to drive
straight into the Mojave?

WM: I never even talked to her. I saw her
at the party—I mean, everyone did. She was
in the tan-line competition. Super hot. But
she didn't have the time of day for me. I
don't know what happened to her. You've got
to believe me, man, I don't know anything
else.

Veronica took photos of the transcript with her phone.
Then she shut the folder, put it on Cliff's desk on a neat
stack of files, and stood up.

Cliff was right. It was a stupid story. A clumsy, terrible, stupid story.

But she couldn't help but feel that it was stupid enough to be true.

She looked down at her phone. It was just 3:30 p.m. She could be in Bakersfield by sunset, easy.

CHAPTER TWENTY-EIGHT

She'd just crossed the L.A. County line and was driving past the gray-green hills of Los Padres National Forest when her phone rang.

"Hello?"

Logan's car was equipped with Bluetooth, and he'd synced it with her phone before he'd deployed. The radio cut out, and Mac's voice came clear and crisp through the BMW's speakers.

"Veronica? Where are you?"

"En route to Bakersfield. I got a lead. What's up?"

"Well, it might be nothing, but I thought you should know. That story about the Meat Loaf song in the ransom message? You know, the proof-of-life stuff?"

"Yeah?" Veronica was suddenly alert. She sat up.

"Well, she posted it on Facebook five years ago."

Veronica's fingers curled more tightly around the steering wheel. She stared intently at the road.

"Still there?"

"Yeah. Sorry, Mac. I'm just thinking."

"That doesn't necessarily mean she's, like . . . not alive. Does it?"

"I don't know what it means yet. Is there anything else?"

"That's all I've got for now. Should I stay in the office in case you need anything?"

"No, there's no sense in that. Go home, Mac. I'll see you tomorrow."

She stopped at the turn-off to Frazier Park and found Oxman's card in her bag. He answered on the third ring.

"Mr. Oxman, this is Veronica Mars. I know you asked me not to interfere until you get Hayley home safe, but I wanted to give you a little information. It looks like the proof-of-life story they offered for Hayley was actually a story she posted on Facebook when she was thirteen years old."

There was a long silence on the line. When he spoke, his voice was low and careful. "I see. That's . . . good information to have. I'll have to look into it." Another pause. "Thanks, kid."

She didn't have Jackson's card, but the Meridian Group's website had a number listed for "general inquiries." A nasal female voice answered.

"Meridian."

"Hi, this is Veronica Mars calling for Lee Jackson. Any way you can patch me through?"

"I'm so sorry, Ms. Mars, but Lee is in the field."

"I know that, but I really need to get in touch. Can you maybe forward me, or give me a number where I can—"

"I can take a message for you."

She gritted her teeth in frustration but left her name and number. For just a moment she considered calling her mother, but the idea of having that conversation with Lianne—of having to discuss everything this new development could mean—made her squirm in her seat. Better to leave it to the professionals. Better to tell Jackson and let him make of it what he would.

There were three truck stops along I-5 just outside of Bakersfield, but only one of them had a twenty-four-hour diner, meaning it had to be the place where Willie Murphy had his breakfast at about 4:00 a.m. the morning Hayley had disappeared.

Murphy's story still didn't make sense. For one thing—why Bakersfield? She hadn't been able to find any evidence that Hayley Dewalt knew anyone at all in Bakersfield—no friends, no family—and it wasn't like it was some spring break mecca. But it was the detail that made her want to believe him. It was too random, too unlikely, to be anything but true. If he was trying to save his butt, he'd have come up with a better story.

She parked outside a low building with dented and dirty aluminum siding. A buzzing neon sign overhead read LUCY'S ALL NITE, with a red neon pie below. A gas station blazed with light on the other side of the parking lot. About fifteen trucks were parked in slanting rows between diner and diesel. It was nearly 6:30 p.m. and the regimented palm trees around the edge of the parking lot sent long shadows across the ground. In the east the sky was already a deepening blue.

She went into the diner, a bundle of sleigh bells on the door handle announcing her arrival. The inside was hot and steamy, the smell of burnt coffee and bacon hanging like a dense fog on the air. The walls were covered in cheap seventies wood paneling. Red-and-white gingham oilcloth covered the tables, and foam stuffing sprouted out of the holes in the vinyl booths like mushrooms.

A few stray travelers loitered at the tables, dragging french fries through globs of ketchup or nursing cups of coffee. At the counter, a wall of plaid flannel faced her, the backs of several men and one particularly barrel-chested woman. It seemed too quiet to Veronica, especially after all the revelry of Neptune. No one was talking except for two men in mesh-backed hats, who were arguing loudly about a boxing match.

"If his damn corner hadn't told him he had to finish it that round, he would've knocked Chavez into next Tuesday."

"You're fucking dreaming."

A waitress with a hard crest of bottle-red hair and a mouth ringed with lines approached Veronica with a menu. She wore a yellow puff-sleeved dress that made her look jaundiced. Her badge said her name was Geena. "What can I do for you, honey?"

"Hi. I'm . . . I'm hoping you can answer a few questions for me. I'm investigating a missing persons case in Neptune, and I'm trying to figure out if this guy came through here. It would have been two weeks ago—the morning of the eleventh." She held up her phone, where she'd loaded a photo of Willie Murphy. In it he wore an aloha shirt hanging open to show off his skinny chest. A tattoo in Gothic lettering spelled out BAD DOG across his sternum. He held a forty-ounce bottle of malt liquor up for the camera in a toast. She'd gotten it from an article on Trish Turley's blog; Turley had probably gotten it from Facebook.

The waitress looked down at the picture, then shook her head. "Lots of people come through here. It's hard to say. Any idea what time he'd have been here?"

"It would have been early in the morning. Four or five a.m."

Geena frowned. "Well, I work four p.m. to midnight, so I wouldn't have seen him. You might come back tomorrow, before eight. One of the graveyard girls may know something."

Disappointment rose up in Veronica's gut. She hadn't considered the time of day, but now it seemed obvious—anyone who would have been on the clock at 4:00 a.m. probably wouldn't be serving the dinner crowd. She turned to go.

"Oh, wait!"

Geena's eyes had gone very round. She smiled, the heavy smoker's pucker of wrinkles bunching around her lips. She turned to look at the counter, where a pretty bronze-skinned girl wearing the same yellow dress was refilling the truckers' coffee. "Rosa usually works the night shift but she's covering evenings this week. Chantelle just had her baby and we had to turn the schedule on its head. Rosa, honey, we've got a question for you when you have a sec."

The girl's dark eyes flickered up over the slouching line of flannel-clad backs. She nodded, finished pouring, and put the carafe back on the warmer. Wiping her hands on the edge of her apron, she pushed her way out from behind the counter.

"What's up, Geena?"

"This little girl has a question about someone who may've come through a week ago."

"Two weeks ago," Veronica cut in, holding out her phone. "This guy. It would have been early."

Rosa stared down at the small screen, her brow crinkling. She was younger than Veronica—maybe even close to Hayley's age—with round, flushed cheeks and a bow tie of a mouth. "Yeah, I remember him. He drank like fifty cups of coffee and stiffed me on the tip. It seemed like he was in a really bad mood."

"Was anyone with him? Did he talk to anyone?"

"No. He sat right over there"—she gestured to a booth beneath the window—"kind of scowling. He just looked out the window and ate breakfast. Didn't say anything to anyone."

Heart beating fast, Veronica pulled one of her flyers from her bag. She showed to it both women. "Have you seen her at all in the past two weeks?"

Both shook their heads.

She thanked them for their time and gave them the flyer, just in case. Some of the people in the diner were watching her now, with hard, curious eyes. She left them to their tired dinner, the bells jingling behind her.

Veronica stood for a few minutes in the parking lot, letting her eyes drift over the surroundings. The ground was parched and cracked, with shoots of green grasping up through chinks in the paving. Across the highway a threadbare-looking motel sat like a squat unfrosted cake, the neon in the vacancy sign stuttering on and off. The hills stretched out behind it, dotted with scrub and low stunted cedars, birds wheeling overhead in the wind. Besides that, there was nothing. The air smelled faintly of manure, and of exhaust, and of something sour and unclean. She took a few steps away from the diner.

Then her eyes settled on the sign. It was one of the plain green markers the California Department of Transportation used to indicate distances. How far to the next landmark, the next rest stop, the next city.

SAN JOSE—239 MILES

SAN FRANCISCO—280 MILES

And even though it wasn't listed on the sign, she could do the math in her head. She'd driven it dozens of times herself:

STANFORD—263 MILES

CHAPTER TWENTY-NINE

Veronica stood rooted to the spot. Distantly, she could hear the sound of traffic, but it wasn't as loud as the sound of the blood in her ears. Chad Cohan didn't have to get to Neptune and back in time for class. He had to get to Bakersfield. Four hours one way. Four hours back.

It worked. The math worked.

She looked up and down the highway. Traffic was light, and after a semi roared past, she hurried across the road toward the Lake Creek Motel, a scraped-looking two-story row of rooms. She pushed her way into the main office.

It was dank and smelled like sweat. The wallpaper, faded and peeling, was printed with roses twining up gold vertical stripes. A completely incongruous deer head hung over the front desk, its antlers lopsided on its forehead. The desk was unattended, but in the room behind it she could hear the sound of a TV.

An old man peeked around the corner, then came tottering out to the desk. He was small and rumpled, in a moth-eaten sweater and saggy jeans. She noticed that he was missing two fingers on his left hand, and when he scratched at his chin it was with his thumb. "Evening, ma'am."

"Hi. I have kind of a strange question for you."

The old man stared at her from a nest of wrinkles. His eyes were dark and shiny and hard to read. "We get some of those from time to time."

"Do you happen to work early mornings? Like, four, five a.m.?"

The old man shook his head. "My son taps me out sometime after midnight, usually works until ten or eleven the next day."

"Is he here at all?"

He shifted his weight, his expression unchanging. "He's asleep, ma'am. We work pretty long nights here. He won't be up for a few more hours."

She nodded. "Well, maybe you can help me. I don't know if you've seen the news, but there are a couple of missing girls in Neptune . . ."

His face lit up. "I saw that! It's been on Trish Turley all week long. Awful thing. I hope that fella they caught gets the death penalty."

"I've been hired to try to find the girls, and I have reason to believe that one of them stayed here on the eleventh of March, checking in during the very early morning. Maybe four or five a.m.? She may have been staying under a false name, or with someone else who footed the bill. Is there any way you can pull up the records for that morning?"

"Well, we don't usually give out names or personal information of our guests without a subpoena." He tapped a complicated tattoo on the desk with his mangled hand—thumb, pinky, ring, thumb, thumb, pinky, ring. He watched her face curiously, as if he was looking for some evidence that this might somehow put him one step closer to being on Trish Turley's show. It gave her an idea.

"I _completely_ understand," Veronica said. "If I were you,

I wouldn't want all the attention either." She leaned in confidingly. "I mean, all those interviews are a huge pain. I've heard Trish Turley is calling anyone with any kind of connection to the case and begging for interviews."

His eyes went wide. For a moment he stood there, thinking. Then he turned to a boxy old computer perched on the edge of his desk, pecking the keys one by one with his good hand.

"What time you say they were here?"

"Between four and five on the morning of the eleventh."

His eyes scanned over the monitor. She didn't breathe.

"Looks like we had one check-in," he said slowly. "At four fifteen a.m."

"Was it a couple?"

He gave her another long deadpan look. She realized right then that he wasn't going to tell her anything else.

"Sorry. Okay. But let me ask you one more favor, and then I'll be out of your hair." She took a deep breath. "Is there any way you could let me in to look around the room?"

The sunlight was a dark burnished gold when she let herself into the first-story room a few minutes later. She swung open the door and turned on the light.

It was shabby and stale smelling, not so much bland as despairing. The walls were papered in the same faded rose-trellis pattern as the lobby was, and the gray carpet was stained and threadbare. The clumsy old furniture seemed weirdly bunched up at one end of the room, a pile of thickly varnished wood, the bedspread pilling and thin.

She stood in the middle of the room for a moment. Déjà

vu. This was every shitty motel that'd ever been someone's undoing—this was the Camelot, where she'd followed philanderers and con artists night after night. This was the Palm Tree Lodge, where she'd long ago looked for another missing girl, poor Amelia DeLongpre. This was the Lake Creek Motel, and she was almost certain Hayley Dewalt had been here.

She started with the obvious, opening drawers, feeling around in the back of the closet, unsure what she hoped she'd find, but looking for it anyway. Perhaps she'd turn up something Chad or Hayley left behind, a clue that would tell her what had happened the morning they arranged to meet halfway between Neptune and Stanford. She ran her hands along the seams of the room—the AC vents, the paneling in the walls, the outlets—trying to feel anything loose, unusual.

When she'd finished she sat on the edge of the bed. She softened her gaze, no longer looking for something but looking at everything. Her mind rolled gently over the objects of the room, the facts she knew, and the suspicions she had. Sometimes you had to see both the forest and the trees.

That was when they sharpened into view: the marks on the wallpaper. Boxy outlines where the wallpaper was brighter, less faded and filthy. As if something had been sitting in front of it, protecting it from the light the rest of the roses were exposed to. The shapes were low on the wall.

Approximately where furniture would usually sit.

She jumped off the bed. First she grabbed the nightstand—it was bulky but surprisingly light. The bed was harder. She had to drag it in fits and starts. It'd been crowded close to the dresser, but based on where the wallpaper had faded it'd recently been moved about three feet. She pulled it back to where it'd once stood. Then she walked around to the other side. And that's when she saw it.

There, in the carpet, was the unmistakable stain of blood.

Someone had tried to clean it up—a wide, pale circle around the spatter showed where it'd been scrubbed. But the rusty splotches were too deep, too rich to be wiped away so easily. A pointillist collection of drops formed a small circle, about six inches in diameter. From there the spray radiated left, fanning out about two feet.

It'd been about ten years since she'd done her FBI internship—and she'd only worked for a few days with blood spatter. But it was obvious someone had been hit, hard. And probably more than once.

Her throat felt raw. She straightened up again, eyes darting over the room. Something frantic scuttled in her chest, a panicked and sharp-nailed feeling. She tried to ignore it. But the only thing that mattered right now was the evidence— the physical facts.

There was nowhere to hide anything large in the motel room. And besides, two weeks out, the smell of a body would have gotten someone's attention. She left the door to the room ajar as she walked back outside. The world seemed suddenly more desolate than it had twenty minutes before, dry and brown beneath the setting sun. Down at the end of the row of rooms, she saw the cool light of a vending machine. Next to it was the icemaker.

She walked toward it as if she were in a dream. Or a memory? How many dead girls drifted in her wake? How many ghosts did she have to carry? She could almost see

Amelia walking ahead of her, translucent and shimmering. Lifting up the flap to the ice machine and climbing inside.

That was where she'd found DeLongpre's body all those years before, covered in ice in another crappy motel courtyard. Murdered by her boyfriend for the money she'd received in a settlement from Kane Software. Lightning couldn't strike twice. It *couldn't*.

She stood in front of the machine for a moment and then lifted the metal flap. Crushed ice glistened inside. She grabbed the scoop and started shifting it around, rummaging toward the back. Then her shoulders collapsed as she exhaled.

Nothing there. Nothing but ice.

Hayley Dewalt could still be alive. Maybe the blood wasn't even hers—or maybe it was and she'd just run off, hoping to get away from everything in her life that had led her to that tawdry room, everything that had led her to a boy who would hurt her when he was supposed to love her. She went back to the room and shut the door, putting the key in her pocket. She turned to head back to the office. And then she saw something that made her jaw go tight.

The birds she'd seen from across the street still wheeled in tight circles behind the motel. She could see them more clearly now—their dark red heads, the silent, focused gliding of their bodies, wings wide and motionless for seconds at a time as they hung on an updraft. The desperate, scared thing in her chest went very still as understanding, irrevocable as the blood on the carpet, settled on her.

The sun was now sinking behind the hills, brilliant as it

died. She walked around the edge of the building. The motel lot extended back half an acre before the land started to climb, dense with buckwheat and sumac. An ancient chain-link fence ran along the property line, but it sagged in several places, and in one spot it'd tumbled altogether. The buzzards dispersed as she approached the site they'd been circling. She stepped over the fallen fence.

Something hot and fetid washed over her in waves, getting stronger as she went. She covered her mouth and nose, breathing against her own palm as shallowly as she could. Her mind spun, throwing out desperate possibilities. It could be a deer, a coyote, even a bear. But she knew it wasn't.

She saw the hair first, a swath dark against the dun-colored earth, curling out from a haphazard tangle of branches. She took a few more steps and could see the body clearly then. She lay facedown under a low bush. It looked as if he had tried to cover her with leaves and twigs, but something—animals, most likely—had disturbed her. She caught a glimpse of a white dress so covered in dirt it blended with the ground. The distant and industrious buzz of insects sent electric prickles over Veronica's skin.

She'd found Hayley Dewalt.

CHAPTER THIRTY

By 10:00 p.m., the area around the motel was swarming with cops. Bright yellow crime scene tape fluttered in the beams of the flood lamps. Three police cruisers made a barrier in the parking lot, their lights slowly rotating red and blue. Beyond the yellow tape a few onlookers loitered, and every so often a helicopter's mosquito whine rose and fell.

Veronica watched through the window of Lucy's All Nite, sipping a cup of coffee. She could see her own reflection superimposed over the crime scene, her lips a pale, downturned curve in the glass. Behind her she could see the bright lights in the kitchen and the row of flannel-clad truckers sneaking looks at her every few minutes.

She'd lingered at the crime scene long enough to make a statement, explaining who she was and how she'd retraced Hayley's steps to the motel. A stocky, bespectacled officer whose name badge read MEEKS had confirmed for her that the body was Hayley's; the girl's purse had been tucked under one arm, with her ID inside.

"That's off the record," he'd said, glancing sidelong at Veronica. "Don't go repeating it to anyone before we have a chance to contact the family. I'm not supposed to talk about an ongoing case. But, as you found her . . ." He gave Veronica a strange look, part pity and part grudging respect.

Meeks had made her sit in the parking lot of the motel while an EMT wrapped a blanket around her shoulders and checked her vitals. After an hour or so, the officer had escorted her across the road to the diner. "Would you mind staying close for a few hours in case we have further questions? If it gets late, we'll get you a room in town and we can speak in the morning."

"Anywhere but the Bates Motel," she'd said, trying to sound wry but coming out strained and shaky instead.

In the diner, Meeks took Geena aside and spoke to her in a whisper, Geena's hands flying to her mouth partway through the story. Then the cop had given Veronica a solemn nod and headed out the door into the darkness. Geena had come to Veronica's table and put a hand on the back of her jacket. Veronica didn't mind. It felt almost motherly. Then that thought made her want to cry.

"What you want to eat, honey?" The waitress had a smoker's voice, hoarse and a little phlegmy. "Anything you like. It's on the house."

More to placate Geena than anything, Veronica had ordered eggs and toast. Now the plate sat untouched where she'd pushed it away, unable even to look at the congealing yolk and slick, greasy sausage. But she was on her third cup of coffee, and while she could feel the caffeine start to rattle her eyeballs in her skull, it felt good to cup the warm mug in her fingers. The hot, bitter liquid helped wake her up from what felt like a long bad dream, and she slowly came back to herself.

Her phone sat to the left of her cup, set to vibrate. As

if on cue, Mac had called her twenty minutes after she'd settled in the diner, talking fast.

"Veronica, I feel like a moron. Chad Cohan's credit cards didn't have anything on them for that night—but his mom's did. Her name's Sharon Ganz—I guess she went back to her maiden name after the divorce. Chad charged the room to a card he has in her name."

"It's okay, Mac." She poured a packet of sugar into her coffee and stirred. A little slopped out onto her saucer. "We couldn't have saved her. She's been dead all along."

She could see a few of the patrons leaning subtly toward her, trying to overhear. She should probably care—she should probably try to protect Hayley's privacy as long as she could. But everyone would know what had happened soon enough.

"The motel clerk who worked that morning has already identified Chad Cohan as the guy who rented the room," Veronica told Mac. "I'm still putting it all together, but I think Cohan saw the pictures of her with Rico and panicked. That was the idea—she was trying to make him jealous so he'd want her back. He called her and asked her to meet him halfway. I bet the idea seemed romantic to her." She couldn't keep the bitterness out of her voice. "Her girlfriends hated Chad. She didn't want to tell them where she was going, so she got a ride from Willie. Willie seemed to be operating under the hope that they'd hook up—I don't know, maybe she hinted they would, or maybe she just let him convince himself. But when they got to the truck stop, she slipped off to the motel."

"So Chad Cohan went down there with intent to kill?"

"I don't think so. Not consciously, anyway. I think he

planned to talk it out, to win her back. But somewhere in the course of the morning he lost his temper. Maybe he talked himself into it all the way down from Stanford. Or maybe she just didn't give him the answers he wanted to hear." She pictured Chad Cohan, his handsome face twisted in anguished rage, his fist slamming into Hayley's jaw and knocking her down on that dingy carpet. And by that time, hitting her felt good. Did he hit her again with his fists, slamming her head hard enough to fracture her skull? Or had he grabbed something to hit her with—a lamp, an ashtray? Something heavy and irrevocable? She supposed the autopsy would tell.

"He must have realized he had to get to that eleven o'clock class. He didn't have time to do anything really creative to the body. So he pulled it as far back into the bushes as he could and hoped no one would find it for a while. It wasn't a bad plan. This is a place people drive past—not a place people go poking around. Maybe he planned to come back and move her when the heat of the investigation died down."

Mac was quiet for a few seconds. When she spoke again, her voice was low and tentative.

"Do you want me to drive up and meet you? Wallace and I can carpool up, and one of us can drive you home in Logan's car. Just so you're not alone."

A rush of gratitude welled up in her. She caught a glimpse of her face in the window again. This time she was smiling, just a little.

"No. Thanks, though. I'm okay. I'll probably start home early tomorrow. We'll have to talk to the Dewalts, obviously, and check in with the Scotts." She paused. "I'm not sure what this means for Aurora. It's pretty obvious the ransom note is a hoax—but it's also pretty obvious Cohan wouldn't have killed both girls. So we're back to the drawing board."

"Have you called your mom yet?"

She winced. "No. Do you think I should?"

She could hear something rustling on the other end of the line, like Mac was shifting her weight uncomfortably. "I don't know. As her PI? Yeah, probably. As her daughter . . . well, that's your call."

Now Veronica stared down at her phone, still and silent on the gingham oilcloth. She knew she should call the Scotts to let them know they had to halt the ransom exchange. She wished Lee fucking Jackson would call her back so she wouldn't have to.

Out beyond the window, cars were slowing as they drove past, and a line of traffic extended down the road. A news van had pulled in across the street. It wouldn't be long before more showed up—and they'd probably try the diner when the cops wouldn't give them any information.

"Look!"

A cry went up from the counter. Everyone in the restaurant was turned now toward the TV bolted just above a framed poster of Buddy Holly with his guitar. On the screen was an aerial view of the freeway. A Range Rover roared up the middle of the road; an entourage of speeding police cruisers, their lights flashing, trailed behind. A caption along the bottom of the screen said BREAKING NEWS.

Rosa picked up a remote control and turned up the volume. The rotating police lights at the motel seemed weirdly echoed by those on the TV.

". . . now we go live to a high-speed chase heading south on

Highway 101 just outside of San Jose. We have reports that the driver is a Stanford student wanted in connection to a murder, though the police are refusing to comment at this time."

Veronica set her cup down with a hard thunk. She hoped someone had gotten in touch with the Dewalts, because if they hadn't, the cat was out of the bag now. That was what happened in a Trish Turley world—everyone was waiting for a new Jodi Arias, a new O.J. They couldn't wait to tell everyone that their worst suspicions about humanity were true.

She rose stiffly to her feet, picking up her bag and her phone. Rosa looked up and met her eyes, giving her a pensive, searching look before turning away to refill a customer's coffee cup.

Outside in the parking lot, Veronica leaned against the BMW and pulled out her phone. The cool night air raised goose pimples along her skin. From here she could hear the crackle of radios across the street where the crime scene had been sealed off.

Lianne's phone rang only once before she picked it up.

"Veronica, what's going on? A reporter just came by the condo saying someone found a . . . a girl. What . . ."

"It was Hayley." Her voice was low and heavy.

Her mother gave a gasping sob. "God. Oh, God." Then, in a high, frail voice: "What's this mean for Aurora?"

"I don't know yet. But, Mom, I don't think kidnappers killed Hayley. I can't talk about the details just yet—but I'm pretty sure her death was an isolated incident." She took a deep breath. Her heart was beating almost as hard as it did in the scrub behind the motel a few short hours ago. "I know this is scary and . . . awful. But try not to panic yet. I'll check in with you tomorrow when I get back to town, okay?"

Her mother's breath was heavy, and Veronica realized she was crying into the phone.

"Did . . . you find her? Hayley? Was it you who found her body?"

She closed her eyes. "Yeah."

Lianne was quiet for a moment. When she spoke, her voice sounded steadier. "Drive carefully, Veronica. I'll see you in the morning."

After hanging up, Veronica stood there for another moment, waiting for her heart to slow down. Across the street, dark figures moved around the motel, casting deep shadows beneath the floodlights.

She couldn't help Hayley. She'd never been able to help Hayley—Hayley had been dead before anyone even knew she was gone. Now, though . . . now she had to focus. Because Aurora Scott was still out there, somewhere. And Veronica needed to find her, more than ever.

CHAPTER THIRTY-ONE

Veronica caught a few hours of shallow sleep in a blessedly sterile Best Western in Bakersfield, five miles from the interstate. She didn't dream, but she woke up several times and lay in the dark, picturing Hayley Dewalt's hair spilling out across the ground, like dark waves rolling off the body. When the clock turned to seven she finally hauled herself out of bed, took a scalding shower, and drove to Officer Meeks's precinct to answer a few final questions. He told her that the San Jose police had finally arrested Chad Cohan in the small hours of the morning. He'd made it as far as Morgan Hill before a hastily erected blockade forced him off the road. Then he sat in his car with a loaded Glock at his temple for three hours, until some smooth-voiced negotiator had talked him down. By 9:00 a.m. he'd hired Leslie Abramson as his defense. Veronica had a nauseated feeling he'd be out on bail in no time.

It was nearly 1:00 p.m. when Veronica left the station. Before she hit the highway she called Margie Dewalt, ready to offer her condolences. It was a relief to get voice mail. She assumed they were en route to Bakersfield to identify the body, or maybe they were on the phone with family members back in Montana. She'd send something—flowers, a letter. She'd have to follow up. But for now, she'd leave them to their grief.

When she arrived at the condo, Lianne was pacing the house like an angry cat, her shoulders back and sharp. Hunter sat at the kitchen counter, shaking a pair of heavy wooden maracas to the samba beat of a little Casio. Tanner occupied one of the deep white leather armchairs, and Lee Jackson stood with his back to the room, looking out over the cityscape beyond the window. She realized with mild annoyance that he hadn't called her back the day before. He looked up and nodded at her when she came in the room, cool and professional as ever.

On the coffee table sat a blue nylon duffel bag, unzipped. Bundles of twenty-dollar bills were neatly stacked inside.

"Anything new?" Veronica asked before even saying hello.

Lianne shook her head. "Nothing. We haven't heard from anyone."

Veronica let out her breath in a sudden exhale.

"Okay." She shrugged out of her leather jacket and draped it over one arm. "How are you guys doing?"

Tanner glanced up from where he'd been staring into space. His eyes looked bruised and exhausted; he didn't look like he'd been to bed the night before. "Oh, Veronica, we're just confused. Confused and worried and tired. None of this makes any sense." He gestured toward the bag on the coffee table. "We'd just gotten the ransom ready to go when we heard the news."

She felt like she should pat his shoulder or offer a hug, but instead she just stood there awkwardly. "Look, I don't know if you heard the news yet, but Hayley's boyfriend has been charged with the murder. So Aurora's disappearance seems to be totally unrelated to Hayley's."

"That poor girl." Lianne covered her face with her hands. "Her poor parents."

A tense silence fell over the room, underscored by the sound of Hunter's maracas.

"Mind if I get a cup of coffee?" Veronica finally asked. Lianne nodded, dabbing at her eyes. Veronica went into the kitchen, stopping on her way to lean over Hunter's Casio and hit a few keys, playing a quick, modified "Chopsticks." She winked at the kid, and he shook one maraca at her. It was painted bright red, with green stars.

"So do you think it was some kind of copycat crime?" Lianne asked, resting her forearms on the kitchen counter. Veronica poured coffee into a pristine white mug, then held the carafe up to ask if Lianne wanted any. Her mother shook her head no and she replaced it in the coffeemaker.

"Maybe. It's possible that whoever took Aurora heard about Hayley going missing from that party and decided to take the opportunity." She dropped a lump of sugar into her mug with a small plop and stirred. "As for the notes, the proof of life on Hayley's ransom message was actually a story from her Facebook feed about five years ago. I'm guessing the notes were sent by someone who had nothing to do with either crime, trying to cash in."

Tanner spoke up. "Or maybe someone really did kidnap Aurora, and they were trying to con an extra paycheck out of the Dewalts in the process." He stood up out of his chair and came toward the kitchen counter, standing between Lianne and Hunter. He held out an empty cup, and Veronica filled it with coffee, feeling a little like a waitress at Lucy's All Nite.

"Mr. Jackson?" she asked, holding up the carafe. He turned away from the window and shook his head.

"Thank you, no." He smoothed his lapels, hovering back by the sofas, away from the counter.

"So what's our next step?" Lianne asked. "What do we do now?"

"Well, I'm going to start going through all the evidence again," Veronica answered. "The party pictures, anything that's come into the tip line. Now that we know this has nothing to do with Hayley, something new may stand out."

Tanner set his coffee mug down on the counter and turned to Lianne. "We need to take the money to the drop. The ransom's due tomorrow."

Lianne turned to face him, her lip curling in contempt. "Tanner, that's insane. There's nothing, *nothing* in those messages to make us believe whoever sent them has Aurora."

"There was the story about my relapse . . ."

"Which she could have told to anyone: Adrian. Her therapist. Her teachers. Hell, I might have told it at AA, right to a whole crowd of drunks and junkies." She shook her head and looked back to Veronica. "We should have listened to you, Veronica. You were right—we should have tried to find her. Not just throw money out there and hope for the best."

"But what if someone *does* have her?" Tanner argued. "What if it's not a fraud? If that money isn't there—"

"Tanner, Jesus Christ. The ransom message was a con."

Hunter's maracas sounded loudly in a syncopated beat.

"God damn it!" Tanner turned on his heel and grabbed the maracas out of Hunter's hands. His chest heaved, and for a single surreal moment Veronica thought he was going to hit the boy with them. But he didn't. He just held them in his clenched fists. "Hunter, go play in your room. Take your keyboard. I can't even hear myself think around this place."

For a moment nobody moved. Hunter looked over at his mother, his eyes large and confused. Lianne gave Tanner an angry, reproachful glance, but then she leaned around him to smile at her son.

"It's okay, sweetheart. Go on. Maybe later we'll call Adrian and see if he'd like to take you to a movie. Right now Mom and Dad are just upset."

Hunter gave Tanner a last, baleful glance before jumping down off the high stool, his Casio in his hands, and disappearing down the hallway.

"Nice," Lianne spat. "Nice way to talk to your son."

Tanner stood for a moment, face rigid. Then all at once, he seemed to deflate.

"I just want my baby back." His mouth writhed as he fought tears. "Lianne, I just want Aurora back. I'll do anything. I'll flush the fucking money down the toilet if that's what it takes. I *know* the ransom is probably a grift. But what if it's not? What if it's our chance to get her back?"

Jackson cleared his throat. He moved slowly, almost leisurely from his position by the window to the kitchen counter. Today he wore a navy blue suit with thin, precise pinstripes, his tie a somewhat flashy lime green.

"Let me interject a minute here. Mrs. Scott is right—it's not a good idea to hand over the money without any substantive proof of life. If Aurora's ransom letter is genuine—if someone is holding her hostage—they'll have seen the news about Hayley, and they'll know they have to follow up with us to convince us they really do have Aurora. They'll want to make sure we know that at least one of their claims is genuine. So I think we can safely wait." He patted Tanner on the back. "I'll put the duffel bag in the safe at the Neptune Grand—we'll have it primed and ready to go if we need it."

Lianne glanced from Jackson to Veronica. "What do you think, Veronica?"

"Seems sound," she said. Privately, she suspected Jackson was indulging Tanner. It didn't seem likely they'd hear from the supposed kidnappers again. It was too risky now to make contact.

Tanner shook his head. "I don't want it to be out of my reach. What if they want it right away? What if those minutes I spend tracking your ass down tomorrow are minutes that matter?"

"Tanner!" Lianne hissed, glancing at Jackson. But the specialist just smiled.

"It's all right, Mrs. Scott. Tempers run high at times like this." He addressed Tanner. "I'm on call day and night until we reach some kind of resolution, Mr. Scott. If you need that money, I'll have it to you in no time. But I don't think it's wise to leave it sitting here on the coffee table."

"He's right, Tanner." Lianne looked relieved. She rested her hand on Tanner's arm, suddenly gentle with him again. "Please, babe. Let him take it."

Tanner stared at Jackson for a moment. Veronica noticed that the maracas were still clenched in his fists, forgotten. After a few seconds ticked by, he nodded grudgingly.

"Fine," he said. "Fine, take it."

Jackson gave a genteel nod. He went to the table and zipped the duffel, then picked up the strap with one hand. "I'll keep it secure. Call me if anything at all changes."

No one saw him to the door.

Veronica sipped her coffee and checked her watch. She needed to get home soon. Her dad was probably by the door, waiting. Lianne and Tanner both seemed exhausted. She wondered vaguely how desperate either of them was for a drink. She wondered if either of them had cracked in the week since Aurora had gone missing.

She was rinsing out her coffee mug when the doorbell rang. Lianne frowned, glancing toward the entry hall. "Maybe Jackson forgot something." She left to answer the door. Veronica went back to the living room and picked up her purse. Tanner had resettled into the same white leather chair.

"I'm going home for a change of clothes, and then I'll be in the office for the rest of the night. Call me right away if you hear anything. I'm going to start looking further back in Aurora's e-mail and phone records. Just in case there's something we missed." She hesitated, then she put a hand on Tanner's shoulder. "We'll find her, Tanner. One way or another."

He reached up and squeezed her fingers, blinking away tears.

Lianne came back into the living room, trailed by Adrian. He wore a Hearst College warm-up jacket over a snug T-shirt that hugged his muscles. He looked pale beneath his gelled shock of hair. Lianne seemed nervous, her eyes flitting every which way without quite meeting anyone else's.

"Adrian says he has something important to tell us," she said, leaning tiredly against the mantel. Tanner looked up.

"What is it?"

Adrian shifted his weight. His finger played absently with the zipper on his track jacket. He opened his mouth to speak but seemed to choke. He swallowed and tried again.

"The thing is," he said. "The thing is . . ."

"What is it, Adrian?" Lianne barely moved her lips to ask the question.

He looked up then, not at Tanner or at Lianne but straight at Veronica.

"The thing is . . . I know where Rory went."

CHAPTER THIRTY-TWO

"What the hell are you talking about?"

Tanner's voice exploded in the still and silent room. The maracas clattered to the floor as he shot to his feet. Adrian held Veronica's gaze for another moment, then dropped his eyes, a light flush creeping up his neck.

"I *swore* I wouldn't tell, but everything's gotten so *crazy*. And I saw that other girl on the news, and now . . ." He gestured wildly with his hands as he spoke, his voice fast and high-pitched. "Rory came out here to meet with a guy. I don't know who he is—she wouldn't tell me. But I guess she was pretty sure you wouldn't like him."

Lianne stared incredulously at him. "What are you saying, Adrian? Aurora's with . . . with a boy?"

He pursed his lips. "I'm not sure 'boy' is the right word. I got the feeling he was . . . older."

Lianne gaped at him. But Tanner was shaking his head.

"There's no way. She wouldn't do this to me. There's no way!"

Veronica took Adrian by the arm and walked him, not particularly gently, to the glass table in the dining area. She pulled out a chair. "Sit."

He did.

Behind them, Tanner was staring at Adrian so hard his eyes bulged. His expression was somewhere between shock, horror, and fury. Lianne's eyes darted between Tanner and Adrian for a moment. She went into the kitchen with forced calm and came back with a few bottles of water.

"Start at the beginning," Veronica said as Lianne set the bottles on the table. "Did you and Aurora have some kind of plan before she came to visit?"

Adrian shifted in his seat. "I wasn't exactly included in the plan. As far as I knew, she was coming out here to see *me*, but as soon as she got off the bus she was hinting about some guy she planned to meet up with. I didn't get a lot of details."

"But she came out here to meet up with him? Does he live in Neptune?"

He shook his head. "No, I think they just arranged to meet here. She knew her parents would let her come to see me." He looked down at the tabletop. "And she knew I'd help her."

Lianne looked like she was about to cry. "Adrian." The word was a simple, sorrowful admonishment. His shoulders hunched around his ears.

"I'm so sorry, Mrs. Scott. Mr. Scott. I know I should have told you. But everything got sort of . . . out of control. And I didn't know what to do." He glanced up. "Rory's my best friend. I mean, we've been through hell together. She was one of the few people in the world who had my back in high school. I owe her everything—and she asked me for a favor." He gave a lame shrug. "So I helped her."

"So you didn't meet this boyfriend? Or see him? Why wouldn't she at least introduce you, if you're her most trusted friend?" Veronica put both her hands on the table and leaned across it.

He smiled slightly. "Rory likes mystery—she thinks it makes her interesting. And honestly, I didn't ask. She's always trying to get me to act shocked or impressed—she loves creating drama. But I get tired of being her sidekick. Sometimes I just refuse to play the game. It really pisses her off." He opened the water bottle in front of him, taking a small sip.

"When was the last time you saw her?"

"That part's the same as what I told the police. She arrived Monday afternoon on the bus. I picked her up, we went to the beach and checked out cute boys. That night she told me she didn't plan to go back to Tucson. She said she'd met a guy, that she was crazy in love, and that her parents wouldn't approve. She said he was picking her up Wednesday night. She begged me not to tell anyone. I told her she was being stupid. But you know Rory. She's kind of . . `. impulsive." This last bit he said to Lianne, almost as if it were an apology. "So Wednesday we went to that party together. Sort of a last hurrah, I guess. Around about two a.m. she gave me a hug and a kiss and told me her ride was there and she'd see me sometime."

For a moment, the only sound was the careless tick of the wall clock over the fireplace. Tanner stood at the window where Jackson had been a few moments before, staring out at the lush balcony, with its jewel-colored plants and heavy furniture. He seemed to be absorbing the information, his hands dangling unsure at his sides. Lianne leaned against the kitchen island.

"Mom? Tanner? I know you told me there's been some

power struggles between you and Aurora in the past few years." She kept her voice carefully neutral. "Was there anything recently that made you feel like she was angry again? Did you ground her or punish her at all in the past few weeks?"

Tanner closed his eyes, but it was Lianne who answered.

"We almost didn't let her go." Her voice was a whisper, low and husky. "She had a week where she kept coming home past curfew. Way past curfew. And she skipped a few days of school. When she brought up the idea of visiting Hearst we almost told her no. Tanner was afraid she was getting wild on us again, that she'd gotten in with a bad crowd. But I thought a visit with Adrian would help. I talked Tanner into saying yes because I thought . . . I thought it'd stabilize her."

Adrian was staring down at the table as if he wanted to crawl under it. Veronica almost felt sorry for him. Letting a missing person search mount when he knew perfectly well where Aurora was? Pretty shitty thing to do. But the more she heard about Aurora Scott, the more she reminded her of Lilly Kane—wild, warmhearted, and sometimes manipulative. And, once upon a time, Veronica would have done almost anything for Lilly.

"Do you have any means of contacting her? Is she answering texts, e-mails?" Veronica asked, turning back to Adrian.

"She hasn't replied to any of my texts so far," Adrian said, biting down on the corner of his lip. "It sounded like they were heading off the grid or something. She kept talking about a cabin. She said Oregon at first, then mentioned Idaho. I don't think she really knew herself. I tried to let her know that everyone was going crazy looking for her, but she might be somewhere she doesn't have service." He shook his head. "She didn't even think about the fact that the other girl was missing. I guess I didn't either."

"Did she have some kind of plan for how this would end?" Lianne asked, her voice hoarse. "Is she coming back? Is she trying to . . . to disappear?"

"I don't know, Mrs. Scott." Adrian finally looked up from where he sat, absently tracing the bubbles in the glass table-top. Tears ran down his cheeks now. "I'm so sorry. I wish I could go back in time and change this. I wish I'd told you where she was from the get-go."

Hesitantly, her own lips trembling, Lianne stepped toward him. She patted his back gently. "Shhh. Shhhhh."

Tanner exhaled then, a hard stream of air all at once.

"I'm going to kill her," he growled. "That spoiled fucking brat. I'll kill her."

Veronica's eyes darted toward him. His usually dun-colored face was red, his shoulders clenched. For the first time, the charming, affable blarney was gone, and Veronica could see a version of Tanner that might lead a free-spirited daughter to run away.

Lianne gave him a shocked look. "Don't say that. Not after what we thought had happened to her. Don't even joke about it."

"God damn it, Lianne, she's has broken your heart time and time again. I'm tired of it. She didn't even stop to think what this would do to us. Or worse . . . she didn't care." He shook his head, ran his fingers through his hair, and left it sticking up in patches. "It's my fault, though. It's my fault for what I put her through, back in the bad old days."

"Don't say that, Tanner. Please, don't say that."

"I think I need to find a meeting tonight." Tanner stood there for another long moment, staring angrily at Adrian. Then he turned on his heel and went into the hall to the bedrooms. A moment later they heard a door slam.

The sound echoed through the living room. Lianne stared after him for a long moment before she turned back to Veronica.

"I'm sorry," she said. "None of us slept last night. We're all just so tired." She shook her head as if trying to clear it. Then a sudden, tremulous smile broke across her face. She gave a short, disbelieving laugh. "But this is good news, right? I mean . . . this means she's alive. She's out there, somewhere, and we just have to find her."

Veronica didn't answer right away. She picked up her bag from where it slouched on the side table and stood, watching as her mother patted Adrian's back.

"I should go," she said. "I'll check in with you guys tomorrow, okay? Give me a call if you find out anything else."

Her thoughts raced as she let herself out. The truth was, she didn't *know* what it all meant—but for now, she had to get home. Keith would be waiting, worried. And she was ready to change out of yesterday's clothes and catch her breath.

CHAPTER THIRTY-THREE

"So does that mean we're off the case?"

Mac kicked the fridge door shut and headed into the living room, beer bottles in hand.

It was an hour later, and Veronica, Mac, and Wallace sat in Mac's apartment. For the first night in what felt like forever, none of Veronica's clients were in actual physical peril. That seemed reason enough to take the night off.

They'd decided to spend the evening in—most of their haunts weren't exactly spring break central, but even so no one felt like facing the crowds. Veronica had done a beer run, Wallace brought tacos, and Mac manifested a batch of organic salsa and tortilla chips. The Alabama Shakes wailed on the stereo. Veronica curled her legs up under her on the couch and took a sip of beer.

"I don't know. I'm guessing as far as Petra Landros is concerned, the job is done. Hayley Dewalt's murder is resolved, and it's hard to imagine she's going to pay me to try to track down a juvenile delinquent who's run off with a boy her dad won't like."

"That's pretty messed up." Wallace shook his head. "I mean, she had to know there'd be some kind of search, right? She just let everyone worry about her."

"I get the feeling 'impulse control' isn't high on the list of Aurora Scott's better qualities." Veronica shrugged. "Honestly, I don't know if she even thought that far ahead."

"I did a little accounting on your behalf today," Mac said. "With the reward money and your hourly we might even be able to convince the power company to stop sending threatening notes."

"You calculated your paycheck in there too, right?"

"Veronica." Mac gave her an oh-please kind of look. "Of course."

They clinked their beer bottles together.

"So this is the last week of spring break?" Veronica asked, looking at Wallace.

"Yeah, this is it." He sighed. "And then it's back to work for Mr. Fennel. Back to an office that smells like dirty socks. Even better, next week my health class is starting on sex ed."

"Come on, Fennel. If there's anything you know about, it's sex ed." Veronica nudged him.

He grimaced. "You have no idea. Trying to get a bunch of sophomores to let me get away with saying 'shaft' without giggling . . ."

"I hear he's a bad mother," Mac said.

Veronica didn't miss a beat. "Shut yo' mouth!"

"I'm just talking about—"

"You two are a laugh a minute, you know that?"

Suddenly Veronica heard her phone, trilling at the bottom of her bag from where it hung on a hook by the door. She got up, Mac and Wallace still mock bickering behind her. The caller ID read UNKNOWN.

"Hello?" As she answered, she cracked open the door

to the apartment and stepped out into the hallway, which smelled like cabbage and industrial-strength cleaner.

"Hi, is this Veronica Mars?"

The voice was female, throaty, and a little hoarse, not someone she recognized.

"Yes, it is. Who's this, please?"

"This is Lee Jackson from the Meridian Group. I'm returning your call."

The phone almost fell right out of Veronica's hand.

"Ms. Mars? Still there? Hello?"

Even taking the sketchiest back roads she knew, it took Veronica almost twenty minutes to get to the Neptune Grand. She'd never been prone to road rage, but she laid on the horn as slow-moving packs of drunken students staggered out into the road ahead of her. They gave her offended, unfocused looks. A wobbly blonde with bundles of Mardi Gras beads dangling around her neck slapped her palm on the hood of the BMW, and for just a split second Veronica imagined running her over.

Back at Mac's she'd asked Lee Jackson if she could call her back. Then she'd stuck her head in the apartment to tell Wallace and Mac she had to go. Their faces barely had a chance to register surprise before she'd slammed the door shut behind her. There'd be time to explain later. Now she had to find the "Lee Jackson" who currently had $600,000 in unmarked, nonsequential bills in an easy-to-transport nylon duffel bag.

The closer she got to the Grand, the worse the traffic got. Downtown was a snarl of cars and pedestrians. Tenth

Avenue was completely shut down for a concert; she could see the lights flashing on the distant stage. People swarmed around the bars, and the souvenir shops were all open late for last-minute purchases. At the '09er, a long line of glittering hopefuls hung back behind the velvet ropes, waiting for entry.

She caught sight of the Grand from a few streets away, its new tall glass tower stretching over the old sandstone façade. She waited impatiently for a light to turn, then roared through the intersection.

After throwing her keys to the valet she ran through the lobby, gentle piano music tinkling from the speakers in an absurd contrast to her pounding heart. She stopped at the desk and leaned toward the startled-looking clerk.

"I need to know which room Lee Jackson is staying in," she said, trying to catch her breath.

The clerk, a young woman whose dark hair was scraped painfully back into the tightest bun Veronica had ever seen, pursed her lips. "I'm sorry, ma'am, we're not able to give out —"

"I'm working for Petra Landros," she snapped. "Veronica Mars? She said if I needed anything I should ask. Well, this is an emergency, and I'm asking."

The woman's mouth dropped open for a half second. Then she was on the phone, speaking in a hushed, urgent voice, apparently to Petra's assistant. "She says her name is Mars? Oh . . . oh, okay. I'm sorry, Gladys, I'll do that right away."

Veronica shifted her weight, glancing around the lobby. It was quiet tonight; the resident spring breakers were already out at the clubs, and any other tourists kept a wide berth from

Neptune this time of year. A bellboy stood gossiping with the concierge near the front door; back in the bar she could just make out that the cocktail waitresses were leaning against the bar, watching the TV. The calm was surreal after the commotion on the streets surrounding the hotel.

Finally the clerk hung up the phone. "I'm so sorry, Miss Mars. Mr. Jackson is in the north tower, room 1201—do you want directions?"

But she was already running, out to the courtyard and around the pool, to the tower.

The elevators stood on both sides of the tower, facing the streets to either side of the hotel. They were glass-fronted and cylindrical, and Veronica felt as if she were stepping into one of the vacuum tubes at the bank as she hit the button for the twelfth floor. Slowly, then quickly, the elevator started to rise.

The city dropped away at her feet. From here she could see the bright, glittering streets around the hotel. A hot-tub limo drifted past like a shark, the bubbling water full to capacity with topless girls. A few streets away, a crowd was forming up around a guy in a cow suit—a moment later she realized he had a T-shirt cannon as white jersey knit went flying through the air. And down at the base of the hotel . . .

She pressed her face against the glass, eyes bulging. Down at the base of the hotel, she just had time to catch an image of a tall black man in a dark suit, hurrying up the street with a blue duffel bag in one hand.

She jammed her thumb against the Stop button on the elevator's panel, then hit the button for the ground floor. Her eyes were glued to Jackson's form as he paused at the corner, then crossed the street, his long legs taking him farther and farther away in enormous strides. The elevator stopped on the fourth floor and let on four boys in tight polo shirts. It seemed to take forever for them all to climb on and select their floor, one seemed to be half in the bag already. The rest nudged one another at the sight of Veronica, and one propped an elbow against the glass to lean down over her. "Hey, there."

"Shut up and get on!" she barked. The boy looked startled, then glanced quickly over to his friends.

"Come on, guys, hurry up. Hurry up."

But by the time the doors closed and the elevator started its quick descent, Lee Jackson had disappeared into the dark side street next to a boutique.

Veronica shoved past the hulking boys and out the doors the moment they slid open. She bolted across the street. Traffic screeched to a stop in front of her, horns blaring, but she didn't slow down. As she approached, she saw that the boutique was closed for the night, the mannequins standing in postures of casual disdain. She put on another burst of speed and veered into the alley.

Almost immediately, the smell of urine and garbage assaulted her nostrils. The alley was unlit, steeped in shadow. She stopped in her tracks, listening. The only sounds came from the surrounding streets, the pulsing bass and screams of laughter. Then she snapped on the Maglite attached to her keys.

Its beam revealed that she was in a service corridor between shops, bars, and restaurants. A clutter of empty boxes and broken bottles filled the spaces between the small concrete loading docks. To one side she could see a large wooden crate lined with blankets and empty bottles—someone's abandoned squat. She made her way slowly, stepping carefully over debris. A cold breeze cut through the alley, sending loose newspapers fluttering like wounded birds. Then a low groan sounded from somewhere to her right.

She turned quickly, sending the tiny circle of light searching over the spot where she'd heard it. It took her a moment before she found him.

The man lay on his side next to an overflowing Dumpster. She couldn't see his face—it was turned toward the ground—but she recognized the navy suit with its narrow white pinstripes, recognized the long and lanky form of the man who'd called himself Lee Jackson. The back of his head was wet with blood, and blood soaked the shoulder of his jacket.

Hands trembling, she called 911.

"Hi. Yes, I'm in the alley just off Seventh Avenue—it's the one just across from the Grand's north tower. There's a man here who's had some kind of head injury. I think he might be unconscious." She knelt down next to him, shining the light closer on his head without touching him. "Looks like some kind of blunt force trauma. Can you please send an ambulance immediately?"

She hung up the phone before they could ask her to stay on the line. She didn't have long before the ambulance would arrive; if she wanted answers, she was going to have to look now.

She felt for the lump of his wallet in his jacket pocket. Carefully, trying not to move him more than necessary, she tugged it free. It was a billfold, made of very soft leather.

All right, Lee Jackson. Just who are you, anyway? She stuck the Maglite in her mouth and opened the wallet.

The compartments were full to bursting. She tugged one of the cards out; it was an Idaho driver's license. She recognized the picture as the man prone before her. The name on the card was Omar Tyrell Mitchell, date of birth 5/12/68. Behind it was an Arizona license for Roy Franklin III, and behind that was a military ID for Reginald Dalton Baker, PFC. They were all like that—licenses and IDs from all over the country, all with the same man's picture. There were at least ten, along with a handful of platinum-grade credit cards in various names.

He was either a con man or a private eye—she had a collection of IDs not much smaller than his. Veronica's money was on the former. Stealing the identity of the real Lee Jackson was short-con behavior; he'd planned to be gone before anyone knew the difference. But had he conned Tanner— or were they in this together? *Tanner* had been the one to bring up hiring a specialist. *Tanner* had been the one who refused to work with the guy the Dewalts hired.

The sound of sirens echoed up the narrow corridor, faint at first but growing louder. She closed the billfold and carefully slid it back into his pocket. Then she saw something that made her freeze in her tracks.

Slowly, cautiously, she reached out and plucked a small, dry object from the ground next to the man's head.

A pinto bean. For a moment she stared at it in the palm of her hand. Then she shined the flashlight around the man's body. There were more, lying around his shoulders, one caught in the collar of his shirt.

She barely had time to process what she was seeing before

red and blue lights came fluttering down the alleyway, the siren echoing painfully off the walls. The cops were here; the ambulance wouldn't be far behind. She shoved the bean, still clutched in her hand, into her pocket. Then she stepped back from the body, turning toward the street to meet the officer who'd almost certainly have questions for her.

CHAPTER THIRTY-FOUR

"I need you to check out Tanner's movements, Mac. Find out if he has a flight, a rented car, anything in the next few days."

The BMW tore up into the hills, tracing along the winding roads with hairpin precision. Veronica kept rubbing the pinto bean between her fingers, her mind churning. She stepped on the gas and urged the car up toward the condo.

"What's going on, Veronica?"

"I'll explain everything as soon as I have a chance, I promise. For now just get me that information."

Neptune was a glittering bracelet spread below the bluffs, every light in town on for another wild spring break night. In the condo's parking lot Veronica killed the engine and was at the door in a flash, first ringing the doorbell, then pounding with her fist.

When Lianne opened the door, Veronica didn't even bother to say hello.

"Where's Tanner?" she asked, walking past her mother, darting her gaze all over the living room.

"What? He's out." Lianne shut the door and turned to her, eyes round. She was still dressed in the short-sleeved sweater and jeans she'd worn earlier, but she had on chenille socks and a pair of reading glasses. Dressed to stay in. "What's wrong?"

"Out where?"

"Out for a run!" A frown creased her forehead. "Hunter's just gone to bed. Can you please keep your voice down?"

"Out for a run after dark? At nine?"

"He always runs at night." Lianne stared at her. "Look, we couldn't find a meeting tonight. An AA meeting? Running helps to calm him down. When he's upset, when he's angry. When he's feeling like picking up a drink. I told him to take as much time as he needs."

Veronica tried to read Lianne's face. Did she know? Did she suspect what her husband had done? Was she in on it? Or was she just like poor Willie Murphy—another dumb patsy in someone else's game?

Lianne had been Veronica's own personal villain for a long time—not because she was evil, but because her father was good. Because Keith was the hero, the one who stayed. Veronica had always known the truth about her mother, the painful, awful truth. Lianne was, like all addicts and drunks, a world-class con. But she always fell for her own trick. She was the only one, in the end, who believed her own lies.

"Mom . . . ," she said, not sure how to start. She closed her eyes, shook her head, opened them. Started again.

"Who hired Lee Jackson? Did you find him? Or did Tanner?"

Lianne's frown deepened. "Tanner found him. I didn't even know there was such a thing as a kidnapping specialist. But Tanner heard about it on some TV show a few years ago."

Veronica shook her head.

"I put in a call to the Meridian Group yesterday, and tonight I finally got a call back. Funny thing . . . it turns out the Lee Jackson who works for Meridian is a woman. I can see why it'd be easy to assume it's a man's name. Kidnapping and ransom is a pretty male-dominated profession, after all. It'd be easy to, say, pick that name off a website, print out a few cards, and run with it. Then anyone who wanted to check your credibility would be able to see a nice CV and a list of pretty heavy-duty accomplishments on the website, but not a picture—pictures are a liability in the security world. Something about blown covers. But if you're a grieving, scared parent, desperate to find your child, that cursory glance would probably be enough to convince you to trust him."

Lianne blinked at Veronica in confusion.

"I went to the Grand to try to confront your fake Lee Jackson, but when I got there he'd already been attacked in the alley. Someone hit him over the head. When the cops checked his wallet there were at least ten different IDs in it—driver's licenses from different states with his picture on each, and credit cards for a handful of identities. I went back and talked to the guy at the front desk and get this— he never checked that money into the safe today. I get the feeling he might have been getting ready to make a getaway. But someone double-crossed the double-crosser. Because that money? It's gone."

Lianne sat down hard in one of the armchairs near the fire. "You mean we hired a . . . a fake?"

Veronica shook her head. "No, Mom. I don't think so." She put both her hands on the winged back of a chair and leaned forward. "I don't think Tanner was taken in by some smooth-talking con man. I think Tanner's working with the guy."

Lianne gave a hot, forced laugh. "You're joking, right?"

"I wish I were."

"If Tanner was working with this guy, why would he steal the money from him?"

Veronica gave Lianne a pitying look. "You know as well as I do there's no honor among thieves. I'm guessing Tanner decided that one hundred percent of the money was preferable to half. Maybe Lee Jackson just outlived his usefulness. Maybe Tanner was planning this the whole time. Either way, I don't think he's coming back."

Her mother's lips tugged downward, a sudden angry sneer. "Where's your evidence, Veronica?"

"Mom, think about it for just a second. Tanner said he called Jackson, right? It wasn't like Jackson cold-called him when news of Aurora's disappearance hit."

"I don't really remember how it all happened," Lianne said, stubborn. Veronica exhaled through closed teeth, fighting to keep her patience.

"Yes, you do. Because the Dewalts had already hired Miles Oxman, and they talked to you about consolidating the investigations and using Oxman for both ransom drops. But Tanner was adamant that he'd heard about this guy Jackson, that he'd already called to hire him. Well, if Tanner had placed the call to Meridian, he would have gotten the real Jackson. The only way this makes sense is if he's in on it."

Suddenly Lianne was on her feet again. "Here's what I think. I think you just can't stand the idea that I've gotten my life back on track, Veronica. I think you can't stand the idea that I might be happy. You're just hoping to find out I've made as big a mess of this marriage as I made of the last one, so you can be right about me. You want to be able to punish me." Her voice shook, but her eyes flashed with anger. "I'm sorry I couldn't do better for you. I'm sorry for it every day. But you can't do this to me. You can't just come in here and try to tell me my family is a sham."

For the span of a breath, Veronica's vision went bloody. She could barely see Lianne through the brilliant red. Then she blinked. Lianne's shoulders were back, her arms clenched close to her body, like she was ready to take a swing.

So like Lianne, to make this a story about poor little her. To make everything she'd done to Veronica and Keith into another way to feel sorry for herself.

So like Lianne too to somehow make Veronica half believe the accusation. That was a drunk's best trick, after all—spread the blame around, let everyone take part in the dysfunction. But didn't Lianne deserve to be punished, just a little? It wasn't fair that she could just decide to move on, easy as that. It wasn't fair that she could build a new life, one where she didn't have to live with what she'd done to Veronica and her father. So maybe some part of Veronica did want to believe Tanner was a crook.

But just because she wanted to believe it didn't make it a delusion.

"I'm not trying to hurt you," she said, fighting to control her voice. "I'm trying to warn you. If you want to keep living in denial, fine by me. It won't be the first time."

She grabbed her purse from where she'd set it down. Then she stopped and turned to face her mother.

"When Tanner doesn't come back tonight—because trust me, he won't—don't bother calling me. Call the sheriff. I'm sure by that time he'll have figured out who the guy with the head injury really is, and he might be very interested to know Tanner and the money both vanished at once."

She spun on her heel, ready to charge toward the door. Then, suddenly, she heard someone come in. She froze in her tracks, her stomach lurching.

Tanner, in nylon shorts and a tank top, came into the room, sweat glistening on the surface of his skin.

"Veronica," he said in surprise, looking up at her as he untied his shoes. "To what do we owe the pleasure?"

"What . . . I . . ." She stared at him, agape, her thoughts swimming. Out of the corner of her eye, she sensed Lianne's attention sharpen. For a moment she expected her mother to say something to her, maybe to kick her out. Maybe just to laugh in her face. But instead, Lianne strode across the cavernous living room and stood inches from Tanner. She stood over him by almost two inches, even in her socked feet.

"What the hell is going on, Tanner?" Her tone was more baffled than anything. "Lee Jackson just got attacked in the parking lot of the Grand. Veronica thinks—"

"Lee got attacked?"

Either Tanner Scott was a world-class actor or Veronica was wrong. A look first of confusion, then of dawning horror, crept over his face. He turned to look at Veronica. "Who attacked him?"

"We don't know yet," Veronica said carefully. She watched him closely as she spoke. "Someone clubbed him from behind. He's alive, but he's in bad shape."

"And the ransom money's gone," Lianne added.

Tanner's eyes bulged slightly, twitching wildly this way and that. "Oh my god."

"I'm just glad you're back." Tears were starting to pour down Lianne's face. "I'm just so glad you're back."

Veronica was about to speak when she heard a soft noise from the hallway to the bedrooms. Hunter, his sandy blond hair sticking up in tufts, came shuffling into the room, pausing just inside the doorway. He wore pajamas with robots printed all over them, and his feet were bare.

"What's going on? Why's everyone yelling?"

Lianne went to scoop him into her arms, while Tanner lowered himself, still looking shocked, into a chair. Veronica stood still, her thoughts racing, her limbs strangely heavy.

Distantly, she heard her text chime on her phone. She pulled it out of her pocket and glanced down at the screen. It was from Mac.

> Tanner on Delta 1792 to Bermuda, tomorrow morning at 6 a.m.

It was when she looked up from her phone that she saw it. Tanner sat, rubbing his hands against his knees, staring nervously toward the fire. Lianne stood in the doorway holding Hunter close, tears pouring down her face. And there, where it'd rolled beneath the coffee table, sat a single maraca, painted in brilliant red and green.

In one fluid movement, she crossed the room and picked it up from where it lay. It rattled in her hand, heavier than she would have expected, the wood thick and quite hard.

She raised it high over her head and brought it down against the edge of the hearth.

With a satisfying crack, the instrument crumpled against the stone. And pinto beans—small, dry, innocuous—spilled out all over the immaculate carpet.

The very same ones that had spilled out beneath Lee Jackson's body at the Neptune Grand.

CHAPTER THIRTY-FIVE

"Look, for the thousandth time, I didn't attack Shep."

It was late Tuesday night, and Veronica watched Tanner's interrogation unfold through a one-way mirror. Lamb hadn't wanted her there— he'd been ready to throw her in the lockup for obstruction, never mind that she hand delivered the perp in question. She'd had to call Petra Landros and remind her that $600,000 was still missing—$600,000 that had been raised in part by Neptune's Chamber of Commerce. "Do you think Lamb's capable of tracking it down?" Veronica had asked.

Within twenty minutes a hulking, concrete-faced deputy was showing her where she could hang her coat. She assumed Petra had put in a call to Lamb to remind him that his campaign funds and endorsements were on the line. *Well, whatever works.* She just wanted to hear what Tanner Scott had to say for himself.

Tanner Scott sat across from Lamb, his forearms flat on the table. Next to him, Cliff McCormack jotted notes onto a legal pad.

"Fine, yes, we were *working* together." Tanner's flat Midwestern drawl was a shade higher than usual. He was nervous. "I mean, I was working *for* him. This whole thing was his idea. I've been out of the game for a long time, living clean and legitimate. But then along come Shep . . ."

"That's Duane Shepherd? The victim?"

"Yeah. He tracked me down in Tucson. I hadn't seen him in eight years. We used to be partners."

At this point Cliff leaned over and whispered something to Tanner, but he shook his head.

"No, look, I'll come clean to anything I'm actually responsible for. But I swear to God, I wasn't anywhere near that hotel tonight. I didn't have anything to do with that maraca."

He pronounced "maraca" with a short "a" on the second syllable, like "rack."

"We used to hustle a little bit, back before I stopped drinking. I got busted nine years ago and served my time. It scared me straight. I got sober, I settled down. By the time I got out of prison, Shep had landed himself in. After that we lost touch. I didn't see him again until last week."

Veronica had already been on and off the phone with Mac for most the night—enough so that she could piece together the parts that Tanner wasn't telling. She already knew about Tanner's check fraud. Shepherd, on the other hand, had a meatier rap sheet. He'd served six months in the nineties for selling forged athletic memorabilia in Sacramento, including a football supposedly signed by "the Juice" himself in the aftermath of the O. J. Simpson trial. A few years after that he was in trouble again, this time for passing off altered lottery tickets in Denver. The last sentence, the one that had come down while Tanner was serving his time, was for identity theft and credit card fraud, a five-year stint in federal prison for maxing out dozens of accounts he'd established with stolen Social Security numbers.

The men had never been implicated in the same set of crimes, but she was willing to bet they'd worked together on and off for a long, long time. Mac had dug deep and found complaints in Reno, Fresno, and Phoenix—cases where victims had come forward claiming fraud but where nothing could be proven. Six women who claimed they'd been recruited by a "modeling firm" that had required them to pay money up front for their portfolios, only to find the firm vanished when they went back; a few socialites who claimed to have met "Denzel Washington's charming brother" and loaned him vast amounts of money. An older couple who'd purchased a houseboat from a "little skinny guy with blue eyes," only to find that the deed was forged. Veronica knew the statistics on swindling—most people never came forward, too ashamed of having been taken in, too ashamed of a situation where their own greed or lust or hunger had been laid bare. For every one complaint, it was worth assuming there were a half dozen other victims who'd stayed hidden in the shadows.

"He had an idea for how to make some money. I told him no, I was out. But the thing about Shep is, he can be very persuasive." He rubbed the back of his neck. "He forced me into it."

"How'd he force you into it?" Lamb's voice was dripping skepticism, his left eyebrow arched over a baby-blue eye. "Did he threaten you with violence?"

"Shep has stuff on me from way back. Enough to get me put away. I mean, nothing violent," he said quickly. "Some scams we ran back in the day that are still technically, uh, unsolved. He threatened to turn me in. I never meant to hurt anyone. I swear."

"You believe him?"

Veronica looked up. Norris Clayton had sidled up next to her, holding two cups of coffee. He handed one to Veronica.

"About being blackmailed by Shepherd? I'll give it a fifty-fifty. It's possible—but Tanner's an established liar, and Shepherd isn't exactly in a position to argue."

"Oh, you didn't hear?" Norris grinned humorlessly. "Shepherd disappeared from his hospital bed about an hour ago. No one's sure how he managed it—but he's vapor."

Veronica turned to stare at him, but she didn't have time to speak. Lamb was still grilling Tanner Scott. She shook her head and turned back to the window.

"Okay, okay. So what was Mr. Shepherd's plan? Walk me through it like I'm stupid," Lamb said.

Norris snorted softly, and Veronica's esteem for the man rose dramatically.

"Well, he'd seen how much money was flooding into that Hayley Dewalt website. I mean, by noon on the first day it hit a hundred thousand. It was unbelievable. So he thought it'd be pretty easy to get in on that. All Aurora had to do was make sure to be seen at the same party the first girl went missing from, and then hole up for a few weeks while the money rolled in. Then we'd do the ransom drop, and a few days later she could stagger into a gas station, dirty and a little worse for wear. Shep would get the money out of town, and we'd meet up later and split it."

Lamb was staring at him now with unmasked skepticism. "Wait, wait. You're saying your sixteen-year-old daughter was in on this?"

Tanner hesitated, then nodded.

The sheriff leaned back in his seat, arms crossed over

his chest. "Look, we have this other kid—Adrian Marks—saying she ran off with some guy. I gotta tell you, that's more plausible to me than the idea of a teenaged girl staying holed up during spring break."

"How many teen girls you know, Sheriff?"

Lamb didn't crack a smile. Tanner sighed.

"Well, that's how the whole thing fell apart. Damn girl told that friend of hers she was running off with a boy so he wouldn't worry about her when she went missing. She was trying to be kind, I guess, but it was an amateur mistake." Tanner erupted in a hoarse laugh. "I thought I taught her better."

"Mr. Scott, forgive me, but I don't see how it's funny to use a minor as an accessory to fraud, theft, obstruction of justice, and tampering with evidence."

Tanner sobered at once. "Look, don't be hard on the kid. She didn't want any part of this, either—but when she found out what Shep was threatening, she was scared. Last time I went to jail she was stuck in foster care for a year and a half. It wasn't a day at the fucking beach. She's terrified of losing me again."

"And what about your wife and your son? Did they know what was going on?"

A strange look flitted across Tanner's face. Veronica couldn't decide if it was regret or relief.

"No. They didn't. They don't."

Which meant, if it was true, that he'd been planning to leave her mom high and dry. The ticket to Bermuda spoke volumes about how he'd planned to end the heist: on a beach, with a daiquiri in hand and no straight-and-narrow wife or noisy six-year-old in sight.

Lianne was being questioned in a different interrogation room even now, a few doors down; Veronica had no desire to listen in on that session.

"So you wrote both ransom notes?"

"Shep did. He's the one with the technical savvy. Knows how to encrypt things, knows how to mask an IP address, all that stuff. He thought we might get lucky and get the ransom for Hayley Dewalt too, but then that girl found the body."

Veronica smiled a little. She'd gone from being "Veronica, honey" to "that girl" in a matter of hours. All things considered, she preferred the latter. At least from Tanner Scott.

"So today when Adrian Marks came forward with his story, you decided to move. You jogged to the Grand with one of your son's maracas, waited for Shepherd to leave the hotel, assaulted him, and took the money."

"No!" Tanner slammed his fist on the table. "No, I didn't. I wasn't anywhere near the hotel. I was checking in on Rory. Room twenty-four in the Pinehurst Lodge, like I've been saying for two hours. Check it if you don't believe me!"

"We did check it."

A look of surprise flashed across Tanner's face, too quick for him to hide it. "So? What'd she say?"

Lamb's chest swelled up, and Veronica could only guess how much he was loving this part—the trap sprung, the cat catching the canary. He'd taken the loss of Willie Murphy hard. But here he had a nice, juicy replacement for his trouble, a swindler who preyed upon the fears of anyone who'd ever seen a picture of a missing girl and imagined his or her own daughter in her place.

"Mr. Scott, no one at the Pinehurst has ever laid eyes on your daughter. Room twenty-four has been vacant for a week. There's no evidence she was ever anywhere near that motel."

Tanner shook his head, his jaw tight. "That's not right. I just saw her there. Three hours ago, I just saw her there!"

"So on top of everything else, I'm starting to have a strong inclination to charge you not just in the assault of Duane Shepherd but also for the murder of Aurora Scott."

"Lamb, get real." Cliff broke in for the first time in a while. "You don't have anything to indicate that Aurora Scott has been murdered—particularly not by my client."

"Not yet," Lamb said, a leering grin spreading across his face. "But until I start getting more satisfied about some of these answers, it's definitely a possibility."

"We've been searching the areas around the condo and around the Camelot," Norris whispered. "I can't figure out where he would have put the cash. I mean, look at him, he doesn't even have pockets on his shorts. He had to hide it somewhere, right?"

For a second, Veronica felt everything stop. The sound of the station, the beating of her heart, the blood in her veins. The earth tilting and swaying. It all went still. Flashes went off in her brain, brilliant and blinding. She closed her eyes. She could feel a smile, incongruous and strange, spreading over her face.

"You won't find that money hidden around the condo. Or the Neptune Grand," Veronica said.

She opened her eyes. Norris was staring at her expectantly.

"How do you know that?"

"Give me an hour and I'll explain everything." She adjusted her purse strap on her shoulder. "Thanks, Norris. I've gotta go."

She was halfway down the hall when she heard Norris calling after her. "Be careful, Veronica!" Veronica held up her hand in acknowledgment and rounded the corner to the exit.

CHAPTER THIRTY-SIX

Adrian Marks lived in a shoddy apartment complex a few blocks from the wide green swaths of Hearst College. When Veronica arrived it was almost eleven. The pool was packed with kids—Hearst was back in session, but it looked like the residents were trying to stretch the party out a little longer. Coolers of beer lined the sides of the pool, and a few empty bottles bobbed like ducks on the water's surface.

Adrian's unit was on the top floor. There was a light in the window, bands of yellow peeking out past the closed blinds. She pressed her ear to the door but she couldn't hear anything over the thump of the music at the pool below. Then she knocked.

The light in the window shifted as someone moved through it. It seemed to take a few minutes. She stood a few extra inches back from the door. She was so short people often had a hard time seeing her through the peephole.

After what felt like a beat too long, the door swung open. Adrian stood silhouetted in the doorway. He wore an inside-out T-shirt and a pair of plaid boxer shorts, his dark hair tousled over one eye. It was the most undressed she'd seen him since she'd met him the week before—he usually gave the impression of being carefully put together, even when he was just wearing jeans and a T-shirt.

"I didn't wake you up, did I?" Veronica's voice was apologetic. "I know it's late."

Adrian rubbed the back of his neck. He gave an awkward smile.

"I wasn't asleep yet. Just getting settled in. It's actually early for me, but it was a royal *night*mare of a day." He held up his hands, palms out in a gesture of exasperation.

"Yeah, I heard you had to make a statement. That must have been tough."

He shuddered. "I never want to have to go through anything like it again."

Veronica smiled sympathetically.

"The thing is, I have a few more questions about Aurora. I was hoping you could help clarify a few things for me."

Adrian glanced behind him into the apartment. "It can't wait for tomorrow? I really was just on my way to bed."

"It'll only take a moment." She paused. "I just want to make sure Aurora's all right."

Behind her she heard a shriek and then a splash from the pool. After another few seconds, Adrian swung open the door to let her in.

The cramped little apartment was a catastrophe. Dirty dishes and empty pizza boxes cascaded across the floor. An overflowing ashtray sat on top of a statistics book, next to a cluster of beer bottles. One of the lightbulbs in the kitchen was out, giving the place a yellowed and dingy look. A smell of unwashed socks mingled with the smell of sour, turning food. Beneath it she could just make out a whiff of something sweeter, like the ghost of a vanilla candle.

"So you said you had questions?" Adrian prompted.

She stuck her hands into her pockets, rocking slightly on the balls of her feet. "Did you hear what happened tonight? Mr. Jackson —you know, that kidnapping expert? Someone attacked him outside the Neptune Grand and disappeared with the ransom money."

Adrian's head jerked backward in a double take. "What?"

"Crazy, right?" She shifted her weight. "The sheriff brought Mr. Scott in for questioning."

"Mr. Scott? But . . . why?" The boy's brow furrowed.

"Apparently Jackson and Tanner were working together all along. Well, Jackson, Tanner, and Aurora. According to Tanner she's been in on it too." She watched Adrian's face carefully. He looked confused, his eyes wide with surprise. "They decided to stage her disappearance when Hayley went missing, then created the ransom notes, hoping to cash in on both Hayley's disappearance and Aurora's. But when it looked like their cover was about to be blown, Jackson tried sneaking off with the money. Lamb thinks it was Tanner who assaulted him and hid the money somewhere."

Adrian sat down hard on a lumpy easy chair. It creaked beneath him. "Oh. My. God." He covered his eyes with one hand for a moment, then looked up, his eyes flashing. "I'm going to *kill* her! She let me sit here and feel like shit for covering her ass, and all this time she's been in on everything? I can't fucking believe her."

Veronica sat down across from him on a sagging sofa, hands in her lap. From where she sat she could see a little way down the darkened hallway— one door was closed, another cracked slightly, too dark to see in. "So you haven't heard from her at all tonight?"

He shook his head. "Have the cops found her yet?"

"That's the thing." She leaned forward. "She's not at the motel where Tanner said she'd be. She really *is* missing this time."

"What are you saying?"

"I don't know." She straightened up again. "Lamb is talking about charging Tanner with her murder, but I don't buy it. For one thing there's no evidence. Not that that'd stop Lamb. But for another, Tanner allegedly hit his partner over the head with a *maraca*. I don't buy that he'd clock Lee Jackson with an amateur bludgeon if he were cold enough to off his own daughter."

"A maraca?" Adrian asked, looking thunderstruck.

"So what I'm wondering," she went on, as if he hadn't spoken at all, "is if you think Aurora has it in her to double-cross her dad."

He stared at her for a moment, his mouth hanging open.

"Because here's the thing," she said. "Tanner may be sketchy, but he seems like a pretty smart guy. So why would he take his child's musical instrument—which I'd just seen him handling a few hours earlier—and use it to assault someone?" She grimaced. "Besides which, where the hell was he keeping it? He was out jogging. I saw his clothes—mesh shorts, T-shirt, no pockets. So did he just jog down to the Grand with the maraca clenched in his fist, then jog off with the duffel of money? I doubt it. But if Tanner didn't do it—and I don't think he did—that means that whoever did do it worked really hard to pin it on him. The only person in the scam who's unaccounted for is Aurora. And if I've learned anything about Aurora in the past week, it's that she's clever, she's ambitious, and she's a damn good liar."

Adrian ran his fingers through his hair. He was quiet for a minute, staring blankly up at the ceiling. When he looked back down, his blue eyes were conflicted.

"I don't know anymore. I mean, a few hours ago, I would have told you no way— that Rory wouldn't do something like that to her own dad. But . . . she's been lying to me all this time. She's been lying to everyone. So I don't know what to think. I'm sorry, I wish I could help you."

She stood up. "It's all right, Adrian. This has got to come as a real shock to you." She smiled and held out her hand. They shook. "Look, give me a call if you hear from her, okay? I just want to know she's safe."

"I will," he promised.

She turned to go but paused near the dark hallway. It was now or never.

"Mind if I use your bathroom before I go?"

Before he could answer, she pushed open the closed door—the one she'd pegged as the bedroom. Immediately a wave of that sweet vanilla smell came wafting out through the open door.

Then a white-hot ripple of pain unfurled in her chest, spreading out through her body. Her muscles seized up. She felt herself falling and she couldn't move—couldn't even put out her hands to brace her fall.

In the moment before she hit the carpet, she just had time to make out the freckled face and straight auburn hair of her attacker, a Taser crackling in her hand.

Hello, Aurora.

CHAPTER THIRTY-SEVEN

"Shit! Shit! What are we going to do?"

"Shut up. Just shut up and let me think for a second."

Veronica found herself on her back, staring across a grimy, khaki-colored carpet at a landscape of dust bunnies and beer caps. She couldn't move to turn her head from where it was crooked to the left, but from where she lay she could make out a bed with a rumpled quilt spilling half on the floor, a single desk lamp casting yellow light around the bedside table. There were dirty clothes all over the room, and just a few feet away, a blue nylon duffel bag slumped on the floor.

That vanilla perfume grew stronger, and she felt warm breath on her cheek. Pain ricocheted through her body as Aurora shocked her again, her nerves screaming. She felt her legs flop against the floor like dying fish, wondering distantly if this was some horrible kind of karma for all the people she'd tased over the years. Then she fell still.

"Hand me her purse," Aurora demanded. "We have to make sure she's not armed."

There was a rustling noise near Veronica's ear as Aurora rifled through Veronica's bag and pulled out her Taser. "Hold on to that. We definitely don't want to be on the receiving end of this thing."

They had Veronica's Taser. Her mouth was dry. She could already feel the pins and needles of sensation returning to her limbs, but before she could move she felt something pressing into her legs.

"We need to get her tied up before the shock wears off."

"Yeah, but what then? She's seen you, Rory—what the fuck are we going to do with her?" Adrian's voice suddenly seemed to have dropped about two octaves in the last few seconds.

"Baby, I love you, but you are not helping." Aurora's voice was a tight, controlled hiss. "Use your exercise bands and *tie her up.*"

There was some scuffling behind her. Veronica wiggled her toes, testing her movement. Suddenly Aurora was in front of her, cocking her head to one side to meet Veronica's eyes. She was in a black bra and panties, her hair loose around her shoulders. Her mascara was smeared beneath her eyes. She held the stun gun in her right hand.

"You wouldn't believe how much I've heard about you," she said. Her voice was tense and excited. "Clever, good Veronica Mars, the daughter so decent and upstanding Lianne couldn't even look her in the eye. It's fucking pathetic. She never had that problem with me." Aurora gave a short, harsh laugh.

"It takes a con to know a con, I guess," Veronica rasped. Her throat was dry, and her muscles were bunched in tense, vicious knots. She groaned, her voice weak and shaky, as Adrian appeared and tugged her arms roughly away from her body. He wound something cool and tight around her wrists. Almost instinctively she pulled her hands slightly apart, hoping against hope that it would help her generate slack in the bindings.

Aurora seemed to be enjoying her discomfort. "So it was Adrian who attacked Duane Shepherd with the maraca and left those beans there for me to find?"

"I knew that doorknob of a sheriff wouldn't put it together, but I thought you might." She started to pace, her bare feet padding back and forth across the carpet. "I never liked Shep. He liked to think he was in charge of the whole operation. Kind of a bummer that I didn't get to smack him myself." She paused, looking behind Veronica at Adrian. "You get it good and tight? Get her legs too."

Next it would be a gag. She didn't have a lot of time left if she wanted to get them talking. She lifted her head slightly to meet Aurora's catlike green eyes.

"So how long have you been sleeping with your gay BFF, Aurora?"

Aurora stopped her pacing for a moment and actually giggled. It sounded absurdly young, almost childish.

"We started the Will and Grace act last year, just after we started dating. At first we did it just to see if we could get away with it. I told Lianne and Dad a couple sad, sad stories about how the kids at school bullied him, about how his own family would disown him if they knew. They ate it right up. Never said a word, not even when I'd come out of my room with Adrian still in there, half naked." She smirked. "I wasn't surprised Lianne bought it, but my dad should've figured it out. He's lost his edge."

"You started the rumor just so you could fool around?" Veronica asked. Adrian quickly wound a towel around her ankles. Again, she kept them almost imperceptibly apart. "That's a long con. I'm impressed."

Aurora shrugged. She stopped her pacing to pick up a long silk scarf from the top of the dresser, balling it up in one fist. "We didn't know it'd end up being useful too. It's not like we've been planning this. But it's come in pretty handy. No one would suspect sweet, limp-wristed Adrian of having anything to do with my disappearance."

"So now you've got the cash," Veronica said. "And as an added bonus, you got to throw your dad under the bus. Pretty cold, Aurora."

The girl's nostrils flared. "He got what was coming to him."

"I think there's about to be a lot of that going around," Veronica said.

The girl dropped down on one knee in front of Veronica. Her smirk had turned to an agitated, angry sneer. "You don't know *anything* about me. You don't get to judge me." She gripped a handful of Veronica's hair and pulled her head up. Veronica cried out in pain, but the instant her mouth was open the girl shoved the scarf into it.

Veronica tried to whip her head away, to writhe out of Aurora's grip, but the girl held on, pinning her down to the floor. Veronica's scalp burned, and the silk scarf filled her dry mouth, stretching her cheeks uncomfortably wide.

Aurora met Veronica's eyes. "Tanner treated me like the dumb little girl I was before he went straight. He never even stopped to think I could do something like this if I wanted to. But I spent the first seven years of my life as a prop in his small-time games. I was a perfect shill—cute as a button and eager to please. He had me return stolen dogs for reward money. Once he and Shep shaved my head and passed me off as a brave little cancer patient." She snorted. "Jesus, for a while, when we were on the road, he'd have me sit alone at the rest stop or outside a gas station. Then if a certain kind of man talked to me or asked if I needed help, I'd scream bloody murder. Dad would come running and accuse the guy of attempted kidnapping. Nine times out of ten, the poor rube would get so freaked out he'd pay anything he had in his pocket to make the problem go away. And then, just because prison scared the shit out of him, he decided to go straight. He just *decided* it for both of us, like I didn't get a vote. Then it was nine years of 'Straighten up and fly right, Aurora,' nine years of, 'You're going down a dangerous path, little missy.'" She was shaking—whether with fury or nerves, Veronica couldn't tell. "So as annoying as Shep is, I was fucking ecstatic when he showed up with a plan. Of course, in his version, I was going to be a good girl and stay put in that scummy motel they had picked out for me. There wasn't even cable TV in there! Instead I stayed right here, right where I wanted to be. I broke into the motel long enough for Dad to see me there and came right back here. Now they've both been caught, and it *serves them right* for underestimating me."

Abruptly she let go of Veronica's hair. Veronica's head hit the carpet again, and for a moment she saw stars.

"Come on, Adrian, the timetable just got moved up." Aurora was on her feet again. "We've got to get out of here."

"What are we gonna do with her?"

"We'll leave her here. Tied up and gagged. Someone will find her in a few days."

The pressure on Veronica's legs disappeared as Adrian stood up. He clenched his fists at his sides, his knuckles white. "That's not gonna work and you know it. People know who she is. They're gonna look for her, and if they find her before we're gone . . ."

"Then what do you recommend?" she hissed.

He gave her a significant look. The girl went pale beneath her freckles.

"No way," she whispered. "That's crazy, Adrian. You think they're gonna let us stay disappeared if we've *killed* someone?"

Veronica's throat went tight. For a moment she felt like she was choking on the scarf. She moved her fingers, testing the bonds that held her. There was a little bit of slack, but it'd take some work to get out.

"We can't risk her getting found." Adrian gripped Aurora by either shoulder, a panicked, wild look in his eyes. "We've got to get rid of her."

The two of them stared at each other in silence. On the floor Veronica tried to slow her breathing, to stay calm. She'd need both her breath and her energy if they decided they were out of options.

Then, cutting through the tense, anxious air, three quick knocks sounded at the door.

Veronica's heart leapt.

Aurora and Adrian exchanged glances, eyes narrowed. Adrian nodded at Aurora and slipped out of the bedroom, shutting the door firmly behind him. Veronica listened to his footsteps trailing across the little apartment.

The door opened. Adrian's voice was muffled through the wall, but the visitor's voice came loud and clear.

"Hi, Mr. Marks. Sorry to disturb you, but I'm looking for my daughter."

It was Keith.

Finally, Veronica thought. *He's here.*

CHAPTER THIRTY-EIGHT

Veronica could hear Adrian's voice through the wall. He'd put the high camp back on —she could picture him, jutting a hip out, cocking his head. "Your daughter?"

"Yeah. I'm pretty sure you know her—blond woman, yay tall. Veronica. The private eye helping with Aurora's case."

Veronica felt tears gathering at the corners of her eyes and blinked them quickly away. When she'd called her dad on the car ride over to explain her theory, he'd told her to wait for him in the parking lot. Worried that Adrian and Aurora could be on their way out of town at any moment, she'd gone in anyway. But she'd underestimated Aurora— badly. And now her dad was in danger too.

"Oh! Yeah, I saw her this afternoon. I haven't seen her since then, though." His voice sounded concerned. "Why, is she missing?"

Aurora crouched frozen by the bedroom door, stun gun in hand. She was so engrossed in eavesdropping she didn't notice Veronica, twisting her wrists, trying to work her hand through the knot.

"Well, that's funny. Her car's in the parking lot. I know she's been working on a case you've been involved with, and she gave me a call not too long ago saying she was coming over here."

"Shit," Aurora breathed.

There was a long pause. Then Adrian's voice came back with false bravado. "I'm sorry, Mr. Mars. I don't know anything about that. Look, I've got an early class tomorrow. I've got to get some sleep. But if I hear anything from Veronica I'll tell her to call you right away."

She heard a clunking sound. The door shutting on a cane?

"I'm sorry, Mr. Marks, but I'd really feel a lot better if you'd let me look around."

"Hey, man, you can't just come in here like—"

"Veronica? Can you hear me?"

"Get the fuck out of my apartment."

"You don't like it?" A beat. "Call the sheriff, kid."

She closed her eyes, trying to breathe slowly around the scarf, to keep from panicking. Trying not to calculate the odds between Adrian Marks, eighteen years old, athletic and fit, and Keith Mars, fifty-one, who'd almost died two months earlier and couldn't make it a block without his cane.

There was a scuffling sound, followed by a dull thud. The wall shook as something fell against it. Aurora was on her feet and out the door in a flash. Veronica gave one final wrench of her hands and pulled her left wrist through the knot.

"Stay down, if you know what's good for you, Grandpa." Aurora's voice was muffled through the wall, but Veronica could hear the triumph in it. There was another thud, and a low groan. Veronica peeled the tubing off her wrist and sat up to untie her ankles.

It was lucky Adrian hadn't patted her down; he'd been in a hurry just to bind her. She pulled the .38 out of the holster at the small of her back and checked to make sure it was loaded. Then she burst through the door, the gun held out in front of her.

This time, her hands were steady.

Keith was on his side on the ground, clutching his stomach. Adrian stood over his body with the titanium cane in his hand, blood pouring from his nose. As Veronica entered he swung it straight into Keith's stomach with an awful *thwack*. Aurora watched from a few feet away, her face rigid with fury. Any hint of the crafty, calculating girl Veronica had glimpsed was obscured now, replaced by a towering rage, the destructive temper tantrum of a teenager.

Veronica didn't stop to think. She aimed the gun at a lamp a few feet to Adrian's left, and she pulled the trigger.

The sound tore through the apartment, the lamp exploding in a shower of ceramic. Adrian dropped the cane and covered his ears. Veronica turned slightly to point the gun straight at Aurora. Slowly, the girl dropped the stun gun and held up her arms.

In the distance, the sound of sirens wailed.

Ten minutes later, Veronica and Keith sat side by side on the steps outside the apartment, watching as Norris Clayton pushed Aurora's head down into the cruiser. Adrian was still upstairs in handcuffs; the EMTs were taking care of his broken nose. Keith's legs were still frail; his right hook, not so much.

"Did you get a confession?" he asked.

"Oh!" She reached into her green corduroy jacket and pulled out her iPhone. It was still recording. She turned it off. "I almost forgot."

"You could have been killed." His voice was sad but resigned. She looked at him, not sure if she was being admonished or not. "I told you to wait for me."

"Aurora and Adrian were about to skip town; every second mattered."

"Veronica, it wasn't worth risking your life over. The cops would have caught them." He frowned. "Not every fight is worth going to the mat for."

She stared out over the pool. When the college kids had heard the sirens they'd fled, leaving nothing behind but their empty beer cans and one forlorn green towel, abandoned over the back of a chair. She knew he was right. And she knew that was the thing that scared him the most— the fact that she couldn't stand the thought of losing her quarry. The fact that, more than anything, she hated the idea that sometimes assholes got away with everything and left other people—people like Hayley Dewalt's family— empty-handed and bereft.

Keith put an arm around her shoulders and hugged her to his side. "Next time I want you to wait for me. I'm your backup, Veronica." He hesitated for a moment. "I'm your *partner.*"

The word took a moment to land. For a second, it sounded foreign, almost forced—like a story they were both trying to believe. She looked at him, wondering if there was any way she'd ever feel less like a kid when she was with him. Wondering if they could actually ever work as equals.

Then she smiled and realized they would. They'd needed each other for a long, long time. They'd already been partners for years.

She rested her head on his shoulder and watched the cruiser pull away from the curb and slip off into the night.

CHAPTER THIRTY-NINE

The sunlight caught the windows of the Warehouse District late Wednesday morning, glittering like ocean spray. Even this far inland, miles from the brilliant Pacific surf, away from the luxurious playgrounds of the lucky and the carefree, it looked like it was going to be another beautiful day in Neptune, California.

Veronica slammed the door of the BMW shut behind her, then stood for a moment looking up at the office building. It'd been less than twenty-four hours since Adrian and Aurora's arrest. Her body ached all over with bruises and her eyes were dry and tired from the run of sleepless nights. If she'd ever deserved a day off, it was now—but she knew there'd be plenty going on at the office. After a major case, things usually blew up in the PI business, and while the Chamber of Commerce's money would keep them solvent for a little while, she had to be on point and ready to snatch up anything else that came her way. She took another breath of fresh air and started inside.

She was almost to the door when it swung open and Petra Landros stepped out, sleek and smooth in a plum-colored sheath dress and spindle-heeled Louboutins. As ever, she seemed to be stepping from some luxurious alternate reality, somewhere between perfume-scented pages. Her lipsticked mouth turned up when she saw Veronica, and she lifted her oversize Jackie O shades off her face to meet Veronica's eyes.

"Ms. Mars. Congratulations on another case closed." They shook hands. "I was just dropping off the check with your assistant."

"Mac's not really my assistant; she's more of a . . ." She paused for a moment, realizing she'd almost said *hacker*. "Colleague," she finished vaguely.

Petra waved one hand as if it didn't make any difference. She leveled her dark brown eyes on Veronica, suddenly thoughtful.

"You know, you're a remarkable young woman." She tapped the corner of her mouth with one manicured index finger. "Bright, resourceful, and about as dogged as anyone I've ever met. I have to confess . . ." She smiled more warmly. "I feel safer knowing that you're in Neptune, looking after us all."

Veronica met the woman's gaze. "Thanks, Ms. Landros. I'm grateful for the work. But I have to wonder: Wouldn't it be cheaper in the long run for the Chamber to back a competent sheriff than to rely on me to fix Lamb's screwups?"

She expected the woman's smile to fade, but if anything, it broadened.

"Still not a saleswoman, I see." She put her shades back on, hiding her eyes once again. "Like I said, Ms. Mars. You're bright, resourceful, and dogged. All admirable qualities, I assure you. But sometimes, it's good to have someone around who does just as he's told."

With that, she walked past Veronica and toward the

street to her black Mercedes-Benz. Veronica watched her fold her legs into the car and shut the door before she turned to climb the stairs to her office.

On the landing outside the office, she caught the sound of Trish Turley's clipped syllables coming through the door. She sighed and went in to find Mac sitting at her desk staring at her big monitor.

". . . speaking to Dan Lamb, the sheriff of Neptune, California, who made several arrests late last night in the Aurora Scott case—including, in a surprise twist, Aurora Scott herself! Tell me, Sheriff, how exactly did you find Aurora?"

Lamb's voice was the height of smugness. "Well, Trish, to be honest, it was just some good old-fashioned detective work."

"Oh, God, turn it off before I throw up," Veronica said, throwing her bag onto the couch. Mac muted the computer and stood up. She grabbed a handful of small pink notes from a basket near her desk and shoved them unceremoniously into Veronica's hands.

"Messages," Mac said. "For you. That's what came in before ten. I turned off the ringer after that. Some of them are news outlets, but there are about six potential clients in there. I'm guessing there are more on the voice mail by now. FYI, you're going to have to find someone with people skills if you want a receptionist." She crossed her arms over her chest and leaned back against her desk. "You might want to call a few of those reporters back. Lamb's busy telling anyone with a microphone that he broke the case. His numbers are already rebounding in the polls."

Veronica sat down on the couch and slung her feet on the

low table in front of her. "Let the idiots vote for him. You get the government you deserve, right?"

"Ah, the misanthropy levels are high in here today." Mac picked up a check from the desk, snapping it briskly. "This should cheer you up. You can pay rent *and* afford a technical-analyst-slash-super-hot secretary for the next few months at the very least."

Veronica smiled. "That does cheer me up. We might just be okay, Mac."

"We're always okay," Mac said. She went to the coffeemaker and poured herself a mug. "I still can't believe Aurora was in on the whole thing. I mean, parting a fool from his money? I respect that. But piggybacking on an actual victim is pretty . . . tasteless, even for Neptune."

Veronica didn't answer. It was all too easy for her to imagine Tanner and Aurora, back before they'd gone straight. Back when they'd each been all the other had. She could picture the way he'd reward her with that warm Midwestern smile when she'd pulled a swindle off. Could picture the way he'd ignore her, then, for weeks at a time, drunk between jobs, no use for the needy child who watched him so closely. It'd been inevitable that Aurora would decide that love was just another way to use someone—just another long con.

She stood up and stretched. "I'd better get on some of those phone calls, I guess. You want to go to Doriola's for lunch? My treat."

"Sure." Mac watched, a strange expression on her face, as Veronica went to the door of her inner office. "Sounds good."

Veronica glanced at her friend over her shoulder as she opened the door. She was just about to ask what was with the weird look when she saw something that stopped her in her tracks.

Keith sat at his desk. He was wearing a trim gray suit and a blue striped tie, his cane hooked over the edge of the desk. A second desk stood adjacent to his. It was neat and orderly, with a small chrome lamp at one corner, a cup of pens and an in-tray bristling with paperwork to one side.

"You're late," Keith said, a mild, deadpan expression on his face. "Last I heard, the American workday starts at nine."

A small, grateful smile spread across her face. She glanced at Mac again, who smirked and turned back to her computer. Then Veronica walked into the office and sat down in her new chair.

"I thought you had physical therapy this morning," she said.

"Assembling furniture is more or less the same thing as physical therapy," he answered. Their eyes met, and his expression said more than words could.

A moment later, Veronica heard the front door open again. She looked up to see Hunter and Lianne standing in reception, just inside the door.

Lianne's eyes were dark with exhaustion. She wore the same gray sweater and jeans she'd worn the day before, rumpled, a fresh coffee stain speckling her thigh. Hunter, somber as ever, stared around the office. For once he didn't have an instrument in hand. Veronica and Keith both stood up and went into the outer office to meet them.

"Lianne." Keith paused a few feet away from his ex-wife. He looked uncertain for a moment, his hands awkward at his sides. Then he held out his arms, and she moved in to hug him, resting her chin on his shoulder for a moment.

When they broke apart, Keith held her by the shoulders and looked down at her. "How're you holding up?"

She glanced at Hunter, then back at Keith. "We're . . . we're all right. Thanks."

Hunter looked around the room, a small skeptical frown on his face. Veronica knelt down to his height. "How are you, Hunter?"

"We were just at jail." There was a mixture of pride and something else in his voice. Resignation, maybe? Sadness? "The police officers gave me a badge. See?"

"That's pretty cool," Veronica said, admiring the pin on the boy's shirt.

"It's plastic," Hunter answered, offhand.

Lianne twisted her wedding ring around and around on her finger, her mouth turned downward. "Do you mind if we talk in your office?" The look on her face was pointed; she didn't want Hunter to overhear.

"Of course. Veronica, can you keep an eye on the little pitcher?" Keith asked.

"Sure." She watched as Keith ushered Lianne into the office, shutting the door firmly behind him. For a moment the only sound in the room was the soft gurgling of the fish tank. She looked at Mac, who shrugged helplessly.

"The sheriff might arrest my mom," Hunter suddenly said. His chin jutted pugnaciously. He scuffed one sneaker back and forth across the floor. "That's why she's talking to your dad."

Veronica sat down on the sofa, where she was more or less at face height with the little boy. "Is that what she told you?"

"No," he said, scornful. "But I heard it."

She stared at him—at this tiny stranger. Her brother. Lianne may have been sober for his lifetime, but he still had the cagey look of an addict's child—stoic, hidden, careful. Maybe that was an effect of growing up with so many secrets, so many lies . . . with a dad who could stop drinking but couldn't seem to stop scamming. With a sister who'd been born and bred a criminal. With a mom who kept her past locked up in her heart, secret and shameful.

"He said she was an . . . accessorary?"

"An accessory?"

"Yup." He nodded. "So she might have to go to jail. And I'll be alone."

She didn't say anything for a moment. Across the room, the little electronic treasure chest in the fish tank opened and closed, rhythmically releasing its bubbles. Beyond the door to the inner office, she could hear her father's low, gentle voice, but she couldn't make out the words he was saying. She didn't know what, exactly, they were talking about— didn't know how Keith could help Lianne this time. But she turned back to Hunter. Quickly, impulsive, she pulled him into a hug. His little shoulders tensed. She leaned close and whispered into his ear.

"Listen, Hunter. I don't know what's going to happen, but I can promise you one thing. You're not going to be alone. If something happens to Mom, if she does have to go to jail, I'll take care of you, okay? You'll have me. And I won't let anything bad happen to you."

She felt a single sob move up his spine. Then, suddenly, he relaxed. He wrapped his arms around her neck and hugged.

A few minutes later, Keith opened the door, and Lianne stepped out ahead of him. Her face was red and damp, but she looked calm, resolved. She smiled when she saw Hunter, sitting close to Veronica on the couch and looking at the pictures in a *National Geographic*.

"Well, come on, Hunter. We should go. I'm sure Keith and Veronica have work to do."

"I'll walk you down to the street." Veronica got up from the sofa. She wasn't sure why, but she wasn't quite ready to say good-bye.

Downstairs, just inside the door, she paused. She was reminded of the afternoon nearly a week ago now, when her mom had walked her to the door of the condo after seeing her for the first time in more than a decade. A loaded moment—one or the other of them anxious to hurry through another door, to put some distance between them, as if the collapse of eleven long years of silence was too much too soon too fast.

For the past week Veronica had been careful with her mother. She'd wrapped her own boundaries in chain link and razor wire, doing her best to stay professional and aloof. That meant she didn't let anything out—didn't show any of her hurt, her grief, any of the old scars Lianne had left. And it meant she didn't have to feel sorry for her mother. She didn't have to feel *anything* for her mother.

But now it was hard not to. Maybe it was just her exhaustion—two weeks of sleep deprivation, bad dreams, waking nightmares. Or maybe it was just Lianne, standing raw and unguarded in the entryway, unsure what to do with her hands. Her mother's life—the life she'd rebuilt from the ashes of a thousand burned bridges—had just been ripped apart. The family she'd thought she had was a lie. She'd been betrayed and abandoned.

It was enough punishment for all of them.

Veronica turned to Lianne, and before she could change her mind, she put her arms around her and pulled her into a hug.

Lianne's back was warm and bony, her vertebrae rigid under Veronica's hand. She trembled a little in her daughter's arms, her breath jerky. Veronica closed her eyes for a moment and exhaled.

It wasn't in her nature to forgive. But she was tired of fighting the war.

"Bye, Mom," she whispered. And then she opened the door.